LEGENDS OF THE AMERICAN INDIANS

D.D. Priest   2-2-91

LEGENDS OF THE AMERICAN INDIANS

By
James Fenimore Cooper
Torry Gredsted
Joseph Altsheller
Georg Goll
Karl May

CHARTWELL
BOOKS, INC.

The publishers wish to acknowledge the kind permission for
the use of the texts provided by:
Mr Wolfgang Goll (Georg Goll: Dakota on Fire,

Chapters: Bloody Sunday, Custer's Doom);
Gyldendal Publishers, Denmark
(Torry Gredsted: Singing Arrow,
Chapters: Smiling Eye, White Bear's Story, The Buffalo Hunt;
Torry Gredsted: Prairie Son,
Chapters: At the Great Pow-Wow, The Battle of Lodge-Trail)

First published in Great Britain in 1988 by
Chancellor Press

This 1988 edition
Published by

CHARTWELL BOOKS, INC.
A Division of **BOOK SALES, INC.**
110 Enterprise Avenue
Secaucus, New Jersey 07094

Illustrated by Zdeněk Burian

Selected by Vladimír Hulpach
Graphic design by Vladimír Šmerda
Texts by Torry Gredsted, Georg Goll and
Karl May translated by Stephen Finn
The extract from Joseph Altsheller
adapted by Stephen Finn
© Artia, Prague 1979

ISBN-1-55521-205-0

Printed in Czechoslovakia by Severografia, Liberec
1/08/08/51—01

Contents

THE LAST
OF THE MOHICANS

James Fenimore Cooper

Chapter III

On that day, two men were lingering on the banks of a small but rapid stream, within an hour's journey of the encampment of Webb, like those who awaited the appearance of an absent person or the approach of some expected event.

While one of these loiterers showed the red skin and wild accoutrements of a native of the woods, the other exhibited, through the mask of his rude and nearly savage equipments, the brighter though sunburned and long-faded complexion of one who might claim descent from a European parentage.

'Even your traditions make the case in my favour, Chingachgook,' he said, speaking in the tongue which was known to all the natives who formerly inhabited the country between the Hudson and the Potomac. 'Your fathers came from the setting sun, crossed the big river, fought the people of the country and took the land; and mine came from the red sky of the morning, over the salt lake, and did their work much after the fashion that had been set them by yours; then let God judge the matter between us, and friends spare their words!'

'My fathers fought with the naked red man!' returned the Indian sternly, in the same language. 'Is there no difference, Hawkeye, between the stone-headed arrow of the warrior and the leaden bullet with which you kill?'

'There is reason in an Indian, though nature has made him with a red skin!' said the white man, shaking his head like one on whom such an appeal to his justice was not thrown away. For a moment he appeared to be conscious of having the worst of the argument, then rallying again, he answered the objection of his antagonist in the best manner his limited information would allow:

'I am no scholar and I care not who knows it, but judging from what I have seen at deer chases and squirrel hunts, of the sparks below, I should think a rifle in the hands of their grandfathers was not so dangerous as a hickory bow and a good flint-head might be, if drawn with Indian judgement and sent by an Indian eye.'

'You have the story told by your fathers,' returned the other coldly, waving his hands. 'What say your old men? Do they tell the young warriors that the pale faces met the red men, painted for war and armed with the stone hatchet and wooden gun?'

'I am not a prejudiced man, nor one who vaunts himself on his natural privileges, though the worst enemy I have, and he is an Iroquois, daren't deny that I am genuine white,' the scout replied surveying, with secret satisfaction, the faded colour of his bony and sinewy hand.

A silence of a minute succeeded, during which the Indian sat mute; than, full of the dignity of his office, he commenced his brief tale, with a solemnity that served to heighten its appearance of truth.

'Listen, Hawkeye, and your ear shall drink no lie. 'Tis what my fathers have said and what the Mohicans have done.' He hesitated a single instant and bending a cautious glance toward his companion, he continued, in a manner that was divided between interrogation and assertion.

'My tribe is the grandfather of nations, but I am an unmixed man. The blood of chiefs is in my veins, where it must stay forever. The Dutch landed and gave my people the fire water; they drank until the heavens and the earth seemed to meet, and they foolishly thought they had found the Great Spirit. Then they parted with their land. Foot by foot, they were driven back from the shore, until I, that am a chief and a Sagamore, have never seen the sun shine but through the trees, and have never visited the graves of my fathers.'

'Graves bring solemn feelings over the mind,' returned the scout, a good deal touched at the calm suffering of his companion; 'and they often aid a man in his good intentions; though, for myself, I expect to leave my own bones unburied, to bleach in the woods or to be torn asunder by the wolves. But where are to be found those of your race who came to their kin in the Delaware country, so many summers since?'

'Where are the blossoms of those summers! — fallen, one by one; so all of my family departed, each in his turn, to the land of spirits. I am on the hilltop and must go down into the valley; and when Uncas follows in my footsteps, there will no longer be any of the blood of the Sagamores, for my boy is the last of the Mohicans.'

'Uncas is here,' said another voice, in the same soft, guttural tones, near his elbow; 'who speaks to Uncas?'

The white man loosened his knife in his leathern sheath and made an involuntary movement of the hand toward his rifle, at this sudden interruption; but the Indian sat composed and without turning his head at the unexpected sounds.

At the next instant, a youthful warrior passed between them, with a noiseless step, and seated himself on the bank of the rapid stream. At length Chingachgook turned his eyes slowly toward his son and demanded.

'Do the Maquas dare to leave the print of their moccasins in these woods?'

'I have been on their trail,' replied the young Indian, 'and know that they number as many as the fingers of my two hands; but they lie hid like cowards.'

'The thieves are outlying for scalps and plunder,' said the white

man, whom we shall call Hawkeye, after the manner of his companions. 'That busy Frenchman, Montcalm, will send his spies into our very camp, but he will know what road we travel!'

''Tis enough,' returned the father, glancing his eye toward the setting sun; 'they shall be driven like deer from their bushes. Hawkeye, let us eat to-night, and show the Maquas that we are men to-morrow.'

'I am as ready to do the one as the other; but to fight the Iroquois, 'tis necessary to find the skulkers; and to eat, 'tis necessary to get the game.'

Adjusting his rifle, he was about to make an exhibition of that skill on which he so much valued himself, when the warrior struck up the piece with his hand, saying:

'Hawkeye! Will you fight the Maquas?'

'These Indians know the nature of the woods, as it might be by instinct!' returned the scout, dropping his rifle, and turning away like a man who was convinced of his error. 'I must leave the buck to your arrow, Uncas, or we may kill a deer for the thieves, the Iroquois, to eat.'

The instant the father seconded this intimation by an expressive gesture of the hand, Uncas threw himself on the ground, and approached the animal with wary movements. When within a few yards of the cover, he fitted an arrow to his bow with the utmost care, while the antlers moved, as if their owner snuffed an enemy in the tainted air. In another moment the twang of the cord was heard, a white streak was seen glancing into the bushes, and the wounded buck plunged from the cover, to the very feet of his hidden enemy. Avoiding the horns of the infuriated animal, Uncas darted to his side and passed his knife across the throat, when bounding to the edge of the river it fell, dyeing the waters with its blood.

''Twas done with Indian skill,' said the scout laughing inwardly, but with vast satisfaction; 'and 'twas a pretty sight to behold! Though an arrow is a near shot and needs a knife to finish the work.'

'Hugh!' ejaculated his companion, turning quickly, like a hound who scented game.

'By the Lord, there is a drove of them!' exclaimed the scout, whose eyes began to glisten with the ardour of his usual occupation; 'if they come within range of a bullet I will drop one, though the whole Six Nations should be lurking within sound! What do you hear, Chingachgook? For to my ears the woods are dumb.'

'There is but one deer and he is dead,' said the Indian, bending his body till his ear nearly touched the earth. 'I hear the sounds of feet!'

'Perhaps the wolves have driven the buck to shelter and are following on his trail.'

'No. The horses of white men are coming!' returned the other, raising himself with dignity, and resuming his seat on the log with his former composure. 'Hawkeye, they are your brothers; speak to them.'

'Who comes?' demanded the scout, throwing his rifle carelessly across his left arm, and keeping the forefinger of his right hand on the trigger, though he avoided all appearance of menace in the act. 'Who comes hither, among the beasts and dangers of the wilderness?'

'Believers in religion and friends to the law and to the king,' returned he who rode foremost. 'Men who have journeyed since the rising sun, in the shades of this forest, without nourishment and are sadly tired of their wayfaring.'

'You are, then, lost,' interrupted the hunter, 'and have found how helpless 'tis not to know whether to take the right hand or the left?'

'Even so; sucking babes are not more dependent on those who guide them than we who are of larger growth, and who may now be said to possess the stature without the knowledge of men. Know you the distance to a post of the crown called William Henry?'

'Hoot!' shouted the scout, who did not spare his open laughter, though, instantly checking the dangerous sounds, he indulged his merriment at less risk of being overheard by any lurking enemies. 'You are as much off the scent as a hound would be, with Horican atwixt him and the deer! William Henry, man! if you are friends to the king, and have business with the army, your better way would be to follow the river down to Edward, and lay the matter before Webb, who tarries there, instead of pushing into the defiles, and driving this saucy Frenchman back across Champlain, into his den again!'

Chapter IV

Before the stranger could make any reply to this unexpected proposition, another horseman dashed the bushes aside, and leaped his charger into the pathway in front of his companion.

'What, then, may be our distance from Fort Edward?' demanded a new speaker; 'the place you advise us to seek we left this morning and our destination is the head of the lake.'

'Then you must have lost your eyesight afore losing your way, for the road across the portage is cut to a good two rods and is as grand a path, I calculate, as any that runs into London, or even before the palace of the king himself.'

'We will not dispute concerning the excellence of the passage,' returned Heyward, smilingly; for, it was he. 'It is enough for the present that we trusted to an Indian guide to take us by a nearer though blinder path, and that we are deceived in his knowledge. In plain words, we know not where we are.'

'An Indian lost in the woods!' said the scout, shaking his head doubtfully; 'when the sun is scorching the tree tops, and the water courses are full; when the moss on every beach he sees will tell him in what quarter the north star will shine at night. The woods are full of deer-paths which run to the streams and licks, places well known to everybody; nor have the geese done their flight to the Canada waters altogether! 'Tis strange that an Indian should be lost atwixt Horican and the bend in the river! Is he a Mohawk?'

'Not by birth, though adopted in that tribe; I think his birthplace was farther north and is one of those you call a Huron.'

'Hugh!' exclaimed the two companions of the scout, who had continued until this part of the dialogue, seated immovable, and apparently indifferent to what passed, but who now sprang to their feet with an activity and interest that had evidently got the better of their reserve, by surprise.

'A Huron!' repeated the sturdy scout, once more shaking his head in open distrust; 'they are a thievish race, nor do I care by whom they are adopted; you can never make anything of them but

skulks and vagabonds. Since you trusted yourself to the care of one of that nation, I only wonder that you have not fallen in with more.'

'Of that there is little danger, since William Henry is so many miles in our front. You forget that I have told you our guide is now a Mohawk, and that he serves with our forces as a friend.'

'And I tell you that he who is born a Mingo will die a Mingo,' returned the other, positively. 'A Mohawk! No, give me a Delaware or a Mohican for honesty; and when they will fight, which they won't all do, having suffered their cunning enemies, the Maquas, to make them women — but when they will fight at all, look to a Delaware, or a Mohican, for a warrior!'

'I wish no contention of idle words with you, friend,' said Heyward, curbing his dissatisfied manner and speaking in a more gentle voice; 'if you tell me the distance to Fort Edward, and conduct me thither, your labour shall not go without its reward.'

'And in so doing, how know I that I don't guide an enemy and a spy of Montcalm to the works of the army? It is not every man who speaks the English tongue that is an honest subject.'

'If you serve with the troops, of whom I judge you to be a scout, you should know of such a regiment of the king as the sixtieth.'

'The sixtieth! you can tell me little of the Royal Americans that I don't know, though I do wear a hunting shirt instead of a scarlet jacket.'

'Well, then, among other things, you may know the name of its major?'

'Its major!' interrupted the hunter, elevating his body like one who was proud of his trust. 'If there is a man in the country who knows Major Effingham, he stands before you.'

'It is a corps which has many majors; the gentleman you name is the senior, but I speak of the junior of them all; he who commands the companies in garrison at William Henry.'

'Yes, yes, I have heard that a young gentleman of vast riches, from one of the provinces far south, has got the place. He is over young, too, to hold such rank, and to be put above men whose heads are beginning to bleach; and yet they say he is a soldier in his knowledge and a gallant gentleman!'

'Whatever he may be, or however he may be qualified for his rank, he now speaks to you and, of course, can be no enemy to dread.'

The scout regarded Heyward in surprise and then lifting his cap, he answered, in a tone less confident than before — though still expressing doubt.

'I have heard a party was to leave the encampment this morning for the lake shore?'

'You have heard the truth, but I preferred a nearer route trusting to the knowledge of the Indian I mentioned.'

'And he deceived you and then deserted?'

'Neither, as I believe; certainly not the latter, for he is to be found in the rear.'

'I should like to look at the creatur'; if it is a true Iroquois I can tell him by his knavish look and by his paint,' said the scout. After shoving aside the bushes and proceeding a few paces, he encountered the females, who awaited the result of the conference with anxiety, and not entirely without apprehension. Behind these, the runner leaned against a tree, where he stood the close examination of the scout with an air unmoved, though with a look so dark and savage that it might in itself excite fear. Satisfied with his scrutiny, the hunter soon left him.

'A Mingo is a Mingo, and God having made him so, neither the Mohawks nor any other tribe can alter him,' he said, when he had regained his former position. 'If we were alone, and you would leave that noble horse at the mercy of the wolves to-night, I could show you the way to Edward myself, within an hour, for it lies only about an hour's journey hence; but with such ladies in your company, 'tis impossible!'

'And why? They are fatigued, but they are quite equal to a ride of a few more miles.'

''Tis a natural impossibility!' repeated the scout; 'I wouldn't walk a mile in these woods after night sets into them in company with that runner, for the best rifle in the colonies. They are full of outlying

Iroquois and your mongrel Mohawk knows where to find them too well, to be my companion.'

'Think you so?' said Heyward, leaning forward in the saddle and dropping his voice nearly to a whisper; 'I confess I have not been without my own suspicions, though I have endeavoured to conceal them and affected a confidence I have not always felt, on account of my companions. It was because I suspected him that I would follow no longer; making him, as you see, follow me.'

'I knew he was one of the cheats as soon as I laid eyes on him!' returned the scout, placing a finger on his nose, in sign of caution. 'The thief is leaning against the foot of the sugar sapling, that you can see over them bushes; his right leg is in a line with the bark of the tree, and,' tapping his rifle, 'I can take him from where I stand, between the ankle and the knee, with a single shot, putting an end to his tramping through the woods, for at least a month to come. If I should go back to him, the cunning varmint would suspect something and be dodging through the trees like a frightened deer.'

'It will not do. He may be innocent and I dislike the act. Though if I felt confident of his treachery —'

''Tis a safe thing to calculate on the knavery of an Iroquois,' said the scout, throwing his rifle forward, by a sort of instinctive movement.

'Hold!' interrupted Heyward, 'it will not do — we must think of some other scheme — and yet, I have much reason to believe the rascal has deceived me.'

The hunter, who had already abandoned his intention of maiming the runner, mused a moment, and then made a gesture, which instantly brought his two red companions to his side.

'Now, go you back,' said the hunter, speaking again to Heyward, 'and hold the imp in talk; these Mohicans here will take him without breaking his paint.'

'Nay,' said Heyward, proudly, 'I will seize him myself.'

'Hist! what could you do mounted against an Indian in the bushes?'

'I will dismount.'

'And, think you, when he saw one of your feet out of the stirrup, he would wait for the other to be free? Whoever comes into the woods to deal with the natives must use Indian fashions, if he would wish to prosper in his undertakings. Go, then; talk openly to the miscreant and seem to believe him the truest friend you have on 'arth.'

Heyward prepared to comply, though with strong disgust at the nature of the office he was compelled to execute. Stimulated by apprehension, he left the scout, who immediately entered into a loud conversation with the stranger that had so unceremoniously enlisted himself with the party of travellers that morning. He spurred his charger and drew the reins when the animal had carried him a few yards of the place where the sullen runner still stood, leaning against the tree.

'You may see, Magua,' he said, endeavouring to assume an air of freedom and confidence, 'that the night is closing around us and yet we are no nearer to William Henry than when we left the encampment of Webb with the rising sun. You have missed the way, nor have I been more fortunate. But, happily, we have fallen in with a hunter, he whom you hear talking to the singer, that is acquainted with the deer-paths and by-ways of the woods and who promises to lead us to a place where we may rest securely till the morning.'

The Indian riveted his glowing eyes on Heyward as he asked, in his imperfect English, 'Is he alone?'

'Alone!' hesitatingly answered Heyward, to whom deception was too new to be assumed without embarrassment. 'Oh! not alone, surely, Magua, for you know that we are with him.'

'Then Le Renard Subtil will go,' returned the runner, coolly raising his little wallet from the place where it had lain at his feet; 'and the pale faces will see none but their own colour.'

'Go! Whom call you Le Renard?'

''Tis the name his Canada fathers have given to Magua,' returned the runner, with an air that manifested his pride at the distinction. 'Night is the same as day to Le Subtil, when Munro waits for him.'

'And what account will Le Renard give the chief of William Henry concerning his daughters? Will he dare to tell the hot-blooded Scotsman that his children are left without a guide, though Magua promised to be one?'

'Though the grey head has a loud voice and a long arm, Le Renard will not hear him, nor feel him, in the woods.'

'But what will the Mohawks say? They will make him petticoats and bid him stay in the wigwam with the women, for he is no longer to be trusted with the business of a man.'

'Le Subtil knows the path to the great lakes and he can find the bones of his fathers,' was the answer of the unmoved runner.

'Enough, Magua,' said Heyward; 'are we not friends? Why should there be bitter words between us? Munro has promised you a gift for your services when performed and I shall be your debtor for another. Rest your weary limbs then, and open your wallet to eat. We have a few moments to spare; let us not waste them in talk like wrangling women. When the ladies are refreshed we will proceed.'

'The pale faces make themselves dogs to their women,' muttered the Indian, in his native language, 'and when they want to eat, their warriors must lay aside the tomahawk to feed their laziness.'

'What say you, Renard?'

'Le Subtil says it is good!'

The Indian then fastened his eyes keenly on the open countenance of Heyward, but meeting his glance, he turned them quickly away, and seating himself deliberately on the ground, he drew forth the remnant of some former repast and began to eat, though not without first bending his looks slowly and cautiously around him.

'This is well,' continued Heyward; 'and Le Renard will have strength and sight to find the path in the morning'; he paused, for sounds like the snapping of a dried stick and the rustling of leaves, rose from the adjacent bushes, but recollecting himself instantly, he continued, 'we must be moving before the sun is seen, or Montcalm may lie in our path and shut us out from the fortress.'

The hand of Magua dropped from his mouth to his side and though his eyes were fastened on the ground, his head was turned aside, his nostrils expanded and his ears seemed even to stand more erect than usual, giving to him the appearance of a statue that was made to represent intense attention.

Heyward, who watched his movements with a vigilant eye, carelessly extricated one of his feet from the stirrup, while he passed a hand toward the bear skin covering of his holsters. Every effort to detect the point most regarded by the runner was completely frustrated by the tremulous glances of his organs, which seemed not to rest a single instant on any particular object, and which, at the same time, could be hardly said to move. While he hesitated how to proceed, Le Subtil cautiously raised himself to his feet, though with a motion so slow and guarded that not the slightest noise was produced by the change. Heyward felt it had now become incumbent on him to act. Throwing his leg over the saddle, he dismounted, with a determination to advance and seize his treacherous companion, trusting the result to his own manhood. In order, however, to prevent unnecessary alarm, he still preserved an air of calmness and friendship.

'Le Renard Subtil does not eat,' he said, using the appellation he had found most flattering to the vanity of the Indian. 'His corn is not well parched, and it seems dry. Let me examine; perhaps something may be found among my own provisions that will help his appetite.'

Magua held out the wallet to the proffer of the other. He even suffered their hands to meet, without betraying the least emotion, or varying his riveted attitude of attention. But when he felt the fingers of Heyward moving gently along his own naked arm, he struck up the limb of the young man and, uttering a piercing cry, he darted beneath it and plunged, at a single bound, into the opposite thicket. At the next instant the form of Chingachgook appeared from the bushes, looking like a spectre in its paint, and glided across the path in swift pursuit. Next followed the shout of Uncas, when the woods were lighted by a sudden flash, that was accompanied by the sharp report of the hunter's rifle.

Chapter V

The suddenness of the flight of his guide, and the wild cries of the pursuers, caused Heyward to remain fixed, for a few moments, in inactive surprise. Then, recollecting the importance of securing the fugitive, he dashed aside the surrounding bushes, and pressed eagerly forward to lend his aid in the chase. Before he had, however, proceeded a hundred yards, he met the three foresters already returning from their unsuccessful pursuit.

'Why so soon disheartened!' he exclaimed; 'the scoundrel must be concealed behind some of these trees and may yet be secured. We are not safe while he goes at large.'

'Would you set a cloud to chase the wind?' returned the disappointed scout; 'I heard the imp brushing over the dry leaves, like a black snake, and blinking a glimpse of him, just over ag'in yon big pine, I pulled as it might be on the scent; but 'twouldn't do! and yet for a reasoning aim, if anybody but myself had touched the trigger, I should call it a quick sight; and I may be accounted to have experience in these matters and one who ought to know. Look at this sumach; its leaves are red, though everybody knows the fruit is in the yellow blossom in the month of July!'

''Tis the blood of Le Subtil! He is hurt and may yet fall.'

'No, no,' returned the scout, in decided disapprobation of this opinion, 'I rubbed the bark off a limb, perhaps, but the creature leaped the longer for it. A rifle bullet acts on a running animal, when it barks him, much the same as one of your spurs on a horse; that is, it quickens motion and puts life into the flesh, instead of taking it away. But when it cuts the ragged hole, after a bound or two, there is commonly a stagnation of further leaping, be it Indian or be it deer!'

'We are four able bodies to one wounded man!'

'Is life grievous to you?' interrupted the scout. 'Yonder red devil would draw you within swing of the tomahawks of his comrades, before you were heated in the chase. It was an unthoughtful act in a man who has so often slept with the war whoop ringing in the air, to let off his piece within sound of an ambushment! But then it was

23

a natural temptation! 'twas very natural! Come, friends, let us move our station and in such fashion, too, as will throw the cunning of a Mingo on a wrong scent, or our scalps will be drying in the wind in front of Montcalm's marquee, ag'in this hour to-morrow.'

'What is to be done?' Heyward said, feeling the utter helplessness of doubt in such a pressing strait; 'desert me not, for God's sake! Remain to defend those I escort and freely name your own reward.'

'Offer your prayers to Him who can give us wisdom to circumvent the cunning of the devils who fill these woods,' calmly interrupted the scout, 'but spare your offers of money, which neither you may live to realise, nor I to profit by. These Mohicans and I will do what man's thoughts can invent, to keep such flowers, which, though so sweet, were never made for the wilderness, from harm, and that without hope of any other recompense but such as God always gives to upright dealings. First, you must promise two things, both in your own name and for your friends, or without serving you, we shall only injure ourselves! The one is to be as still as these sleeping woods, let what will happen; and the other is to keep the place where we shall take you forever a secret from all mortal men.'

'I will do my utmost to see both these conditions fulfilled.'

'Then follow, for we are losing moments that are as precious as the heart's blood to a stricken deer!'

Heyward could distinguish the impatient gesture of the scout, through the increasing shadows of the evening, and he moved in his footsteps, swiftly toward the place where he had left the remainder of his party. When they rejoined the expecting and anxious females, he briefly acquainted them with the conditions of their new guide and with the necessity that existed for their hushing every apprehension in instant and serious exertions. Silently and without a moment's delay they permitted him to assist them from their saddles, when they descended quickly to the water's edge, where the scout had collected the rest of the party, more by the agency of expressive gestures than by any use of words.

'What to do with these dumb creatures!' muttered the white man, on whom the sole control of their future movements appeared to devolve; 'it would be time lost to cut their throats and cast them into the river; and to leave them here would be to tell the Mingoes that they have not far to seek their owners!'

'Then give them their bridles and let them range the woods,' Heyward ventured to suggest.

'No; it would be better to mislead the imps and make them believe they must equal a horse's speed to run down their chase. Ay, ay, that will blind their fire balls of eyes! Chingach — Hist! what stirs the bush?'

'The colt.'

'That colt, at least, must die,' muttered the scout, grasping at the mane of the nimble beast, which easily eluded his hand; 'Uncas, your arrows!'

'Hold!' exclaimed the proprietor of the condemned animal, aloud, without regard to the whispering tones used by the others; 'spare the foal of Miriam! it is the comely offspring of a faithful dam, and would willingly injure naught.'

'When men struggle for the single life God has given them,' said the scout, sternly, 'even their own kind seem no more than beasts of the wood. If you speak again, I shall leave you to the mercy of the Maquas! Draw to your arrow's head, Uncas; we have no time for second blows.'

This deed of apparent cruelty, but of real necessity, fell upon the spirits of the travellers like a terrific warning of the peril in which they stood, heightened as it was by the calm though steady resolution of the actors in the scene.

The Indians led the frightened and reluctant horses into the bed of the river.

At a short distance from the shore they turned and were soon concealed by the projection of the bank, under the brow of which they moved, in a direction opposite to the course of the waters. In the meantime, the scout drew a canoe of bark from its place of concealment beneath some low bushes, whose branches were waving with the eddies of the current, into which he silently motioned for the females to enter.

So soon as Cora and Alice were seated, the scout, without regarding the element, directed Heyward to support one side of the frail vessel, and posting himself at the other, they bore it up against the stream, followed by the dejected owner of the dead foal. In this manner they proceeded, for many rods, in a silence that was only interrupted by the rippling of the water, as its eddies played around them, or the low dash made by their own cautious footsteps. At length they reached a point in the river where the roving eye of Heyward became riveted on a cluster of black objects, collected at a spot where the high bank threw a deeper shadow than usual on the dark waters. Hesitating to advance, he pointed out the place to the attention of his companion.

'Ay,' returned the composed scout, 'the Indians have hid the beasts with the judgment of natives! Water leaves no trail and an owl's eyes would be blinded by the darkness of such a hole.'

The whole party was soon reunited, and another consultation was held between the scout and his new comrades, during which, they, whose fates depended on the faith and ingenuity of these unknown foresters, had a little leisure to observe their situation more minutely.

The horses had been secured to some scattering shrubs that grew in the fissures of the rocks, where, standing in the water, they were left to pass the night. The scout directed Heyward and his disconsolate fellow travellers to seat themselves in the forward end of the canoe, and took possession of the other himself, as erect and steady as if he floated in a vessel of much firmer materials. The Indians warily retraced their steps toward the place they had left, when the scout, placing his pole against a rock, by a powerful shove, sent his frail bark directly into the centre of the turbulent stream.

'Where are we! and what is next to be done?' demanded Heyward, perceiving that the exertions of the scout had finally ceased.

'You are at the foot of Glenn's,' returned the other, speaking aloud, without fear of consequences within the roar of the cataract; 'and the next thing is to make a steady landing, lest the canoe upset and you should go down again the hard road we have travelled faster than you came up; 'tis a hard rift to stem, when the river is a little swelled and five is an unnatural number to keep dry, in a hurry-skurry, with a little birchen bark and gum. There, go you all on the rock and I will bring up the Mohicans with the venison. A man had better sleep without his scalp, than famish in the midst of plenty.'

His passengers gladly complied with these directions. As the last foot touched the rock, the canoe whirled from its station, when the tall form of the scout was seen, for an instant, gliding above the waters, before it disappeared in the impenetrable darkness that rested on the bed of the river. Left by their guide, the travellers remained a few minutes in helpless ignorance, afraid even to move along the broken rocks, lest a false step should precipitate them down some one of the many deep and roaring caverns, into which the water seemed to tumble, on every side of them. Their suspense, however, was soon relieved; for, aided by the skill of the natives, the canoe shot back into the eddy and floated again at the side of the low rock, before they thought the scout had even time to rejoin his companions.

'We are now fortified, garrisoned and provisioned,' cried Heyward, cheerfully, 'and may set Montcalm and his allies at defiance. How, now, my vigilant sentinel, can you see anything of those you call the Iroquois, on the main land?'

'I call them Iroquois, because to me every native who speaks a foreign tongue, is accounted an enemy, though he may pretend to serve the king! If Webb wants faith and honesty in an Indian, let him bring out the tribes of the Delaware, and send these greedy and lying Mohawks and Oneidas, with their six nations of varlets, where in nature they belong, among the French!'

'We should then exchange a warlike for a useless friend! I have heard that the Delawares have laid aside the hatchet and are content to be called women!'

'Ay, shame on the Hollanders and Iroquois, who circumvented them by their deviltries into such a treaty! But I have known them for twenty years and I call him liar that says cowardly blood runs in the veins of a Delaware. You have driven their tribes from the seashore and would now believe what their enemies say, that you may sleep at night upon an easy pillow. No, no; to me, every Indian who speaks a foreign tongue is an Iroquois, whether the castle of his tribe be in Canada, or be in York.'

Heyward, perceiving that the stubborn adherence of the scout to the cause of his friends the Delawares or Mohicans, for they were branches of the same numerous people, was likely to prolong a useless discussion, changed the subject.

'Treaty or no treaty, I know full well that your two companions are brave and cautious warriors! Have they heard or seen anything of our enemies?'

'I should be sorry to think that they had, though this is a spot that stout courage might hold for a smart scrimmage. I will not deny, however, but the horses cowered when I passed them as though they scented the wolves, and a wolf is a beast that is apt to hover about an Indian ambushment, craving the offals of the deer the savages kill.'

The scout was busied in collecting certain necessary implements; as he concluded, he moved silently by the group of travellers, accompanied by the Mohicans, who seemed to comprehend his intentions with instinctive readiness, when the whole three disappeared in succession, seeming to vanish against the dark face of a perpendicular rock that rose to the height of a few yards of the water's edge.

Chapter VI

Heyward and his female companions witnessed this mysterious movement with secret uneasiness; for, though the conduct of the white man had hitherto been above reproach, his rude equipments, blunt address and strong antipathies, together with the character of his silent associates, were all causes for exciting distrust in minds that had been so recently alarmed by Indian treachery.

At the further extremity of a narrow, deep cavern in the rock, whose length appeared much extended by the perspective and the nature of the light by which it was seen, was seated the scout, holding a blazing knot of pine. At a little distance in advance stood Uncas, his whole person thrown powerfully into view. The travellers anxiously regarded the upright, flexible figure of the young Mohican, graceful and unrestrained in the attitudes and movements of nature.

'I could sleep in peace,' whispered lovely Alice, 'with such a fearless and generous-looking youth for my sentinel. Surely, Duncan, those cruel murders, those terrific scenes of torture, of which we read and hear so much, are never acted in the presence of such as he!'

'This certainly is a rare and brilliant instance of those natural qualities in which these peculiar people are said to excel,' he answered. 'I agree with you, Alice, in thinking that such a front and eye were formed rather to intimidate than to deceive. Let us then hope that this Mohican may not disappoint our wishes, but prove what his looks assert him to be, a brave and constant friend.'

'Now Major Heyward speaks as Major Heyward should,' said Cora; 'who that looks at this creature of nature, remembers the shade of his skin?'

A short and apparently an embarrassed silence succeeded this remark, which was interrupted by the scout calling to them, aloud, to enter.

'This fire begins to show too bright a flame,' he continued, as they complied, 'and might light the Mingoes to our undoing. Uncas, drop the blanket and show the knaves its dark side.'

Uncas did as the other had directed, and when the voice of Hawkeye ceased, the roar of the cataract sounded like the rumbling of distant thunder.

The repast, which was greatly aided by the addition of a few delicacies that Heyward had the precaution to bring with him when they left their horses, was exceedingly refreshing to the weary party.

'Come, friend,' said Hawkeye, drawing out a keg from beneath a cover of leaves, toward the close of the repast, and addressing the stranger who sat at his elbow, doing great justice to his culinary skill, 'try a little spruce; 'twill wash away thoughts of the colt, and quicken the life in your bosom. I drink to our better friendship, hoping that a little horse flesh may leave no heart burnings atween us. How do you name yourself?'

'Gamut — David Gamut,' returned the singing master, preparing to wash down his sorrows in a powerful draught of the woodman's high-flavoured and well-laced compound.

'A very good name and, I dare say, handed down from honest forefathers.'

'What can be more fitting and consolatory than to offer up evening praise, after a day of such exceeding jeopardy!'

Alice smiled; but regarding Heyward, she blushed and hesitated.

'Indulge yourself,' he whispered; 'ought not the suggestion of the worthy namesake of the Psalmist to have its weight at such a moment?'

Encouraged by his opinion, Alice did what her pious inclinations and her keen relish for gentle sounds had before so strongly urged. The singers were dwelling on one of those low, dying chords, which the ear devours with such greedy rapture, as if conscious that it is about to lose them, when a cry, that seemed neither human nor earth-

ly, rose in the outward air, penetrating not only the recesses of the
cavern, but to the inmost hearts of all who heard it. It was followed by
a stillness apparently as deep as if the waters had been checked in
their furious progress, at such a horrid and unusual interruption.

'What is it?' murmured Alice, after a few moments of terrible
suspense.

'What is it?' repeated Heyward aloud.

Neither Hawkeye nor the Indian made any reply. They listened, as
if expecting the sound would be repeated, with a manner that expressed their own astonishment. At length they spoke together, earnestly, in the Delaware language, when Uncas, passing by the inner
and most concealed aperture, cautiously left the cavern. When he had
gone, the scout first spoke in English.

'What it is, or what it is not, none here can tell, though two of
us have ranged the woods for more than thirty years. I did believe
there was no cry that Indian or beast could make that my ears had
not heard; but this has proved that I was only a vain and conceited
mortal.'

'Was it not, then, the shout the warriors make when they wish to
intimidate their enemies?' asked Cora.

'No, no; this was bad and shocking and had a sort of unhuman
sound; but when you once hear the war whoop, you will never mistake it for anything else. Well, Uncas!' speaking in Delaware to the
young chief as he re-entered, 'what see you? Do our lights shine
through the blankets?'

The answer was short and apparently decided, being given in the
same tongue.

'There is nothing to be seen without,' continued Hawkeye, shaking
his head in discontent; 'and our hiding place is still in darkness. Pass
into the other cave, you that need it, and seek for sleep; we must be
afoot long before the sun, and make the most of our time to get to
Edward, while the Mingoes are taking their morning nap.'

Cora set the example of compliance, with a steadiness that taught
the more timid Alice the necessity of obedience. Before leaving the
place, she whispered a request to Duncan that he would follow.

Heyward took with him a blazing knot, which threw a dim light through the narrow vista of their new apartment. Placing it in a favourable position, he joined the females, who now found themselves alone with him for the first time since they had left the friendly ramparts of Fort Edward.

'Leave us not, Duncan,' said Alice; 'we cannot sleep in such a place as this, with that horrid cry still ringing in our ears.'

'First let us examine into the security of your fortress,' he answered, 'and then we will speak of rest.'

He approached the further end of the cavern to an outlet which, like the others, was concealed by blankets; and removing the heavy screen, breathed the fresh and reviving air from the cataract.

'Nature has made an impenetrable barrier on this side,' he continued, pointing down the perpendicular declivity into the dark current, before he dropped the blanket; 'and as you know that good men and true are on guard in front, I see no reason why the advice of our honest host should be disregarded. I am certain Cora will join me in saying that sleep is necessary to you both.'

'Cora may submit to the justice of your opinion, though she cannot put it in practice,' returned the elder sister, who had placed herself by the side of Alice, on a couch of sassafras; 'there would be other causes to chase away sleep, though we had been spared the shock of this mysterious noise. Ask yourself, Heyward, can daughters forget the anxiety a father must endure, whose children lodge he knows not where or how, in such a wilderness, and in the midst of so many perils?'

'He is a soldier, and knows how to estimate the chances of the woods.'

'He is a father and cannot deny his nature.'

'How kind has he ever been to all my follies, how tender and indulgent to all my wishes,' sobbed Alice. 'We have been selfish, sister, in urging our visit at such hazard.'

'I may have been rash in pressing his consent in a moment of much embarrassment, but I would have proved to him, that however others might neglect him in his strait, his children at least were faithful.'

'When he heard of your arrival at Edward,' said Heyward, kindly, 'there was a powerful struggle in his bosom between fear and love; though the latter, heightened, if possible, by so long a separation, quickly prevailed. "It is the spirit of my noble-minded Cora that leads them, Duncan," he said, "and I will not balk it. Would to God that he who holds the honour of our royal master in his guardianship would show but half her firmness!"'

'And did he not speak of me, Heyward?' demanded Alice, with jealous affection. 'Surely, he forgot not altogether his little Elsie?'

'That were impossible,' returned the young man; 'he called you by a thousand endearing epithets that I may not presume to use, but to the justice of which I can warmly testify. Once, indeed, he said —'

Duncan ceased speaking; for while his eyes were riveted on those of Alice, who had turned toward him with the eagerness of filial affection, to catch his words, the same strong, horrid cry, as before, filled the air and rendered him mute. A long, breathless silence succeeded, during which each looked at the other in fearful expectation of hearing the sound repeated. At length, the blanket was slowly raised and the scout stood in the aperture with a countenance whose firmness evidently began to give way before a mystery that seemed to threaten some danger, against which all his cunning and experience might prove of no avail.

Chapter VII

"Twould be neglecting a warning that is given for our good to lie hid any longer,' said Hawkeye, 'when such sounds are raised in the forests. These gentle ones may keep close, but the Mohicans and I will watch upon the rock, where I suppose a major of the Sixtieth would wish to keep us company.'

'Is then our danger so pressing?' asked Cora.

'He who makes strange sounds and gives them out for man's information, alone knows our danger. I should think myself wicked, unto rebellion against His will, was I to burrow with such warnings in the air! Even the weak soul who passes his day in singing is stirred by the cry and, as he says, is "ready to go forth to the battle." If 'twere only a battle, it would be a thing understood by us all, and easily managed; but I have heard that when such shrieks are atween heaven and 'arth, it betokens another sort of warfare!'

'If all our reasons for fear, my friend, are confined to such as proceed from supernatural causes, we have but little occasion to be alarmed,' continued the undisturbed Cora; 'are you certain that our enemies have not invented some new and ingenious method to strike us with terror, that their conquest may become more easy?'

'Lady,' returned the scout, solemnly, 'I have listened to all the sounds of the woods for thirty years, as a man will listen whose life and death depend on the quickness of his ears. There is no whine of the panther, no whistle of the catbird, nor any invention of the devilish Mingoes that can cheat me! I have heard the forest moan like mortal men in their affliction; often, and again, have I listened to the wind playing its music in the branches of the girdled trees; and I have heard the lightning cracking in the air like the snapping of blazing brush as it spitted forth sparks and forked flames; but never have I thought that I heard more than the pleasure of him who sported the things of his hand. But neither the Mohicans, nor I, who am a white man without a cross, can explain the cry just heard. We, therefore, believe it a sign given for our good.'

'It is extraordinary!' said Heyward, taking his pistols from the place where he had laid them on entering; 'be it a sign of peace or a signal of war, it must be looked to. Lead the way, my friend; I follow.'

On issuing from their place of confinement, the whole party instantly experienced a grateful renovation of spirits, by exchanging the pent air of the hiding place for the cool and invigorating atmosphere which played around the whirlpools and pitches of the cataract. The moon had risen and its light was already glancing here and there on the waters above them; but the extremity of the rock where they stood still lay in shadow.

34

'Here is nothing to be seen but the gloom and quiet of a lovely evening,' whispered Duncan; 'how much should we prize such a scene and all this breathing solitude at any other moment, Cora! Fancy yourselves in security and what now, perhaps, increases your terror, may be made conducive to enjoyment —'

'Listen!' interrupted Alice.

The caution was unnecessary. Once more the same sound arose, as if from the bed of the river, and having broken out of the narrow bounds of the cliffs, was heard undulating through the forest.

'Can any here give a name to such a cry?' demanded Hawkeye, when the last echo was lost in the woods; 'if so, let him speak; for myself, I judge it not to belong to 'arth!'

'Here, then, is one who can undeceive you,' said Duncan; 'I know the sound full well, for often have I heard it on the field of battle and in situations which are frequent in a soldier's life. 'Tis the horrid shriek that a horse will give in his agony; oftener drawn from him in pain, though sometimes in terror. My charger is either a prey to the beasts of the forest or he sees his danger, without the power to avoid it. The sound might deceive me in the cavern, but in the open air I know it too well to be wrong.'

The scout and his companions listened to this simple explanation with the interest of men who imbibe new ideas, at the same time that they get rid of old ones, which had proved disagreeable inmates. The two latter uttered their usual expressive exclamation, 'hugh!' as the truth first glanced upon their minds, while the former, after a short, musing pause, took upon himself to reply.

'I cannot deny your words,' he said, 'for I am little skilled in horses, though born where they abound. The wolves must be hovering above their heads on the bank, and the timorsome creatures are calling on man for help in the best manner they are able. Uncas' — he spoke in Delaware — 'Uncas, drop down in the canoe and whirl a brand among the pack; or fear may do what the wolves can't get at to perform and leave us without horses in the morning, when we shall have so much need to journey swiftly!'

The young native had already descended to the water to comply, when a long howl was raised on the edge of the river, and was borne swiftly off into the depths of the forest, as though the beasts, of their own accord, were abandoning their prey in sudden terror. Uncas, with instinctive quickness, receded, and the three foresters held another of their low, earnest conferences.

'We have been like hunters who have lost the points of the heavens and from whom the sun has been hid for days,' said Hawkeye, turning away from his companions; 'now we begin again to know the signs of our course and the paths are cleared from briars! Seat yourselves in the shade which the moon throws from yonder beech —'tis thicker than that of the pines — and let us wait for that which the Lord may choose to send next. Let all your conversation be in whispers; though it would be better and, perhaps in the end, wiser, if each one held discourse with his own thoughts for a time.'

In this manner hours passed without further interruption. The moon reached the zenith and shed its mild light perpendicularly on the lovely sight of the sisters slumbering peacefully in each other's arms. Duncan cast the wide shawl of Cora before a spectacle he so much loved to contemplate and then suffered his own head to seek a pillow on the rock. David began to utter sounds that would have shocked his delicate organs in more wakeful moments; in short, all but Hawkeye and his Mohicans lost every idea of consciousness in uncontrollable drowsiness. But the watchfulness of these vigilant protectors neither tired nor slumbered. Immovable as that rock, of which each appeared to form a part, they lay, with their eyes roving, without intermission, along the dark margin of trees that formed the adjacent shores of the narrow stream. Not a sound escaped them; the most subtle examination could not have told they breathed. It was evident that this excess of caution proceeded from an experience that no subtlety on the part of their enemies could deceive. It was, however, continued without any apparent consequences, until the moon had set, and a pale streak above the tree tops, at the bend of the river a little below, announced the approach of day.

Then, for the first time, Hawkeye was seen to stir. He crawled along the rock and shook Duncan from his heavy slumbers.

'Now is the time to journey,' he whispered; 'awake the gentle ones and be ready to get into the canoe when I bring it to the landing place.'

'Have you had a quiet night?' said Heyward; 'for myself, I believe sleep has got the better of my vigilance.'

'All is yet still as midnight. Be silent, but be quick.'

By this time Duncan was thoroughly awake and he immediately lifted the shawl from the sleeping females. The motion caused Cora to raise her hand as if to repulse him, while Alice murmured, in her soft, gentle voice, 'No, no, dear father, we were not deserted; Duncan was with us!'

'Yes, sweet innocence,' whispered the youth; 'Duncan is here and while life continues or danger remains, he will never quit thee. Cora! Alice! awake! The hour has come to move!'

A loud shriek from the younger of the sisters and the form of the other standing upright before him, in bewildered horror, was the unexpected answer he received.

While the words were still on the lips of Heyward, there had arisen such a tumult of yells and cries as served to drive the swift currents of his own blood back from its bounding course into the fountains of his heart. It seemed, for near a minute, as if the demons of hell had possessed themselves of the air about them and were venting their savage humours in barbarous sounds. The cries came from no particular direction, though it was evident they filled the woods and, as the appalled listeners easily imagined, the caverns of the falls, the bed of the river and the upper air. David raised his tall person in the midst of the infernal din, with a hand on either ear, exclaiming:

'Whence comes this discord! Has hell broke loose, that man should utter sounds like these?'

The bright flashes and the quick report of a dozen rifles, from the opposite banks of the stream, followed this incautious exposure of his person and left the unfortunate singing master senseless on that rock where he had been so long slumbering. The Mohicans boldly sent back the intimidating yell of their enemies, who raised a shout of savage triumph at the fall of Gamut. The flash of rifles was quick and close between them, but either party was too well skilled to leave even a limb exposed to the hostile aim. Duncan listened with intense anxiety for the strokes of the paddle, believing that flight was now their only refuge. The river glanced by with its ordinary velocity, but the canoe was nowhere to be seen on its dark waters. He had just fancied they were cruelly deserted by the scout, as a stream of flame issued from the rock beneath him, and a fierce yell, blended with a shriek of agony, announced that the messenger of death, sent from the fatal weapon of Hawkeye, had found a victim. At this slight repulse the assailants instantly withdrew and gradually the place became as still as before the sudden tumult.

Duncan seized the favourable moment to spring to the body of Gamut, which he bore within the shelter of the narrow chasm that protected the sisters. In another minute the whole party was collected in this spot of comparative safety.

'The poor fellow has saved his scalp,' said Hawkeye, coolly passing his hand over the head of David; 'but he is a proof that a man may be born with too long a tongue! 'Twas downright madness to show six feet of flesh and blood, on a naked rock, to the raging savages. I only wonder he has escaped with life.'

'Is he not dead?' demanded Cora, in a voice whose husky tones showed how powerfully natural horror struggled with her assumed firmness. 'Can we do aught to assist the wretched man?'

'No, no! the life is in his heart yet, and after he has slept a while he will come to himself and be a wiser man for it, till the hour of his real time shall come,' returned Hawkeye, casting another oblique glance at the insensible body, while he filled his charger with admirable nicety. 'Carry him in, Uncas, and lay him in the sassafras. The longer his nap lasts the better it will be for him, as I doubt whether he can find a proper cover for such a shape on these rocks; and singing won't do any good with the Iroquois.'

'You believe, then, the attack will be renewed?' asked Heyward.

'Do I expect a hungry wolf will satisfy his craving with a mouthful! They have lost a man and 'tis their fashion, when they meet a loss and fail in the surprise, to fall back, but we shall have them on again, with new expedients to circumvent us and master our scalps. Our main hope,' he continued, raising his rugged countenance, across which a shade of anxiety just then passed like a darkening cloud, 'will be to keep the rock until Munro can send a party to our help! God send it soon and under a leader that knows the Indian customs!'

'You hear our probable fortunes, Cora,' said Duncan, 'and you know we have everything to hope from the anxiety and experience of your father. Come then, with Alice, into this cavern, where you, at least, will be safe from the murderous rifles of our enemies and where you may bestow a care suited to your gentle natures on our unfortunate comrade.'

The sisters followed him into the outer cave, where David was beginning, by his sighs, to give symptoms of returning consciousness; and then commending the wounded man to their attention, he immediately prepared to leave them.

'Duncan!' said the tremulous voice of Cora, when he had reached the mouth of the cavern. He turned and beheld the speaker, whose colour had changed to a deadly paleness, and whose lip quivered, gazing after him, with an expression of interest which immediately recalled him to her side. 'Remember, Duncan, how necessary your safety is to our own — how you bear a father's trust — how much depends on your discretion and care — in short,' she added, while the tell-tale blood stole over her features, crimsoning her very temples, 'how very deservedly dear you are to all of the name of Munro.'

'If anything could add to my own base love of life,' said Heyward, suffering his unconscious eyes to wander to the youthful form of the silent Alice, 'it would be so kind and assurance. As major of the 60th, our honest host will tell you I must take my share of the fray; but our task will be easy: it is merely to keep these bloodhounds at bay for a few hours.'

Without waiting for a reply, he tore himself from the presence of the sisters and joined the scout and his companions who still lay within the protection of the little chasm between the two caves.

'I tell you, Uncas,' said the former, as Heyward joined them, 'you are wasteful of your powder and the kick of the rifle disconcerts your aim! Little powder, light lead and a long arm seldom fail of bringing the death screech from a Mingo! At least, such has been my experience with the creatur's. Come, friends; let us to our covers, for no man can tell when or where a Maqua will strike his blow.'

A long and anxious watch succeeded, but without any further evidences of a renewed attack; and Duncan began to hope that their fire had proved more fatal than was supposed, and that their enemies had been effectually repulsed. When he ventured to utter this impression to his companion, it was met by Hawkeye with an incredulous shake of the head.

'You know not the nature of a Maqua, if you think he is easily beaten back without a scalp!' he answered. 'If there was one of the imps yelling this morning, there were forty! and they know our number and quality too well to give up the chase so soon. Hist! look into the water above, just where it breaks over the rocks. I am no mortal, if the risky devils haven't swam down upon the very pitch and, as bad luck would have it, they have hit the head of the island. Hist! man, keep close! or the hair will be off your crown in the turning of a knife!'

Heyward lifted his head from the cover and beheld what he justly considered a prodigy of rashness and skill. The river had worn away the edge of the soft rock in such a manner as to render its first pitch less abrupt and perpendicular than is usual at waterfalls. With no other guide than the ripple of the stream where it met the head of the island, a party of their insatiable foes had ventured into the current and swam down upon this point, knowing the ready access it would give, if successful, to their intended victims.

As Hawkeye ceased speaking, four human heads could be seen peering above a few logs of driftwood that had lodged on these naked rocks and which had probably suggested the idea of the practicability of the hazardous undertaking. At the next moment, a fifth form was seen floating over the green edge of the fall, a little from the line of the island. The savage struggled powerfully to gain the point of safety and, favoured by the glancing water, he was already stretching forth an arm to meet the grasp of his companions, when he shot away again with the whirling current, appeared to rise in the air, with uplifted arms and starting eyeballs, and fell, with a sullen plunge, into that deep and yawning abyss over which he hovered. A wild, despairing shriek rose from the cavern and all was hushed again as the grave.

The first generous impulse of Duncan was to rush to the rescue of the hapless wretch; but he felt himself bound to the spot by the iron grasp of the immovable scout.

'Would ye bring certain death upon us, by telling the Mingoes where we lie?' demanded Hawkeye, sternly; "tis a charge of powder saved and ammunition is as precious now as breath to a worried deer! Freshen the priming of your pistols — the mist of the falls is apt to dampen the brimstone — and stand firm for a close struggle, while I fire on their rush.'

He placed a finger in his mouth and drew a long, shrill whistle, which was answered from the rocks that were guarded by the Mohicans. Duncan caught glimpses of heads above the scattered driftwood, as this signal rose on the air, but they disappeared again as suddenly as they had glanced upon his sight. A low, rustling sound next drew his attention behind him, and turning his head, he beheld Uncas within a few feet, creeping to his side. Hawkeye spoke to him in Delaware, when the young chief took his position with singular caution and undisturbed coolness. To Heyward this was a moment of feverish and impatient suspense; though the scout saw fit to select it as a fit occasion to read a lecture to his more youthful associates on the art of using firearms with discretion.

He was interrupted by the low but expressive 'hugh' of Uncas.

'I see them, boy, I see them!' continued Hawkeye; 'they are gathering for the rush, or they would keep their dingy backs below the logs. Well, let them,' he added, examining his flint; 'the leading man certainly comes on to his death, though it should be Montcalm himself!'

At that moment the woods were filled with another burst of cries, and at the signal four savages sprang from the cover of the driftwood. Heyward felt a burning desire to rush forward to meet them, so intense was the delirious anxiety of the moment; but he was restrained by the deliberate examples of the scout and Uncas.

When their foes, who leaped over the black rocks that divided them, with long bounds, uttering the wildest yells, were within a few rods, the rifle of Hawkeye slowly rose among the shrubs and poured out its fatal contents. The foremost Indian bounded like a stricken deer and fell headlong among the clefts of the island.

'Now, Uncas!' cried the scout, drawing his long knife, while his quick eyes began to flash with ardour, 'take the last of the screeching imps; of the other two we are sartain!'

He was obeyed; and but two enemies remained to be overcome. Heyward had given one of his pistols to Hawkeye, and together they rushed down a little declivity toward their foes; they discharged their weapons at the same instant and equally without success.

'I know'd it! and I said it!' muttered the scout, whirling the despised little implement over the falls with bitter disdain. 'Come on, ye bloody minded hell-hounds! ye meet a man without a cross!'

The words were barely uttered when he encountered a savage of gigantic stature and of the fiercest mien. At the same moment, Duncan found himself engaged with the other, in a similar contest of hand to hand. With ready skill, Hawkeye and his antagonist each grasped that uplifted arm of the other which held the dangerous knife. For near a minute they stood looking at one another in the eye and gradually exerting the power of their muscles for the mastery.

At length, the toughened sinews of the white man prevailed over the less practised limbs of the native. The arm of the latter slowly gave way before the increasing force of the scout, who, suddenly wresting his armed hand from the grasp of the foe, drove the sharp weapon through his naked bosom to the heart. In the meantime, Heyward had been pressed in a more deadly struggle. His slight sword was snapped in the first encounter. As he was destitute of any other means of defence, his safety now depended entirely on bodily strength and resolution. Though deficient in neither of these qualities, he had met an enemy every way his equal. Happily, he soon succeeded in disarming his adversary, whose knife fell on the rock at their feet; and from this moment it became a fierce struggle who should cast the other over the dizzy height into a neighbouring cavern of the falls. Every successive struggle brought them nearer to the

verge, where Duncan perceived the final and conquering effort must be made. Each of the combatants threw all his energies into that effort and the result was that both tottered on the brink of the precipice. Heyward felt the grasp of the other at his throat and saw the grim smile the savage gave, under the revengeful hope that he hurried his enemy to a fate similar to his own, as he felt his body slowly yielding to a resistless power, and the young man experienced the passing agony of such a moment, in all its horrors. At that instant of extreme danger, a dark hand and glancing knife appeared before him; the Indian released his hold, as the blood flowed freely from around the severed tendons of the wrist; and while Duncan was drawn backward by the saving arm of Uncas, his charmed eyes were still riveted on the fierce and disappointed countenance of his foe, who fell sullenly and disappointed down the irrecoverable precipice.

'To cover! to cover!' cried Hawkeye, who just then had despatched

the enemy; 'to cover, for your lives! The work is but half ended!'

The young Mohican gave a shout of triumph and, followed by Duncan, he glided up the acclivity they had descended to the combat, and sought the friendly shelter of the rocks and shrubs.

Chapter VIII

The warning call of the scout was not uttered without occasion. During the occurrence of the deadly encounter just related, the roar of the falls was unbroken by any human sound whatever. It would seem that interest in the result had kept the natives on the opposite shores in breathless suspense, while the quick evolutions and swift changes in the positions of the combatants effectually prevented a fire that might prove dangerous alike to friend and enemy. But the moment the struggle was decided, a yell arose as fierce and savage as wild and revengeful passions could throw into the air. It was followed by the swift flashes of the rifles, which sent their leaden messengers across the rock in volleys, as though the assailants would pour out their impotent fury on the insensible scene of the fatal contest.

A steady, though deliberate return was made from the rifle of Chingachgook, who had maintained his post throughout the fray with unmoved resolution. When the triumphant shout of Uncas was borne to his ears, the gratified father raised his voice in a single responsive cry, after which his busy piece alone proved that he still guarded his pass with unwearied diligence. In this manner many minutes flew by with the swiftness of thought.

'Let them burn their powder,' said the deliberate scout, while bullet after bullet whizzed by the place where he securely lay; 'the life lies low in a Mingo, and humanity teaches us to make a quick end of the sarpents.'

'That bullet was better aimed than common!' exclaimed Duncan, involuntarily shrinking from a shot which struck the rock at his side.

Hawkeye laid his hand on the shapeless metal and shook his head as he examined it, saying, 'Falling lead is never flattened, had it come from the clouds this might have happened.'

But the rifle of Uncas was deliberately raised towards the heavens, directing the eyes of his companions to a point, where the mystery was immediately explained. An oak grew on the right bank of the river, nearly opposite to their position, which, seeking the freedom of the open space, had inclined so far forward that its upper branches overhung that arm of the stream which flowed nearest its own shore. Among the topmost leaves, which scantily concealed the gnarled and stunted limbs, a savage was nestled, partly concealed by the tree and partly exposed, as though looking down upon them to ascertain the effect produced by his treacherous aim.

'These devils will scale heaven to circumvent us to our ruin,' said Hawkeye, 'keep him in play, boy, until I can bring "Killdeer" to bear, when we will try his metal on each side of the tree at once.'

Uncas delayed his fire until the scout uttered the word. The rifles flashed, the leaves and bark of the oak flew into the air and were scattered by the wind, but the Indian answered their assault by a taunting laugh, sending down upon them another bullet in return, that struck the cap of Hawkeye from his head. Once more the savage yells burst out of the woods and the leaden hail whistled above the heads of the besieged, as if to confine them to a place where they might become easy victims of the warrior who had mounted the tree.

'This must be looked to,' said the scout, glancing about him with an anxious eye. 'Uncas, call up your father; we have need of all our we'pons to bring the cunning varmint from his roost.'

The signal was instantly given, and before Hawkeye had reloaded his rifle they were joined by Chingachgook. When his son pointed out to the experienced warrior the situation of their dangerous enemy, the usual exclamatory 'hugh' burst from his lips; after which, no further expression of surprise or alarm was suffered to escape him. Hawkeye and the Mohicans conversed earnestly together in Delaware for a few moments, when each quietly took his post in order to execute the plan they had speedily devised.

The warrior in the oak had maintained a quick, though ineffectual fire, from the moment of his discovery. But his aim was interrupted by the vigilance of his enemies, whose rifles instantaneously bore on any part of his person that was left exposed. Still his bullets fell in the centre of the crouching party. The clothes of Heyward, which rendered him peculiarly conspicuous, were repeatedly cut, and once blood was drawn from a slight wound in his arm.

At length, emboldened by the long and patient watchfulness of his enemies, the Huron attempted a better and more fatal aim. The quick eyes of the Mohicans caught the dark line of his lower limbs incautiously exposed through the thin foliage, a few inches from the trunk of the tree. Their rifles made a common report, when, sinking on his wounded limb, part of the savage came into view. Swift as thought, Hawkeye seized the advantage and discharged his fatal weapon into the top of the oak. The leaves were unusually agitated; the dangerous rifle fell from its commanding elevation and after a few moments of vain struggling, the form of the savage was seen swinging in the wind, while he still grasped a ragged and naked branch of the tree with hands clenched in desperation.

'Give him, in pity give him the contents of another rifle,' cried Duncan, turning away his eyes in horror from the spectacle of a fellow creature in such awful jeopardy.

'Nat a karnel,' exclaimed the obdurate Hawkeye; 'his death is certain and we have no powder to spare, for Indian fights sometimes last for days; 'tis their scalps or ours! and God, who made us, has put into our natures the craving to keep the skin on the head.'

Against this stern and unyielding morality, supported as it was by such visible policy, there was no appeal. From that moment the yells in the forest once more ceased, the fire was suffered to decline and all eyes, those of friends as well as enemies, became fixed on the hopeless condition of the wretch who was dangling between heaven and earth. Three several times the scout raised the piece in mercy and as often, prudence getting the better of his intention, it was again silently lowered. At length one hand of the Huron lost its hold and dropped exhausted to his side. A desperate and fruitless struggle was seen for a fleeting instant, grasping wildly at the empty air. The lightning is not quicker than was the flame from the rifle of Hawkeye; the limbs of the victim trembled and contracted, the head fell to the bosom, and the body parted the foaming waters like lead, when the elements closed above it in its ceaseless velocity, and every vestige of the unhappy Huron was lost forever.

No shout of triumph succeeded this important advantage, but even the Mohicans gazed at each other in silent horror. A single yell burst from the woods and all was again still. Hawkeye, who alone appeared to reason on the occasion, shook his head at his own momentary weakness, even uttering his self-disapprobation aloud.

"Twas the last charge in my horn and the last bullet in my pouch, and 'twas the act of a boy!' he said; 'what mattered it whether he struck the rock living or dead! Feeling would soon be over. Uncas, lad, go down to the canoe and bring up the big horn; it was all the powder we have left and we shall need it to the last grain or I am ignorant of the Mingo nature.'

The young Mohican complied, leaving the scout turning over the useless contents of his pouch and shaking the empty horn with renewed discontent. From this unsatisfactory examination, however, he was soon called by a loud and piercing exclamation from Uncas, that sounded, even to the unpractised ears of Duncan, as the signal of some new and unexpected calamity. Every thought filled with apprehension for the previous treasure he had concealed in the cavern, the

young man started to his feet, totally regardless of the hazard he incurred by such an exposure. As if actuated by a common impulse, his movement was imitated by his friends, and together they rushed down the pass to the friendly chasm, with a rapidity that rendered the scattering fire of their enemies perfectly harmless. The unwonted cry had brought the sisters, together with the wounded David, from their place of refuge; and the whole party, at a single glance, was made acquainted with the nature of the disaster that had disturbed even the practised stoicism of their youthful Indian protector.

At a short distance from the rock, their little bark was to be seen floating across the eddy, toward the swift current of the river, in a manner which proved that its course was directed by some hidden agent. The instant this unwelcome sight caught the eye of the scout, his rifle was levelled as by instinct, but the barrel gave no answer to the bright sparks of the flint.

"Tis too late, 'tis too late!' Hawkeye exclaimed, ;'the miscreant has struck the rapid; and had we powder, it could hardly send the lead swifter than he now goes!'

The adventurous Huron raised his head above the shelter of the canoe and while it glided swiftly down the stream, he waved his hand, and gave forth the shout, which was the known signal of success. His cry was answered by a yell and a laugh from the woods, as tauntingly exulting as if fifty demons were uttering their blasphemies at the fall of some Christian soul.

'Well may you laugh, ye children of the devil!' said the scout, seating himself on a projection of the rock and suffering his gun to fall neglected at his feet, 'for the three quickest and truest rifles in these woods are no better than so many stalks of mullein or the last year's horns of a buck!'

'What is to be done?' demanded Duncan, losing the first feeling of disappointment in a more manly desire for exertion; 'what will become of us?'

Hawkeye made no other reply than by passing his finger around the crown of his head, in a manner so significant, that none who witnessed the action could mistake its meaning.

'Surely, surely, our case is not so desperate!' exclaimed the youth; 'the Hurons are not here; we may make good the caverns, we may oppose their landing.'

'With what?' coolly demanded the scout. 'The arrows of Uncas, or such tears as women shed! No, no; you are young, and rich, and have friends, and at such an age I know it is hard to die! But,' glancing his eyes at the Mohicans, 'let us remember we are men without a cross and let us teach these natives of the forest that white blood can run as freely as red, when the appointed hour is come.'

Duncan turned quickly in the direction indicated by the other's eyes and read a confirmation of his worst apprehensions in the conduct of the Indians. Chingachgook, placing himself in a dignified posture on another fragment of the rock had already laid aside his knife and tomahawk and was in the act of taking the eagle's plume from his head, and smoothing the solitary tuft of hair in readiness to perform its last and revolting office. His countenance was composed, though thoughtful, while his dark, gleaming eyes were gradually losing the fierceness of the combat in an expression better suited to the change he expected momentarily to undergo.

'Our case is not, cannot be so hopeless!' said Duncan; 'even at this very moment succour may be at hand. I see no enemies! They have sickened of a struggle in which they risk so much with so little prospect of gain!'

'It may be a minute, or it may be an hour, afore the wily sarpents

steal upon us, and it is quite in natur' for them to be lying within hearing at this very moment,' said Hawkeye; 'but come they will and in such a fashion as will leave us nothing to hope! Chingachgook' — he spoke in Delaware — 'my brother, we have fought our last battle together and the Maquas will triumph in the death of the sage man of the Mohicans and of the pale face, whose eyes can make night as day and level the clouds to the mists of the springs!'

'Why die at all!' said Cora, advancing from the place where natural horror had, until this moment, held her riveted to the rock; 'the path is open on every side; fly, then, to the woods, and call on God for succour. Go, brave men, we owe you too much already; let us no longer involve you in our hapless fortunes!'

'You but little know the craft of the Iroquois, lady, if you judge they have left the path open to the woods!' returned Hawkeye, who, however, immediately added in his simplicity, 'the down stream current, it is certain, might soon sweep us beyond the reach of their rifles or the sound of their voices.'

'Then try the river. Why linger to add to the number of the victims of our merciless enemies?'

'Why,' repeated the scout, looking about him proudly; 'because it is better for a man to die at peace with himself then to live haunted by an evil conscience! What answer could we give Munro, when he asked us where and how we left his children?'

'Go to him and say that you left them with a message to hasten to their aid,' returned Cora, advancing nigher to the scout in her generous ardour; 'that the Hurons bear them into the northern wilds, but that by vigilance and speed they may yet be rescued; and if, after all, it should please heaven that his assistance come too late, bear to him,' she continued, her voice gradually lowering, until it seemed nearly choked, 'the love, the blessings, the final prayers of his daughters and bid him not to mourn their early fate, but to look forward with humble confidence to the Christian's goal to meet his children.'

The hard, weather-beaten features of the scout began to work and when she had ended, he dropped his chin to his hand, like a man musing profoundly on the nature of the proposal.

'There is reason in her words!' at length broke from his compressed and trembling lips; 'and they bear the spirit of Christianity; what might be right and proper in a redskin, may be sinful in a man who has not even a cross in blood to plead for his ignorance. Chingachgook! Uncas! Hear you the talk of the dark-eyed woman?'

He now spoke in Delaware to his companions and his address, though calm and deliberate, seemed very decided. The elder Mohican heard with deep gravity and appeared to ponder on his words, as though he felt the importance of their import. After a moment of hesitation, he waved his hand in assent and uttered the word 'Good!' with the peculiar emphasis of his people. Then replacing his knife and tomahawk in his girdle, the warrior moved silently to the edge of the rock which was most concealed from the banks of the river. Here he paused a moment, pointed significantly to the woods below and, saying a few words in his own language, as if indicating his intended route, he dropped into the water, and sank from before the eyes of the witnesses of his movements.

The scout delayed his departure to speak to the generous girl, whose breathing became lighter as she saw the success of her remonstrance.

'Wisdom is sometimes given to the young, as well as to the old,' he said; 'and what you have spoken is wise, not to call it by a better word. If you are led into the woods, that is, such as you as may be spared for awhile, break the twigs on the bushes as you pass, and make the marks of your trail as broad as you can, when, if mortal eyes can see them, depend on having a friend who will follow to the ends of the 'arth afore he deserts you.'

He gave Cora an affectionate shake of the hand, lifted his rifle, after regarding it a moment with melancholy solicitude, laid it carefully aside, and descended to the place where Chingachgook had just disappeared. For an instant he hung suspended by the rock and looking about him, with a countenance of peculiar care, he added, bitterly, 'had the powder held out, this disgrace could never have befallen!' Then loosening his hold, the water closed above his head and he also became lost to view.

All eyes were now turned on Uncas, who stood leaning against the ragged rock, in immovable composure. After waiting a short time, Cora pointed down the river and said:

'Your friends have not been seen and are now, most probably, in safety. Is it not time for you to follow?'

'Uncas will stay,' the young Mohican calmly answered in English.

'To increase the horror of our capture and to diminish the chances of our release! Go, generous young man,' Cora continued, lowering her eyes under the gaze of the Mohican, and perhaps, with an intuitive consciousness of her power; 'go to my father, as I have said, and be the most confidential of my messengers. Tell him to trust you with the means to buy the freedom of his daughters. Go! 'Tis my wish, 'tis my prayer, that you will go!'

The settled, calm look of the young chief changed to an expression of gloom, but he no longer hesitated. With a noiseless step he crossed the rock and dropped into the troubled stream. Hardly a breath was drawn by those he left behind, until they caught a glimpse of his head emerging for air, far down the current, when he again sank and was seen no more.

These sudden and apparently successful experiments had all taken place in a few minutes of that time which had now become so precious. After a last look at Uncas, Cora turned, and with a quivering lip, addressed herself to Heyward:

'I have heard of your boasted skill in the water, too, Duncan,' she said; 'follow, then, the wise example set you by these faithful beings.'

'Is such the faith that Cora Munro would exact from her protector?' said the young man, smiling mournfully, but with bitterness.

'This is not a time for idle subtleties and false opinions,' she answered; 'but a moment when every duty should be equally considered. To us you can be of no further service here, but your precious life may be saved for other and nearer friends.'

He made no reply, though his eye fell wistfully on the beautiful form of Alice, who was clinging to his arm with the dependency of an infant.

'Consider,' continued Cora, after a pause, during which she seemed to struggle with a pang even more acute than any that her fears had excited, 'that the worst to us can be but death; a tribute that all must pay at the good time of God's appointment.'

'There are evils worse than death,' said Duncan, speaking hoarsely, and as if fretful at her importunity, 'but which the presence of one who would die in your behalf may avert.'

Cora ceased her entreaties; and veiling her face in her shawl, drew the nearly insensible Alice after her into the deepest recess of the inner cavern.

Chapter IX

The sudden and almost magical change, from the stirring incidents of the combat to the stillness that now reigned around him, acted on the heated imagination of Heyward like some exciting dream. While all the events he had witnessed remained deeply impressed on his memory, he felt a difficulty in persuading himself of their truth.

'The Hurons are not to be seen,' he said, addressing David, who had by no means recovered from the effects of the stunning blow he had received; 'let us conceal ourselves in the cavern and trust the rest to Providence.'

Suddenly a yell burst into the air without.

'We are lost!' exclaimed Alice, throwing herself into Cora's arms.

'Not yet, not yet,' returned the agitated but undaunted Heyward; 'the sound came from the centre of the island and it has been produced by the sight of their dead companions. We are not yet discovered and there is still hope.'

A second yell soon followed the first, when a rush of voices was heard pouring down the island, from its upper to its lower extremity, until they reached the naked rock above the caverns, where, after a shout of savage triumph, the air continued full of horrible cries and screams, such as man alone can utter and only he when in a state of the fiercest barbarity.

In the midst of this tumult, a triumphant yell was raised within a few yards of the hidden entrance to the cave. Heyward abandoned every hope, with the belief it was the signal that they were discovered. Again the impression passed away, as he heard the voices collect near the spot where the white man had so reluctantly abandoned his rifle. Amid the jargon of Indian dialects that he now plainly heard, it was easy to distinguish not only words, but sentences, in the patois of the Canadas. A burst of voices had shouted simultaneously, 'La Longue Carabine!' causing the opposite woods to re-echo with a name which, Heyward well remembered, had been given by his enemies to a celebrated hunter and scout of the English camp, and who, he now learned for the first time, had been his late companion.

'Now,' he whispered to the trembling sisters, 'now is the moment of uncertainty! If our place of retreat escapes this scrutiny, we are still safe! In every event, we are assured, by what has fallen from our enemies, that our friends have escaped and in two short hours we may look for succour from Webb.'

There were now a few minutes of fearful stillness, during which Heyward well knew that the savages conducted their search with greater vigilance and method. More than once he could distinguish their footsteps, as they brushed the sassafras, causing the faded leaves to rustle and the branches to snap. At length, the pile yielded a little, lighting a part of the cave. Cora folded Alice to her bosom in agony, and Duncan sprang to his feet. A shout was at that moment heard, as if issuing from the centre of the rock, announcing that the neighbouring cavern had at length been entered. In a minute, the number and loudness of the voices indicated that the whole party was collected in and around that secret place. As the inner passages to the two caves were so close to each other, Duncan, believing that escape was no longer possible, passed David and the sisters, to place himself between the latter and the first onset of the terrible meeting.

Grown desperate by his situation, he drew nigh the slight barrier which separated him only by a few feet from his relentless pursuers, and placing his face to the casual opening, he even looked out with a sort of desperate indifference on their movements.

Within reach of his arm was the brawny shoulder of a gigantic Indian, whose deep and authoritative voice appeared to give directions to the proceedings of his fellows. Beyond him again, Duncan could look into the vault opposite, which was filled with savages, upturning and rifling the humble furniture of the scout. The wound of David had dyed the leaves of sassafras with a colour that the natives well knew was anticipating the season. Over this sign of their success, they sent up a howl, like an opening from so many hounds who had recovered a lost trail. After this yell of victory, they tore up the fragrant bed of the cavern, and bore the branches into the chasm, scattering the boughs, as if they suspected them of concealing the person of the man they had so long hated and feared. One fierce and wild-looking

warrior approached the chief, bearing a load of the brush, and pointing exultingly to the deep red stains with which it was sprinkled,
uttered his joy in Indian yells, whose meaning Heyward was only
enabled to comprehend by the repetition of the name of 'La Longue
Carabine!' When his triumph had ceased, he cast the brush on the
slight heap Duncan had made before the entrance of the second cavern and closed the view. His example was followed by others, who, as
they drew the branches from the cave of the scout, threw them into
one pile, adding, unconsciously, to the security of those they sought.
The very slightness of the defence was its chief merit, for no one
thought of disturbing a mass of brush, which all of them believed, in
that moment of hurry and confusion, had been accidently raised by
the hands of their own party.

As the blankets yielded before the outward pressure and the
branches settled in the fissure of the rock by their own weight, forming a compact body, Duncan once more breathed freely. With a light
step and lighter heart, he returned to the centre of the cave and took
the place he had left, where he could command a view of the opening
next to the river. While he was in the act of making the movement,
the Indians, as if changing their purpose by a common impulse,
broke away from the chasm in a body, and were heard rushing up the
island again, toward the point whence they had originally descended.
Here another wailing cry betrayed that they were again collected
around the bodies of their dead comrades.

'They are gone, Cora!' he whispered; 'Alice, they are returned
whence they came and we are saved! To Heaven, that has alone delivered us from the grasp of so merciless an enemy, be all the praise!'

'Then to Heaven will I return my thanks!' exclaimed the younger
sister, rising from the encircling arm of Cora, and casting herself with
enthusiastic gratitude on the naked rock; 'to that Heaven who has
spared the tears of a gray-headed father; has saved the lives of those
I so much love.'

Both Heyward and the more tempered Cora witnessed the act of
involuntary emotion with powerful sympathy, the former secretly believing that piety had never worn a form so lovely as it had now as-

sumed in the youthful person of Alice. Her eyes were radiant with the glow of grateful feelings; the flush of her beauty was again seated on her cheeks, and her whole soul seemed ready and anxious to pour out its thanksgivings through the medium of her eloquent gestures. But where her lips moved, the words they should have uttered appeared frozen by some new and sudden chill. Her bloom gave place to the paleness of death; her soft and melting eyes grew hard and seemed contracting with horror; while those hands, which she had raised, clasped in each other, toward heaven, dropped in horizontal lines before her, the fingers pointed forward in convulsed motion. Heyward turned the instant she gave a direction to his suspicions and peering just above the ledge which formed the threshold of the open outlet of the cavern, he beheld the malignant, fierce and savage features of Le Renard Subtil.

In that moment of surprise, the self-possession of Heyward did not desert him. He observed by the vacant expression of the Indian's countenance, that his eye, accustomed to the open air, had not been yet able to penetrate the dusky light which pervaded the depth of the cavern. He had even thought of retreating beyond a curvature in the natural wall, which might still conceal him and his companions, when by the sudden gleam of intelligence that shot across the features of the savage, he saw it was too late, and that they were betrayed.

The look of exultation and brutal triumph which announced this terrible truth was irresistibly irritating. Forgetful of everything but the impulses of his hot blood, Duncan levelled his pistol and fired. The report of the weapon made the cavern bellow like an eruption from a volcano; and when the smoke it vomited had been driven away by the current of air which issued from the ravine, the place so lately occupied by the features of his treacherous guide was vacant. Rushing to the outlet, Heyward caught a glimpse of his dark figure stealing around a low and narrow ledge, which soon hid him entirely from sight.

Among the savages a frightful stillness succeeded the explosion, which had just been heard bursting from the bowels of the rock. But when Le Renard raised his voice in a long and intelligible whoop, it was answered by a spontaneous yell from the mouth of every Indian within hearing of the sound. The clamorous noises again rushed down the island; and before Duncan had time to recover from the shock, his feeble barrier of brush was scattered to the winds, the cavern was entered at both its extremities, and he and his companions were dragged from their shelter and borne into the day, where they stood surrounded by the whole band of the triumphant Hurons.

Chapter X

The instant the shock of this sudden misfortune had abated, Duncan began to make his observations on the appearance and proceedings of their captors. Contrary to the usages of the natives in the wantonness of their success they had respected, not only the persons of the trembling sisters, but his own. The ornaments of his military attire had indeed been repeatedly handled by different individuals of the tribe with eyes expressing a savage longing to possess the baubles; but before the customary violence could be resorted to, a mandate in the authoritative voice of the large warrior already mentioned, stayed the uplifted hand, and convinced Heyward that they were to be reserved for some object of particular moment.

While the others were busily occupied in seeking to gratify their childish passion for finery, by plundering even the miserable effects of the scout, or had been searching with such bloodthirsty vengeance in their looks for their absent owner, Le Renard had stood at a little distance from the prisoners, with a demeanour so quiet and satisfied, as to betray that he had already effected the grand purpose of his treachery. When the eyes of Heyward first met those of his recent guide, he turned them away in horror at the sinister though calm look he encountered. Conquering his disgust, however, he was able, with an averted face, to address his successful enemy.

'Le Renard Subtil is too much of a warrior,' said the reluctant Heyward, 'to refuse telling an unarmed man what his conquerors say.'

'They ask for the hunter who knows the paths through the woods,' returned Magua, in his broken English, laying his hand, at the same time, with a ferocious smile, on the bundle of leaves with which a wound on his own shoulder was bandaged. 'La Longue Carabine! His rifle is good and his eye never shut; but, like the short gun of the white chief, it is nothing against the life of Le Subtil.'

'Le Renard is too brave to remember the hurts received in war or the hands that gave them.'

'Was it war, when the tired Indian rested at the sugar tree to taste his corn! who filled the bushes with creeping enemies! who drew the knife! whose tongue was peace, while his heart was coloured with blood! Did Magua say that the hatchet was out of the ground and that his hand had dug it up?'

As Duncan dared not retort upon his accuser by reminding him of his unpremeditated treachery and disdained to deprecate his resentment by any words of apology, he remained silent. But the cry of 'La Longue Carabine' was renewed the instant the impatient savages perceived that the short dialogue was ended.

'You hear,' said Magua, with stubborn indifference; 'the Hurons call for the life of "The Long Rifle", or they will have the blood of them that keep him hid!'

'He is gone — escaped; he is far beyond their reach.'

Renard smiled with cold contempt, as he answered:

'When the white man dies, he thinks he is at peace; but the red men know how to torture even the ghosts of their enemies. Where is his body? Let the Hurons see his scalp.'

'He is not dead, but escaped.'

Magua shook his head incredulously.

'Is he a bird, to spread his wings; or is he a fish, to swim without air! The white chief reads in his books, and he believes the Hurons are fools!'

'Though no fish, "The Long Rifle" can swim. He floated down the stream when the powder was all burned and when the eyes of the Hurons were behind a cloud.'

'And why did the white chief stay?' demanded the still incredulous

Indian. 'Is he a stone that goes to the bottom, or does the scalp burn his head?'

'That I am not stone, your dead comrade, who fell into the falls, might answer, were the life still in him,' said the provoked young man, using, in his anger, that boastful language which was most likely to excite the admiration of an Indian. 'The white man thinks none but cowards desert their women.'

Magua muttered a few words, inaudibly, between his teeth, before he continued, aloud:

'Can the Delawares swim, too, as well as crawl in the bushes? Where is "Le Gros Serpent?"'

Duncan, who perceived by the use of these Canadian appellations, that his late companions were much better known to his enemies than to himself, answered: 'He also is gone down with the water.'

'"Le Cerf Agile" is not here?'

'I know not whom you call "The Nimble Deer,"' said Duncan, gladly profiting by any excuse to create delay.

'Uncas,' returned Magua, pronouncing the Delaware name with even greater difficulty than he spoke his English words. ' "Bounding Elk" is what the white man says, when he calls to the young Mohican.'

'Here is some confusion in names between us, Le Renard,' said Duncan, hoping to provoke a discussion. 'Daim is the French for deer, and cerf for stag, elan is the true term, when one would speak of an elk.'

'Yes,' muttered the Indian, in his native tongue; 'the pale faces are prattling women! They have two words for each thing, while a red-skin will make the sound of his voice speak for him.' Then changing his language, he continued, adhering to the imperfect nomenclature of his provincial instructors. 'The deer is swift, but weak; the elk is swift, but strong; and the son of "Le Serpent" is "Le Cerf Agile." Has he leaped the river to the woods?'

'If you mean the younger Delaware, he, too, has gone down with the water.'

As there was nothing improbable to an Indian in the manner of the escape, Magua admitted the truth of what he had heard, with a readiness that afforded additional evidence how little he would prize such worthless captives. With his companions, however, the feeling was manifestly different.

The Hurons had awaited the result of this short dialogue with characteristic patience, and with a silence that increased until there was a general stillness in the band. When Heyward ceased to speak, they turned their eyes, as one man, on Magua, demanding, in their expressive manner, an explanation of what had been said. Their interpreter pointed to the river, and made them acquainted with the result, as much by the action as by the words he uttered. When the fact was generally understood, the savages raised a frightful yell, which declared the extent of disappointment. Some ran furiously to the water's edge, beating the air with frantic gestures, while others spat upon the element, to resent the supposed treason it had committed against their acknowledged rights as conquerors. A few, and they not the least powerful and terrific of the band, threw lowering looks, in which the fiercest passion was only tempered by habitual self-command, at those captives who still remained in their power, while one or two even gave vent to their malignant feelings by the most menacing gestures, against which neither the sex nor the beauty of the sisters was any protection. The young soldier made a desperate but fruitless effort to spring to the side of Alice, when he saw the dark hand of a savage twisted in the rich tresses which were flowing in volumes over her shoulders, while a knife was passed around the head from which they feel, as if to denote the horrid manner in which it was about to be robbed of its beautiful ornament. But his hands were bound; and at the first movement he made, he felt the grasp of the powerful Indian who directed the band, pressing his shoulder like a vice. Immediately conscious how unavailing any struggle against such an overwhelming force must prove, he submitted to his fate, encouraging his gentle companions by a few low and tender assurances, that the natives seldom failed to threaten more than they performed.

But while Duncan resorted to these words of consolation to quiet the apprehensions of the sisters, he was not so weak as to deceive himself. He well knew that the authority of an Indian chief was so little conventional that it was oftener maintained by physical superiority than by any moral supremacy he might possess.

His apprehensions were, however, greatly relieved, when he saw that the leader had summoned his warriors to himself in counsel. Their deliberations were short and it would seem, by the silence of most of the party, the decision unanimous.

During this short conference, Heyward, finding a respite from his greater fears, had leisure to admire the cautious manner in which the Hurons had made their approaches, even after hostilities had ceased.

It has already been stated that the upper half of the island was a naked rock and destitute of any other defences than a few scattered logs of driftwood. They had selected this point to make their descent, having borne the canoe through the woods around the cataract for that purpose. Placing their arms in the little vessel, a half dozen men clinging to its sides had trusted themselves to the direction of the canoe, which was controlled by two skilful warriors, in attitudes that enabled them to command a view of the dangerous passage. Favoured by this arrangement, they touched the head of the island at that point which had proved so fatal to their first adventurers, but with the advantages of superior numbers and the possession of firearms. That such had been the manner of their descent was rendered quite apparent to Duncan; for they now bore the light bark from the upper end of the rock and placed it in the water, near the mouth of the outer cavern. When this change was made, the leader made signs to the prisoners to descend and enter.

As resistance was impossible and remonstrance useless, Heyward set the example of submission by leading the way into the canoe, where he was soon seated with the sisters and the still wondering David. Notwithstanding the Hurons were necessarily ignorant of the little channels among the eddies and rapids of the stream, they knew the common signs of such a navigation too well to commit any material blunder. When the pilot chosen for the task of guiding the canoe had taken his station, the whole band plunged again into the river, the vessel glided down the current and in a few moments the captives found themselves on the south bank of the stream, nearly opposite to the point where they had struck it the preceding evening.

Here was held another short but earnest consultation, during which the horses, to whose panic their owners ascribed their heaviest misfortune, were led from the cover of the woods and brought to the sheltered spot. The band now divided. The great chief so often mentioned, mounting the charger of Heyward, led the way directly across the river, followed by most of his people, and disappeared in the woods, leaving the prisoners in charge of six savages, at whose head was Le Renard Subtil. Duncan witnessed all their movements with renewed uneasiness.

He had been fond of believing, from the uncommon forbearance of the savages, that he was reserved as a prisoner to be delivered to Montcalm. As the thoughts of those who are in misery seldom slumber, and the invention is never more lively than when it is stimulated by hope, however feeble and remote, he had even imagined that the parental feelings of Munro were to be made instrumental in seducing him from his duty to the king. For though the French commander bore a high character for courage and enterprise, he was also thought to be expert in those political practices which do not always respect the nicer obligations of morality and which so generally disgraced the European diplomacy of that period.

All those busy and ingenious speculations were now annihilated by the conduct of his captors. That portion of the band who had followed the huge warrior took the route toward the foot of the Horican and no other expectation was left for himself and companions than that they were to be retained as hopeless captives by their savage conquerors.

When all were prepared, Magua made the signal to proceed, advancing in front to lead the party in person. Next followed David, who was gradually coming to a true sense of his condition, as the effects of the wound became less and less apparent. The sisters rode in his rear, with Heyward at their side, while the Indian flanked the party and brought up the close of the march, with a caution that seemed never to tire.

64

In this manner they proceeded in uninterrupted silence, except when Heyward addressed some solitary word of comfort to the females, or David gave vent to the moaning of his spirit, in piteous exclamations, which he intended should express the humility of resignation.

Cora alone remembered the parting injunctions of the scout and whenever an opportunity offered, she stretched forth her arm to bend aside the twigs that met her hands. But the vigilance of the Indians rendered this act of precaution both difficult and dangerous. She was often defeated in her purpose, by encountering their watchful eyes, when it became necessary to feign an alarm she did not feel and occupy the limb by some gesture of feminine apprehension. Once, and once only, was she completely successful; when she broke down the bough of a large sumach, and by a sudden thought let her glove fall at the same instant. This sign, intended for those that might follow, was observed by one of her conductors, who restored the glove, broke the remaining branches of the bush in such a manner that it appeared to proceed from the struggling of some beast in its branches, and then laid his hand on his tomahawk, with a look so significant, that it put an effectual end to these stolen memorials of their passage.

As there were horses, to leave the prints of their footsteps, in both bands of the Indians, this interruption cut off any probable hopes of assistance being conveyed through the means of their trail.

Heyward would have ventured a remonstrance had there been anything encouraging in the gloomy reserve of Magua. Whenever the eyes of the wearied travellers rose from the decayed leaves over which they trod, his dark form was to be seen glancing along the stems of the trees in front, his head immovably fastened in a forward position, with the light plume on his crest fluttering in a current of air, made solely by the swiftness of his own motion.

But all this diligence and speed were not without an object. After crossing a low vale, through which a gushing brook meandered, he suddenly ascended a hill, so steep and difficult of ascent that the sisters were compelled to alight in order to follow. When the summit was gained, they found themselves on a level spot, but thinly covered with trees, under one of which Magua had thrown his dark form, as if willing and ready to seek that rest which was so much needed by the whole party.

Chapter XI

Notwithstanding the swiftness of their flight, one of the Indians had found an opportunity to strike a straggling fawn an arrow and had borne the more preferable fragments of the victim, patiently on his shoulders, to the stopping place. Without any aid from the science of cookery, he was immediately employed in common with his fellows, in gorging himself with this digestible sustenance. Magua alone sat apart, without participating in the revolting meal, and apparently buried in the deepest thought.

This abstinence, so remarkable in an Indian, when he possessed the means of satisfying hunger, at length attracted the notice of Heyward.

The young man willingly believed that the Huron deliberated on the most eligible manner of eluding the vigilance of his associates. With a view to assist his plans by any suggestion of his own and to strengthen the temptation, he left the beech and straggled, as if without an object, to the spot where Le Renard was seated.

'Has not Magua kept the sun in his face long enough to escape all danger from the Canadians?' he asked, as though no longer doubtful of the good intelligence established between them; 'and will not the chief of William Henry be better pleased to see his daughters before another night may have hardened his heart to their loss, to make him less liberal in his reward?'

'Do the pale faces love their children less in the morning than at night?' asked the Indian coldly.

'By no means,' returned Heyward, anxious to recall his error, if he had made one; 'the white man may, and does often, forget the burial place of his fathers; he sometimes ceases to remember those he should love and has promised to cherish; but the affection of a parent for his child is never permitted to die.'

'And is the heart of the white-headed chief soft and will he think of the babes that his squaws have given him? He is hard on his warriors, and his eyes are made of stone.'

'He is severe to the idle and wicked, but to the sober and deserving he is a leader, both just and humane. I have known many fond and tender parents, but never have I seen a man whose heart was softer toward his child. You have seen the gray-head in front of his warriors, Magua; but I have seen his eyes swimming in water, when he spoke of those children who are now in your power!'

Heyward paused, for he knew not how to construe the remarkable expression that gleamed across the swarthy features of the attentive Indian. At first it seemed as if the remembrance of the promised reward grew vivid in his mind, while he listened to the sources of parental feeling which were to assure its possession; but as Duncan proceeded, the expression of joy became so fiercely malignant that it was impossible not to apprehend it proceeded from some passion more sinister than avarice.

'Go,' said the Huron, suppressing the alarming exhibition in an instant, in a death-like calmness of countenance; 'go to the dark-haired daughter and say, Magua waits to speak. The father will remember what the child promises.'

Duncan, who interrupted this speech to express a wish for some additional pledge that the promised gifts be not withheld, and reluctantly repaired to the place where the sisters were now resting from their fatigue, to communicate its purport to Cora.

'You understand the nature of an Indian's wishes,' he concluded, as he led her toward the place where she was expected, 'and must be prodigal of your offers of powder and blankets. Ardent spirits are, however, the most prized by such as he; nor would it be amiss to add some boon from your own hand, with that grace you so well know how to practice. Remember, Cora, that on your presence of mind and ingenuity, even your life, as well as that of Alice, may in some measure depend.'

'Heyward, and yours!'

'Mine is of little moment; it is already sold to my king, and is a prize to be seized by any enemy who may possess the power. I have no father to expect me, and but few friends to lament a fate which I have courted with the insatiable longing of youth after distinction. But hush! We approach the Indian. Magua, the lady with whom you wish to speak is here.'

The Indian rose slowly from his seat and stood for near a minute silent and motionless. He then signed with his hand for Heyward to retire, saying, coolly:

'When the Huron talks to the women, his tribes shut their ears.'

'You hear, Heyward, and delicacy at least should urge you to retire. Go to Alice and comfort her with our reviving prospects.'

She waited until he had departed and then turning to the native with the dignity of her sex in her voice and manner, she added: 'What would Le Renard say to the daughter of Munro?'

'Listen,' said the Indian, laying his hand firmly upon her arm, as if willing to draw her utmost attention to his words; a movement that Cora as firmly but quietly repulsed by extricating the limb from his grasp: 'Magua was born a chief and a warrior among the red Hurons of the lakes; he saw the suns twenty summers make the snows of twenty winters run off in the stream before he saw a pale face; and he was happy! Then his Canada fathers came into the woods and taught him to drink the fire water and he became a rascal. The Hurons drove him from the graves of his fathers, as they would chase the hunted buffalo. He ran down the shores of the lake, and followed their outlet to the "city of cannon." There he hunted and fished, till the people chased him again through the woods into the arms of his enemies. The chief, who was born a Huron, was at last a warrior among the Mohawks!'

'Something like this I had heard before,' said Cora, observing that he paused to suppress those passions which began to burn with too bright a flame, as he recalled the recollection of his supposed injuries.

'Was it the fault of Le Renard that his head was not made of rock? Who gave him the fire water? Who made him a villain? 'Twas the pale faces, the people of your own colour.'

'And am I answerable that thoughtless and unprincipled men exist, whose shades of countenance may resemble mine?' Cora calmly demanded of the excited savage.

'No; Magua is a man, and not a fool; such as you never open their lips to the burning stream; the Great Spirit has given you Wisdom!'

'What, then, have I to do, or say, in the matter of your misfortunes, not to say of your errors?'

'Listen,' repeated the Indian, resuming his earnest attitude; 'when his English and French fathers dug up the hatchet, Le Renard struck the war post of the Mohawks and went out against his own nation. The pale faces have driven the red skins from their hunting grounds, and now when they fight, a white man leads the way. The old chief at Horican, your father, was the great captain of our war party. He said to the Mohawks do this, and do that, and he was minded. He made a law that if an Indian swallowed the fire water and came into the cloth wigwams of his warriors, it should not be forgotten. Magua foolishly opened his mouth and the hot liquor led him into the cabin of Munro. What did the gray-head? Let his daughter say.'

THE LAST OF THE MOHICANS

'He forgot not his words and did justice by punishing the offender,' said the undaunted daughter.

'Justice!' repeated the Indian, casting an oblique glance of the most ferocious expression at her unyielding countenance; 'is it justice to make evil and then punish for it? Magua was not himself; it was the fire water that spoke and acted for him! But Munro did not believe it. The Huron chief was tied up before all the pale-faced warriors and whipped like a dog.'

Cora remained silent, for she knew not how to palliate this imprudent severity on the part of her father, in a manner to suit the comprehension of an Indian.

'See!' continued Magua, tearing aside the slight calico that very imperfectly concealed his painted breast; 'here are scars given by knives and bullets — of these a warrior may boast before his nation; but the grey-head has left marks on the back of the Huron chief that he must hide like a squaw, under this painted cloth of the whites.'

'I had thought,' resumed Cora, 'that an Indian warrior was patient and that his spirit felt not and knew not the pain his body suffered.'

'When the Chippewas tied Magua to the stake and cut this gash,' said the other, laying his finger on a deep scar, 'the Huron laughed in their faces and told them, Women struck so light! His spirit was then in the clouds! But when he felt the blows of Munro, his spirit lay under the birch. The spirit of a Huron is never drunk; it remembers forever!'

'But it may be appeased. If my father has done you this injustice, show him how an Indian can forgive an injury and take back his daughters. You have heard from Major Heyward —'

Magua shook his head, forbidding the repetition of offers he so much despised.

'What would you have?' continued Cora, after a most painful pause, while the conviction forced itself on her mind that the too sanguine and generous Duncan had been cruelly deceived by the cunning of the savage.

'What a Huron loves — good for good; bad for bad!'

'You would, then, revenge the injury inflicted by Munro on his helpless daughters. Would it not be more like a man to go before his face and take the satisfaction of a warrior?'

'The arms of the pale faces are long and their knives sharp!' returned the savage, with a malignant laugh; 'why should Le Renard go among the muskets of his warriors, when he holds the spirit of the grey-head in his hand?'

'Name your intention, Magua,' said Cora, struggling with herself to speak with steady calmness. 'Is it to lead us prisoners to the woods, or do you contemplate even some greater evil? Is there no reward, no means of palliating the injury and of softening your heart? At least, release my gentle sister and pour out all your malice on me. Purchase wealth by her safety and satisfy your revenge with a single victim. The loss of both his daughters might bring the aged man to his grave and where would then be the satisfaction of Le Renard!'

'Listen,' said the Indian again. 'The light eyes can go back to the Horican and tell the old chief what has been done, if the dark-haired woman will swear by the Great Spirit of her fathers to tell no lie.'

'What must I promise?' demanded Cora, still maintaining a secret ascendancy over the fierce native by the collected and feminine dignity of her presence.

'When Magua left his people his wife was given to another chief; he has now made friends with the Hurons and will go back to the graves of his tribe, on the shores of the great lake. Let the daughter of the English chief follow and live in his wigwam forever.'

However revolting a proposal of such a character might prove to Cora, she retained, notwithstanding her powerful disgust, sufficient self-command to reply, without betraying the weakness.

'And what pleasure would Magua find in sharing his cabin with a wife he did not love; one who would be of a nation and colour different from his own? It would be better to take the gold of Munro and buy the heart of some Huron maid with his gifts.'

The Indian made no reply for near a minute, but bent his fierce looks on the countenance of Cora, in such wavering glances, that her eyes sank with shame, under an impression that for the first time they had encountered an expression that no chaste female might endure.

While she was shrinking within herself, in dread of having her ears wounded by some proposal still more shocking than the last, the voice of Magua answered, in its tones of deepest malignancy:

'When the blows scorched the back of the Huron, he would know where to find a woman to feel the smart. The daughter of Munro would draw his water, hoe his corn and cook his venison. The body of the gray-head would sleep among his cannon, but his heart would lie within reach of the knife of Le Subtil.'

'Monster! Well dost thou deserve thy treacherous name,' cried Cora, in an ungovernable burst of filial indignation. 'None but a fiend could meditate such a vengeance. But thou overratest thy power! Thou shall find it is, in truth, the heart of Munro you hold and that it will defy your utmost malice!'

The Indian answered this bold defiance by a ghastly smile that showed an unaltered purpose, while he motioned her away, as if to close the conference forever. Cora, already regretting her precipitation, was obliged to comply, for Magua instantly left the spot and approached his gluttonous comrades. Heyward flew to the side of the agitated maiden and demanded the result of a dialogue that he had watched at a distance with so much interest. But unwilling to alarm the fears of Alice, she evaded a direct reply, betraying only by her countenance her utter want of success, and keeping her anxious looks fastened on the slightest movements of their captors. To the reiterated and earnest questions of her sister concerning their probable destination, she made no other answer than by pointing toward the dark group, with an agitation she could not control and murmuring as she folded Alice to her bosom:

'There, there; read our fortunes in their faces; we shall see; we shall see!'

The action, and the choked utterance of Cora, spoke more impressively than any words, and quickly drew the attention of her companions on that spot where her own was riveted with an intenseness that nothing but the importance of the stake could create.

When Magua reached the cluster of lolling savages who, gorged with their disgusting meal, lay stretched on the earth in brutal indulgence, he commenced speaking with the dignity of an Indian chief. The first syllables he uttered had the effect to cause his listeners to raise themselves in attitudes of respectful attention. As the Huron used his native language, the prisoners, notwithstanding the caution of the natives had kept them within the swing of their tomahawks, could only conjecture the substance of his harangue from the nature of those significant gestures with which an Indian always illustrates his eloquence.

At first, the language, as well as the action of Magua, appeared calm and deliberate. When he had succeeded in sufficiently awakening the attention of his comrades, Heyward fancied, by his pointing so frequently toward the direction of the great lakes, that he spoke of the land of their fathers and of their distant tribe. Frequent indications of applause escaped the listeners, who, as they uttered the expressive 'Hugh!' looked at each other in commendation of the speaker. Le Renard was too skilful to neglect his advantage. He spoke of the long and painful route by which they had left those spacious grounds and happy villages, to come and battle against the enemies of their Canadian fathers.

When he spoke of courage, their looks were firm and responsive; when he alluded to their injuries, their eyes kindled with fury; when he mentioned the taunts of the women, they dropped their heads in shame; but when he pointed out their means of vengeance, he struck a chord which never failed to thrill in the breast of an Indian. With the first intimation that it was within their reach, the whole band sprang upon their feet as one man; giving utterance to their rage in the most frantic cries, they rushed upon their prisoners in a body with drawn knives and uplifted tomahawks. Heyward threw himself between the sisters and the foremost, whom he grappled with a desperate strength that for a moment checked his violence. This unexpected resistance gave Magua time to interpose, and with rapid enunciation and animated gesture, he drew the attention of the band again to himself. In that language he knew so well how to assume, he diverted his comrades from their instant purpose, and invited them to prolong the misery of their victims. His proposal was received with acclamations, and executed with the swiftness of thought.

Two powerful warriors cast themselves on Heyward, while another was occupied in securing the less active singing master. Neither of the captives, however, submitted without a desperate though fruitless struggle. Even David hurled his assailant to the earth; nor was Heyward secured until the victory over his companions enabled the Indians to direct their united force to that object. He was then bound and fastened to the body of a pine tree. When the young soldier regained his recollection, he had the painful certainty before his eyes that a common fate was intended for the whole party. On his right was Cora in a durance similar to his own, pale and agitated, but with an eye whose steady look still read the proceedings of their enemies. On his left, the withes which bound her to a pine, performed that office for Alice which her trembling limbs refused, and alone kept her fragile form from sinking. Her hands were clasped before her in prayer, but instead of looking upward toward that power which alone could rescue them, her unconscious looks wandered to the countenance of Duncan with infantile dependency. David had contended, and the novelty of the circumstance held him silent.

The vengeance of the Huron had now taken a new direction. They prepared to execute it with that barbarous ingenuity with which they were familiarised by the practice of centuries. Some sought knots to raise the blazing pile; one was riveting the splinters of pine, in order to pierce the flesh of their captives with the burning fragments; and others bent the tops of two saplings to the earth, in order to suspend Heyward by the arms between the recoiling branches. But the vengeance of Magua sought a deeper and more malignant enjoyment.

While the less refined monsters of the band prepared, before the eyes of those who were to suffer, these well-known and vulgar means of torture, he approached Cora, and pointed out, with the most malign expression of countenance the speedy fate that awaited her:

'Ha!' he added, 'what says the daughter of Munro? Her head is too good to find a pillow in the wigwam of Le Renard; will she like it better when it rolls about this hill a plaything for the wolves? Her bosom cannot nurse the children of a Huron; she will see it spit upon by Indians!'

'What means the monster!' demanded the astonished Heyward.

'Nothing!' was the firm reply. 'He is a savage, a barbarous and ignorant savage and knows not what he does. Let us find leisure, with our dying breath, to ask for him penitence and pardon.'

'Pardon!' echoed the fierce Huron, mistaking in his anger the meaning of her words; 'the memory of an Indian is longer than the arm of the pale faces; his mercy shorter than their justice! Say; shall I send the yellow hair to her father and will you follow Magua to the great lakes, to carry his water and feed him with corn?'

Cora beckoned him away, with an emotion of disgust she could not control.

'Leave me,' she said, with a solemnity that for a moment checked the barbarity of the Indian; 'you mingle bitterness in my prayers; you stand between me and my God!'

The slight impression produced on the savage was, however, soon forgotten, and he continued pointing, with taunting irony, toward Alice.

'Look! The child weeps! She is young to die! Send her to Munro, to comb his grey hairs and keep life in the heart of the old man.'

Cora could not resist the desire to look upon her youthful sister, in whose eyes she met an imploring glance, that betrayed the longings of nature.

'What says he, dearest Cora?' asked the trembling voice of Alice. 'Did he speak of sending me to our father?'

For many moments the elder sister looked upon the younger, with a countenance that wavered with powerful and contending emotions. At length she spoke, though her tones had lost their rich and calm fullness, in an expression of tenderness that seemed maternal.

'Alice,' she said, 'the Huron offers us both life, nay, more than both; he offers to restore Duncan, our invaluable Duncan, as well as you, to our friends — to our father — to our heart-stricken, childless father, if I will bow down this rebellious, stubborn pride of mine and consent —'

Her voice became choked, and clasping her hands, she looked upward, as if seeking, in her agony, intelligence from a wisdom that was infinite.

'Say on,' cried Alice; 'to what, dearest Cora? Oh! that the proffer were made to me! to save you, to cheer our aged father, to restore Duncan; how cheerfully could I die!'

'Die!' repeated Cora, with a calmer and firmer voice, 'that were easy! Perhaps the alternative may not be less so. He would have me,' she continued, her accents sinking under a deep consciousness of the degradation of the proposal 'follow him to the wilderness: go to the habitations of the Hurons; to remain there; in short, to become his wife! Speak, then, Alice; child of my affections! sister of my love! And you, too, Major Heyward, aid my weak reason with your counsel. Is life to be purchased by such a sacrifice? Will you, Alice, receive it at my hands at such a price? And you, Duncan, guide me; control me between you; for I am wholly yours!'

'Would I!' echoed the indignant and astonished youth. 'Cora! Cora! You jest with our misery! Name not the horrid alternative again; the thought itself is worse than a thousand deaths.'

'That such would be your answer, I well knew!' exclaimed Cora, her cheeks flushing and her dark eyes once more sparkling with the lingering emotions of a woman. 'What says my Alice? For her will I submit without another murmur.'

Although both Heyward and Cora listened with painful suspense and the deepest attention, no sounds were heard in reply. It appeared as if the delicate and sensitive form of Alice would shrink into itself, as she listened to this proposal. In a few moments, however, her head began to move slowly, in a sign of deep, unconquerable disapprobation.

'No, no, no; better that we die as we have lived, together!'

'Then die!' shouted Magua, hurling his tomahawk with violence at the unresisting speaker and gnashing his teeth with a rage that could no longer be bridled, at this sudden exhibition of firmness in the one he believed the weakest of the party. The axe cleaved the air in front of Heyward, and cutting some of the flowing ringlets of Alice, quiv-

ered in the tree above her head. The sight maddened Duncan to desperation. Collecting all his energies in one effort, he snapped the twigs which bound him and rushed upon another savage, who was preparing, with loud yells and a more deliberate aim, to repeat the blow. They encountered, grappled, and fell to the earth together. The naked body of his antagonist afforded Heyward no means of holding his adversary, who glided from his grasp and rose again with one knee on his chest, pressing him down with the weight of a giant. Duncan already saw the knife gleaming in the air, when a whistling sound swept past him and was rather accompanied than followed by the sharp crack of a rifle. He felt his breast relieved from the load it had endured; he saw the savage expression of his adversary's countenance change to a look of vacant wildness, when the Indian fell dead on the faded leaves by his side.

Chapter XII

The Hurons stood aghast at this sudden visitation of death on one of their band. But as they regarded the fatal accuracy of an aim which had dared to immolate an enemy at so much hazard to a friend, the name of 'La Longue Carabine' burst simultaneously from every lip and was succeeded by a wild and a sort of plaintive howl. The cry was answered by a loud shout from a little thicket, where the incautious party had piled their arms; and at the next moment, Hawkeye, too eager to load the rifle he had regained, was seen advancing upon them, brandishing the clubbed weapon and cutting the air with wide and powerful sweeps. Bold and rapid as was the progress of the scout, it was exceeded by that of a light and vigorous form which, bounding past him, leaped, with incredible activity and daring, into the very centre of the Hurons, where it stood, whirling a tomahawk and flourishing a glittering knife, with fearful menaces in front of Cora. Quicker than the thoughts could follow those unexpected and audacious movements, an image, armed in the emblematic panoply of death, glided before their eyes and assumed a threatening attitude at the other's side. The savage tormentors recoiled before these warlike intruders and uttered, as they appeared in such quick succession, the often repeated and peculiar exclamations of surprise, followed by the well-known and dreaded appellations of:

'Le Cerf Agile! Le Gros Serpent!'

But the wary and vigilant leader of the Hurons was not so easily disconcerted. Casting his keen eyes around the little plain, he comprehended the nature of the assault at a glance, and encouraging his followers by his voice as well as by his example, he unsheathed his long and dangerous knife, and rushed with a loud whoop upon the expecting Chingachgook. It was the signal for a general combat. Neither party had firearms and the contest was to be decided in the deadliest manner, with weapons of offence, and none of defence.

Uncas answered the whoop and leaping on an enemy, with a well-directed blow of his tomahawk, cleft him to the brain. Heyward tore the weapon of Magua from the pine and rushed eagerly toward the fray. As the combatants were now equal in number, each singled an opponent from the adverse band. The rush and blows passed with the fury of a whirlwind and the swiftness of lightning.

When Uncas had brained his first antagonist, he turned like a hungry lion, to seek another. The fifth and only Huron disengaged at the first onset had paused a moment and then seeing that all around him were employed in the deadly strife, he had sought, with hellish vengeance, to complete the work of revenge. Raising a shout of triumph, he sprang toward the defenceless Cora, sending his keen axe as the dreadful precursor of his approach. The tomahawk grazed her shoulder and cutting the withes which bound her to the tree, left the maiden at liberty to fly. She eluded the grasp of the savage, and reckless of her own safety threw herself on the bosom of Alice, striving with convulsed and ill-directed fingers to tear assunder the twigs which confined the person of her sister. Any other than a monster would have relented at such an act of generous devotion to the best and purest affection; but the breast of the Huron was a stranger to sympathy. Seizing Cora by the rich tresses which fell in confusion about her form, he tore her from her frantic hold and bowed her down with brutal violence to her knees. The savage drew the flowing curls through his hand and raising them on high with an outstretched arm, passed the knife around the exquisitely moulded head of his victim, with a taunting and exulting laugh. But he purchased this moment of fierce gratification with the loss of the fatal opportunity. It was just then the sight caught the eye of Uncas. Bounding from his footsteps he appeared for an instant darting through the air and descending in a ball he fell on the chest of his enemy, driving him many yards from the spot, headlong and prostrate. The violence of the exertion cast the young Mohican at his side. They arose together, fought and bled, each in his turn. But the conflict was soon decided; the tomahawk of Heyward and the rifle of Hawkeye descended on the skull of the Huron, at the same moment that the knife of Uncas reached his heart.

The battle was now entirely terminated with the exception of the protracted struggle between 'Le Renard Subtil' and 'Le Gros Serpent'. Suddenly darting on each other, they closed and came to the earth, twisted together like twining serpents, in pliant and subtle folds. Urged by the different motives of filial affection, friendship and gratitude, Heyward and his companions rushed with one accord to the place, encircling the little canopy of dust which hung above the warriors. In vain did Uncas dart around the cloud, with a wish to strike his knife into the heart of his father's foe; the threatening rifle of Hawkeye was raised and suspended in vain, while Duncan endeavoured to seize the limbs of the Huron with hands that appeared to have lost their power. Covered as they were with dust and blood, the swift evolutions of the combatants seemed to incorporate their bodies into one. The Mohican now found an opportunity to make a powerful thrust with his knife; Magua suddenly relinquished his grasp and fell backward without motion and seemingly without life. His adversary leaped on his feet, making the arches of the forest ring with the sounds of triumph.

'Well done for the Delawares! Victory to the Mohicans!' cried Hawkeye, once more elevating the butt of the long and fatal rifle;

'a finish blow from a man without a cross will never tell against his honour, nor rob him of his right to the scalp.'

But at the very moment when the dangerous weapon was in the act of descending, the subtle Huron rolled swiftly from beneath the danger, over the edge of the precipice and, falling on his feet, was seen leaping, with a single bound, into the centre of a thicket of low bushes, which clung along its sides. The Delawares, who had believed their enemy dead, uttered their exclamation of surprise, and were following with speed and clamour, like hounds in open view of the deer, when a shrill and peculiar cry from the scout instantly changed their purpose and recalled them to the summit of the hill.

''Twas like himself!' cried the inveterate forester, whose prejudices contributed so largely to veil his natural sense of justice in all matters which concerned the Mingoes; 'a lying and deceitful varlet as he is. An honest Delaware now, being fairly vanquished, would have lain still and been knocked on the head, but these knavish Maquas cling to life like so many cats-o'-the-mountain. Let him go — let him go; 'tis but one man, and he without rifle or bow, many a long mile from his French commerades; and like a rattler that has lost his fangs, he can do no further mischief until such time as he, and we too, may leave the prints of our moccasins over a long reach of sandy plain. See, Uncas,' he added, in Delaware, 'your father is flaying the scalps already. It may be well to go round and feel the vagabonds that are left, or we may have another of them loping through the woods and screeching like a jay that has been winged.'

So saying the honest but implacable scout made the circuit of the dead, into whose senseless bosoms he thrust his long knife, with as much coolness as though they had been so many brute carcasses. He had, however, been anticipated by the elder Mohican, who had already torn the emblems of victory from the unresisting heads of the slain.

But Uncas, denying his habits, we had almost said his nature, flew with instinctive delicacy, accompanied by Heyward, to the assistance of the females, and quickly releasing Alice, placed her in the arms of Cora. We shall not attempt to describe the gratitude to the Almighty

Disposer of events which glowed in the bosoms of the sisters who were thus unexpectedly restored to life and to each other. As Alice rose from her knees, where she had sunk by the side of Cora, she threw herself on the bosom of the latter, and sobbed aloud the name of their aged father, while her soft, dove-like eyes sparkled with the rays of hope.

'We are saved! We are saved!' she murmured; 'to return to the arms of our dear, dear father, and his heart will not be broken with grief. And you, too, Cora, my sister, my more than sister, my mother; you, too, are spared. And Duncan,' she added, looking round upon the youth with a smile, 'even our own brave and noble Duncan has escaped without a hurt.'

To these ardent and nearly inco-
herent words Cora made no other
answer than by straining the youthful speaker to her heart, as she bent
over her in melting tenderness. The
manhood of Heyward felt no shame
in dropping tears over this spectacle
of affectionate rapture; and Uncas
stood, fresh and blood-stained from
the combat, a calm and apparently
an unmoved looker-on, it is true,
but with eyes that had already lost
their fierceness, and were beaming
with a sympathy that elevated him
far above the intelligence and ad-

vanced him probably centuries beyond the practices of his nation.

During this display of emotions so natural in their situation, Hawkeye, whose vigilant distrust had satisfied itself that the Hurons, who disfigured the heavenly scene, no longer possessed the power to interrupt its harmony, approached David, and liberated him from the bonds he had, until that moment, endured with the most exemplary patience.

'There,' exclaimed the scout, casting the last withe behind him, 'you are once more master of your own limbs, though you seem not to use them with much greater judgment than that in which they were first fashioned. If advice from one who is not older than yourself, but who, having lived most of his time in the wilderness, may be said to have experience beyond his years, will give no offence, you are welcome to my thoughts; and these are to part with the little tooting instrument in your jacket to the first fool you meet with and buy some we'pon with the money, if it be only the barrel of a horseman's pistol. By industry and care, you might thus come to some prefarment; for by this time, I should think, your eyes would plainly tell you that a carrion crow is a better bird than a mocking thresher. The one will, at least, remove foul sights from before the face of man, while the other is only good to brew disturbances in the woods, by cheating the ears of all that hear them.'

'Arms and the clarion for the battle, but the song of thanksgiving to the victory!' answered the liberated David. 'I invite you, friends, to join in praise for this signal deliverance from the hands of barbarians and infidels, to the comfortable and solemn tones of the tune called "Northampton."'

The scout shook his head, and muttering some unintelligible words, walked away to collect and examine into the state of the captured arsenal of the Hurons. Even Heyward and David were furnished with weapons; nor was ammunition wanting to render them all effectual.

When the foresters had made their selection and distributed their prizes, the scout announced that the hour had arrived when it was necessary to move. By this time the song of Gamut had ceased and the sisters had learned to still the exhibition of their emotions. Aided by Duncan and the younger Mohican, the two latter descended the precipitous sides of that hill which they had so lately ascended under so very different circumstances and whose summit had so nearly proved the scene of their massacre. At the foot they found their Narragansetts browsing the herbage of the bushes, and having mounted, they followed the movements of a guide, who, in the most deadly straits, had so often proved himself their friend. The journey was, however, short. Hawkeye, leaving the blind path that the Hurons had followed, turned short to his right, and entering the thicket, he crossed a babbling brook, and halted in a narrow dell under the shade of a few water elms. Their distance from the base of the fatal hill was but a few rods, and the steeds had been serviceable only in crossing the shallow stream.

The scout and the Indians appeared to be familiar with the sequestered place where they now were; for, leaning their rifles against the trees, they commenced throwing aside the dried leaves and opening the blue clay, out of which a clear and sparkling spring of bright, glancing water quickly bubbled. The white man then looked about him, as though seeking for some object which was not to be found as readily as he expected.

'Them careless imps, the Mohawks, with their Tuscarora and Onandaga brethren, have been here slaking their thirst,' he muttered, 'and the vagabonds have thrown away the gourd! This is the way with benefits, when they are bestowed on such disremembering hounds! Here has the Lord laid his hand, in the midst of the howling wilderness, for their good, and raised a fountain of water from the bowels of the 'arth, that might laugh at the richest shop of apothecary's ware in all the colonies; and see! The knaves have trodden in the clay and deformed the cleanliness of the place, as though they were brute beasts, instead of human men.'

Uncas silently extended toward him the desired gourd, which the spleen of Hawkeye had hitherto prevented him from observing, on a branch of an elm. Filling it with water, he retired a short distance to a place where the ground was more firm and dry; here he coolly seated himself, and after taking a long and apparently a grateful draught, he commenced a very strict examination of the fragments of food left by the Hurons, which had hung in a wallet on his arm.

'Thank you,' he continued, returning the empty gourd to Uncas; 'now we will see how these rampaging Hurons lived, when outlying in ambushments. Look at this! The varlets know the better pieces of the deer; and one would think they might carve and roast a saddle, equal to the best cook in the land! But everything is raw, for them Iroquois are thorough savages. Uncas, take my steel and kindle a fire, a mouthful of a tender broil will give nature a helping hand after so long a trail.'

Heyward, perceiving that their guides now set about their repast in sober earnest, assisted the ladies to alight and placed himself at their side, not unwilling to enjoy a few moments of grateful rest after the bloody scene he had just gone through. While the culinary process was in hand, curiosity induced him to inquire into the circumstances which had led to their timely and unexpected rescue.

'How is it that we see you so soon, my generous friend,' he asked, 'and without aid from the garrison of Edward?'

'Had we gone to the bend in the river, we might have been in time to rake the leaves over your bodies, but too late to have saved your scalps,' coolly answered the scout. 'No, no; instead of throwing away strength and opportunity by crossing to the fort, we lay by, under the bank of the Hudson, waiting to watch the movements of the Hurons.'

'You were, then, witnesses of all that passed?'

'Not of all; for Indian sight is too keen to be easily cheated, and we kept close. A difficult matter it was, too, to keep this Mohican boy snug in the ambushment. Ah! Uncas, Uncas, your behaviour was more like that of a curious woman than of a warrior on his scent.'

Uncas permitted his eyes to turn for an instant on the sturdy countenance of the speaker, but he neither spoke nor gave any indication of repentance.

'You saw our capture?' Heyward next demanded.

'We heard it,' was the significant answer. 'An Indian yell is plain language to men who have passed their days in the woods. But when you landed, we were driven to crawl like sarpents, beneath the leaves; and then we lost sight of you entirely, until we clapped eyes on you again trussed to the trees and ready for an Indian massacre.'

'Our rescue was the deed of Providence. It was nearly a miracle that you did not mistake the path, for the Hurons divided and each band had its horses.'

'Ay! There we were thrown off the scent and might, indeed, have lost the trail had it not been for Uncas; we took the path, however, that led into the wilderness; for we judged, and judged rightly, that the savages would hold that course with their prisoners. But when we had followed it for many miles, without finding a single twig broken, as I had advised, my mind misgave me; especially as all the footsteps had the prints of moccasins.'

'Our captors had the precaution to see us shod like themselves,' said Duncan, raising a foot and exhibiting the buckskin he wore.

'Aye, 'twas judgmatical, and like themselves; though we were too expart to be thrown from a trail by so common an invention.'

'To what, then, are we indebted for our safety?'

'To what, as a white man who has no taint of Indian blood, I should be ashamed to own; to the judgment of the young Mohicans, in matters which I should know better than he, but which I can now hardly believe to be true, though my own eyes tell me it is so.'

''Tis extraordinary! Will you not name the reason?'

'Uncas was bold enough to say that the beasts ridden by the gentle ones,' continued Hawkeye, glancing his eyes, not without curious interest, on the fillies of the ladies, 'planted the legs of one side on the ground at the same time, which is contrary to the movements of all trotting four-footed animals of my knowledge, except the bear. And yet here are horses that always journey in this manner, as my own eyes have seen and as their trail has shown for twenty long miles.'

''Tis the merit of the animal! They come from the shores of Narragansett Bay, in the small province of Providence Plantations, and are celebrated for their hardihood and the ease of this peculiar movement; though other horses are not unfrequently trained to the same.'

'It may be—it may be,' said Hawkeye, who had listened with singular attention to this explanation; 'though I am a man who has the full blood of the whites, my judgment in deer and beaver is greater than in beasts of burden. Major Effingham has many noble chargers, but I have never seen one travel after such a sideling gait.'

'True; for he would value the animals for very different properties. Still is this a breed highly esteemed, and as you witness, much honoured with the burdens it is often destined to bear.'

The Mohicans had suspended their operations about the glittering fire to listen; and when Duncan had done, they looked at each other significantly, the father uttering the never failing exclamation of surprise. The scout ruminated, like a man digesting his newly-acquired knowledge, and once more stole a curious glance at the horses.

'I dare to say there are even stranger sights to be seen in the settlements!' he said, at length; 'natur' is sadly abused by man, when he once gets the mastery. But, go sideling or go straight, Uncas had seen the movement and their trail led us on to the broken bush. The outer branch, near the prints of one of the horses, was bent upward, as a lady breaks a flower from its stem, but all the rest were ragged and broken down, as if the strong hand of a man had been tearing them! So I concluded that the cunning varments had seen the twig bent, and had torn the rest, to make us believe a buck had been feeling the boughs with his antlers.'

'I do believe your sagacity did not deceive you; for some such thing occurred!'

'That was easy to see,' added the scout, in no degree conscious of having exhibited any extraordinary sagacity; 'and a very different matter it was from a waddling horse! It then struck me the Mingoes would push for this spring, for the knaves well know the vartue of its waters!'

'Is it then so famous?' demanded Heyward, examining with a more curious eye the secluded dell with its bubbling fountain, surrounded, as it was, by earth of a deep, dingy brown.

'Few red skins who travel south and east of the great lakes but have heard of its qualities. Will you taste for yourself?'

Heyward took the gourd, and after swallowing a little of the water, threw it aside with grimaces of discontent. The scout laughed in his silent but heartfelt manner and shook his head with vast satisfaction.

'Ah! You want the flavour that one gets by habit, the time was when I liked it as little as yourself; but I have come to my taste, and I now crave it as a deer does the licks. Your high-spiced wines are not better than a red skin relishes this water; especially when his natur' is ailing. But Uncas has made his fire and it is time we think of eating, for our journey is long and all before us.'

Interrupting the dialogue by this abrupt transition, the scout had instant recourse to the fragments of food which had escaped the voracity of the Hurons. A very summary process completed the

simple cookery, when he and the Mohicans commenced their humble meal, with the silence and characteristic diligence of men who ate in order to enable themselves to endure great and unremitting toil.

When this necessary, and, happily, grateful duty had been performed, each of the foresters stooped and took a long and parting draught at that solitary and silent spring, around which and its sister fountains, within fifty years, the wealth, beauty and talents of a hemisphere were to assemble in throngs, in pursuit of health and pleasure. Then Hawkeye announced his determination to proceed. The sisters resumed their saddles; Duncan and David grasped their rifles and followed on their footsteps; the scout leading the advance and the Mohicans bringing up the rear. The whole party moved swiftly through the narrow path toward the north, leaving the healing waters to mingle unheeded with the adjacent brooks and the bodies of the dead to fester on the neighbouring mount without the rites of sepulchre, a fate but too common to the warriors of the woods to excite either commiseration or comment.

Chapter XIII

The route taken by Hawkeye lay across those sandy plains, relieved by occasional valleys and swells of land, which had been traversed by their party on the morning of the same day, with the baffled Magua for their guide. The sun had now fallen low toward the distant mountains; and as their journey lay through the interminable forest, the heat was no longer oppressive. Their progress, in consequence, was proportionate; and long before the twilight gathered about them, they had made good many toilsome miles on their return.

While the eyes of the sisters were endeavouring to catch glimpses through the trees of the flood of golden glory which formed a glittering halo around the sun, tinging here and there with ruby streaks, or bordering with narrow edgings of shining yellow, a mass of clouds that lay piled at no great distance above the western hills, Hawkeye turned suddenly, and pointing upward toward the gorgeous heavens, he spoke:

'Yonder is the signal given to man to seek his food and natural rest,' he said; 'better and wiser would it be, if he could understand the signs of nature and take a lesson from the fowls of the air and the beasts of the fields! Our night, however, will soon be over; for with the moon we must be up and moving again. I remember to have fou't the Maquas, here-aways, in the first war in which I ever drew blood from man; and we threw up a work of blocks to keep the ravenous varments from handling our scalps. If my marks do not fail me, we shall find the place a few rods further to our left.'

Without waiting for an assent, or indeed, for any reply, the sturdy hunter moved boldly into a dense thicket of young chestnuts, shoving aside the branches of the exuberant shoots which nearly covered the ground, like a man who expected, at each step, to discover some object he had formerly known. The recollection of the scout did not deceive him. After penetrating through the brush, matted as it was with briers, for a few hundred feet, he entered an open space, that surrounded a low, green hillock, which was crowned by the decayed blockhouse in question. This rude and neglected building was one of those deserted works which, having been thrown up in an emergency, had been abandoned with the disappearance of danger, and was now quietly crumbling in the solitude of the forest, neglected and forgotten, like the circumstances which had caused it to be reared.

A spring, which many years before had induced the natives to select the place for their temporary fortification, was soon cleared of leaves and a fountain of crystal gushed from the bed, diffusing its waters over the verdant hillock. A corner of the building was then roofed in such a manner as to exclude the heavy dew of the climate and piles of sweet shrubs and dried leaves were laid beneath it for the sisters to repose on.

While the diligent woodsmen were employed in this manner, Cora and Alice partook of that refreshment which duty required more than inclination prompted them to accept. They then retired within the walls and soon sank into those slumbers which nature so imperiously demanded, and which were sweetened by hopes for the morrow. Duncan had prepared himself to pass the night in watchfulness near them, just without the ruin, but the scout, perceiving his intention, pointed toward Chingachgook, as he coolly disposed his own person on the grass, and said:

'The eyes of a white man are too heavy and too blind for such a watch as this! The Mohicans will be our sentinel, so let us sleep.'

'I proved myself a sluggard on my post during the past night,' said Heyward, 'and have less need of repose than you, who did more credit to the character of a soldier. Let all the party seek their rest then, while I hold the guard.'

'If we lay among the white tents of the 60th and in front of an en-emy like the French, I could not ask for a better watchman,' returned the scout; 'but in the darkness and among the signs of the wilderness your judgment would be like the folly of a child and your vigilance thrown away. Do then, like Uncas and myself, sleep, and sleep in safety.'

Heyward perceived, in truth, that the younger Indian had thrown his form on the other side of the hillock while they were talking, like one who sought to make the most of the time allotted to rest and that his example had been followed by David, whose voice literally 'clove to his jaws', with the fever of his wound, heightened, as it was, by their toilsome march. Unwilling to prolong a useless discussion, the young man affected to comply by posting his back against the logs of the block house, in a half recumbent posture, though resolutely deter-mined in his own mind not to close an eye until he had delivered his precious charges into the arms of Munro himself. Hawkeye, believing he had prevailed, soon fell asleep, and a silence as deep as the solitude in which they had found it pervaded the retired spot.

For many minutes Duncan succeeded in keeping his senses on the alert and alive to every moaning sound that arose from the forest. At length, however, the mournful notes of the whip-poor-will became blended with the moanings of an owl; his heavy eyes occasionally sought the bright rays of the stars and he then fancied he saw them through the fallen lids. At instants of momentary wakefulness he mis-took a bush for his associate sentinel; his head next sank upon his shoulder, which, in its turn, sought the support of the ground; and finally his whole person became relaxed and pliant and the young man sank into a deep sleep, dreaming that he was a knight of ancient chivalry holding his midnight vigils before the tent of a recaptured princess, whose favour he did not despair of gaining by such a proof of devotion and watchfulness.

How long the tired Duncan lay in this insensible state he never knew himself, but his slumbering visions had been long lost in total forgetfulness, when he was awakened by a light tap on the shoulder. Aroused by this signal, slight as it was, he sprang upon his feet with a confused recollection of the self-imposed duty he had assumed with the commencement of the night.

'Who comes?' he demanded, feeling for his sword, at the place where it was usually suspended. 'Speak! Friend or enemy?'

'Friend,' replied the low voice of Chingachgook; who, pointing upward at the luminary which was shedding its mild light through the opening in the trees directly on their bivouac, immediately added in his rude English: 'Moon comes and white man's fort far—far off; time to move, while sleep shuts both eyes of the Frenchmen!'

'You say true! Call up your friends and bridle the horses while I prepare my own companions for the march!'

'We are awake, Duncan,' said the soft, silvery tones of Alice within the building, 'and ready to travel very fast after so refreshing a sleep; but you have watched through the tedious night in our behalf, after having endured so much fatigue the livelong day!'

'Say, rather, I would have watched, but my treacherous eyes betrayed me; twice have I proved myself unfit for the trust I bear.'

The young man was relieved from the awkwardness of making any further protestations of his own demerits, by an exclamation from Chingachgook, and the attitude of riveted attention assumed by his son.

'The Mohicans hear an enemy!' whispered Hawkeye, who, by this time, in common with the whole party, was awake and stirring. 'They scent danger in the wind!'

'God forbid!' exclaimed Heyward. 'Surely we have had enough of bloodshed!'

While he spoke, however, the young soldier seized his rifle, and advancing toward the front, prepared to atone for his venial remissness by freely exposing his life in defence of those he attended.

''Tis some creature of the forest prowling around us in quest of food,' he said, in a whisper, as soon as the low and apparently distant sounds which had startled the Mohicans reached his own ears.

'Hist!' returned the attentive scout; ''tis man; even I can now tell his tread, poor as my senses are when compared to an Indian's! That Scampering Huron has fallen in with one of Montcalm's outlying parties and they have struck upon our tent. I shouldn't like, myself, to spill more human blood in this spot,' he added, looking around with anxiety in his features at the dim objects by which he was surrounded; 'but what must be, must! Lead the horses into the block-house, Uncas; and friends, do you follow to the same shelter. Poor and old as it is, it offers a cover and has rung with the crack of a rifle afore to-night!'

He was instantly obeyed, the Mohicans leading the Narragansetts within the ruin, whither the whole party repaired with the most guarded silence.

The sound of approaching footsteps were now too distinctly audible to leave any doubt as to the nature of the interruption. They were soon mingled with voices calling to each other in an Indian dialect, which the hunter, in a whisper, affirmed to Heyward was the language of the Hurons. When the party reached the point where the horses had entered the thicket which surrounded the block-house, they were evidently at fault, having lost those marks which until that moment had directed their pursuit.

It would seem by the voices that twenty men were soon collected at that one spot, mingling their different opinions and advice in noisy clamour.

'The knaves know our weakness,' whispered Hawkeye, who stood by the side of Heyward, in deep shade, looking through an opening in the logs, 'or they wouldn't indulge their idleness in such a squaw's march. Listen to the reptiles! Each man among them seems to have two tongues and but a single leg.'

Duncan, brave as he was in the combat, could not, in such a moment of painful suspense, make any reply to the cool and characteristic remark of the scout. He only grasped his rifle more firmly and fastened his eyes upon the narrow opening, through which he gazed upon the moonlight view with increasing anxiety. The deeper tones of one who spoke as having authority were next heard, amid a silence that denoted the respect with which his orders, or rather advice, was received. After which, by the rustling of leaves and crackling of dried twigs, it was apparent the savages were separating in pursuit of the lost trail. Fortunately for the pursued, the light of the moon, while it shed a flood of wild lustre upon the little area around the ruin, was not sufficiently strong to penetrate the deep arches of the forest, when the objects still lay in deceptive shadow. The search proved fruitless; for so short and sudden had been the passage from the faint path the travellers had journeyed into the thicket that every trace of their footsteps was lost in the obscurity of the woods.

It was not long, however, before the restless savages were heard beating the brush, and gradually approaching the inner edge of that dense border of young chestnuts which encircled the little area.

'They are coming,' muttered Heyward, endeavouring to thrust his rifle through the chink in the logs; 'let us fire on their approach.'

'Keep everything in the shade,' returned the scout; 'the snapping of a flint, or even the smell of a single karnel of the brimstone, would bring the hungry varlets upon us in a body. Should it please God that we must give battle for the scalps, trust to the experience of men who know the ways of savages and who are not often backward when the war whoop is howled.'

Duncan cast his eyes behind him and saw that the trembling sisters were cowering in the far corner of the building, while the Mohicans stood in the shadow, like two upright posts, ready and apparently willing to strike when the blow should be needed.

The savages were so near that the least motion in one of the horses, or even a breath louder than common, would have betrayed the fugitives. But in discovering the character of the mound, the attention of the Hurons appeared directed to a different object. They spoke together and the sounds of their voices were low and solemn, as if influenced by a reverence that was deeply blended with awe. Then they drew warily back, keeping their eyes riveted on the ruin, as if they expected to see the apparitions of the dead issue from its silent walls, until, having reached the boundary of the area, they moved slowly into the thicket and disappeared.

Hawkeye dropped the breech of his rifle to the earth, and drawing a long, free breath, exclaimed, in an audible whisper:

'Ay! They respect the dead and it has this time saved their own lives, and, it may be, the lives of better men too.'

Heyward lent his attention for a single moment to his companion, but without replying, he again turned toward those who just then interested him more. He heard the two Hurons leave the bushes, and it was soon plain that all the pursuers were gathered about them in deep attention to their report. After a few minutes of earnest and solemn dialogue, altogether different from the noisy clamour with which they had first collected about the spot, the sounds grew fainter and more distant and finally were lost in the depths of the forest.

Hawkeye waited until a signal from the listening Chingachgook assured him that every sound from the retiring party was completely swallowed by the distance, when he motioned to Heyward to lead forth the horses and to assist the sisters into their saddles. The instant this was done they issued through the broken gateway, and stealing out by a direction opposite to the one by which they had entered, they quitted the spot, the sisters casting furtive glances at the silent grave and crumbling ruin, as they left the soft light of the moon to bury themselves in the gloom of the woods.

Chapter XIV

During the rapid movement from the block-house and until the party was deeply buried in the forest, each individual was too much interested in the escape to hazard a word, even in whispers. The scout resumed his post in the advance, though his steps, after he had thrown a safe distance between himself and his enemies, were more deliberate than in their previous march, in consequence of his utter ignorance of the localities of the surrounding woods. More than once he halted to consult with his confederates, the Mohicans, pointing upward at the moon, and examining the barks of the trees with care.

When the banks of the little stream were gained, Hawkeye made another halt; and taking the moccasins from his feet, he invited Heyward and Gamut to follow his example. He then entered the water, and for near an hour they travelled in the bed of the brook, leaving no trail. The moon had already sunk into an immense pile of black clouds, which lay impending above the western horizon, when they issued from the low and devious water-course to rise again to the light and level of the sandy but wooded plain. Here the scout seemed to be once more at home, for he held on his way with the certainty and diligence of a man who moved in the security of his own knowledge. The path soon became more uneven, and the travellers could plainly perceive that the mountains drew nigher to them on each hand, and that they were, in truth about entering one of their gorges. Suddenly, Hawkeye made a pause, and, waiting until he was joined by the whole party, he spoke, though in tones so low and cautious, that they added to the solemnity of his words, in the quiet and darkness of the place.

‘It is easy to know the pathways, and to find the licks and watercourses of the wilderness,’ he said; ‘but who that saw this spot could venture to say that a mighty army was at rest among yonder silent trees and barren mountains?’

‘We are, then, at no great distance from William Henry?’ said Heyward, advancing nigher to the scout.

‘It is yet a long and weary path, and when and where to strike it is now our greatest difficulty. See,’ he said, pointing through the trees toward a spot where a little basin of water reflected the stars from its placid bosom, ‘here is the “bloody pond”; and I am on ground that I have not only often travelled, but over which I have fou’t the enemy, from the rising to the setting sun.’

‘By heaven, there is a human form, and it approaches! Stand to your arms, my friend; for we know not whom we encounter.’

‘Qui vive?’ demanded a stern, quick voice, which sounded like a challenge from another world, issuing out of that solitary place.

‘What says it?’ whispered the scout; ‘it speaks neither Indian or English.’

‘Qui vive?’ repeated the same voice, which was quickly followed by the rattling of arms, and a menacing attitude.

'France!' cried Heyward, advancing from the shadow of the trees to the shore of the pond, within a few yards of the sentinel.

'D'où venez-vous — où allez-vous, d'aussi bonne heure?' demanded the grenadier, in the language and with the accent of a man from old France.

'Je viens de la découverte, et je vais me coucher.'

'Etes-vous officier du roi?'

'Sans doute, mon camarade; me prends-tu pour un provincial! Je suis capitaine de chasseurs (Heyward well knew that the other was of a regiment in the line;) j'ai ici avec moi les filles du commandant de la fortification. Aha! tu en as entendu parler! je les ai fait prisonnières près de l'autre fort, et je les conduis au général.'

'Ma foi! mesdames; j'en suis faché pour vous,' exclaimed the young soldier, touching his cap with grace; 'mais — fortune de guerre! vous trouverez notre général un brave homme, et bien poli avec les dames.'

'C'est le caractère des gens de guerre,' said Cora, with admirable self-possession. 'Adieu, mon ami; je vous souhaiterais un devoir plus agréable à remplir.'

The soldier made a low and humble acknowledgment for her civility; and Heyward adding a 'Bonne nuit, mon camarade,' they moved deliberately onward, leaving the sentinel pacing the banks of the silent pool, little suspecting an enemy of so much effrontery, and humming to himself those words which were recalled to his mind by the sight of women, and perhaps, by recollections of his own distant and beautiful France:

'Vive le vin, vive l'amour,' etc., etc.

''Tis well you understood the knave!' whispered the scout, when they had gained a little distance from the place, and letting his rifle fall into the hollow of his arm again; 'I soon saw that he was one of them uneasy Frenchers, and well for him it was that his speech was friendly and his wishes kind, or a place might have been found for his bones among those of his countrymen.'

He was interrupted by a long and heavy groan which arose from the little basin, as though, in truth, the spirits of the departed lingered about their watery sepulchre.

'Surely, it was of flesh,' continued the scout; 'no spirit could handle its arms so steadily.'

'It was of flesh; but whether the poor fellow still belongs to this world may well be doubted,' said Heyward, glancing his eyes around him, and missing Chingachgook from their little band. Another groan more faint than the former was succeeded by a heavy and sullen plunge into the water, and all was still again as if the borders of the dreary pool had never been awakened from the silence of creation. While they yet hesitated in uncertainty, the form of the Indian was seen gliding out of the thicket. As the chief rejoined them, with one hand he attached the reeking scalp of the unfortunate young Frenchman to his girdle and with the other he replaced the knife and tomahawk that had drunk his blood. He then took his wonted station, with the air of a man who believed he had done a deed of merit.

The scout dropped one end of his rifle to the earth and leaning his hands on the other, he stood musing in profound silence. Then shaking his head in a mournful manner, he muttered:

"'Twould have been a cruel and an unhuman act for a white skin; but 'tis the gift and natur' of an Indian and I suppose it should not be denied. I could wish, though, it had befallen an accursed Mingo, rather than that gay young boy from the old countries.'

'Enough!' said Heyward, apprehensive lest the unconscious sisters might comprehend the nature of the detention, and conquering his disgust by a train of reflections very much like that of the hunter; 'tis done; and though better it were left undone, cannot be amended. You see, we are too obviously within the sentinels of the enemy.'

'Yes,' said Hawkeye, rousing himself again; "tis as you say, too late to harbour further thoughts about it. Aye, the French have gathered around the fort in good earnest and we have a delicate needle to thread in passing them.'

'And but little time to do it in,' added Heyward, glancing his eyes towards the bank of vapour that concealed the setting moon.

'The thing may be done in two fashions, by the help of Providence, without which it may not be done at all.'

'Name them quickly, for time presses.'

'One would be to dismount the gentle ones and let their beasts range the plain, by sending the Mohicans in front, we might then cut a lane through their sentries and enter the fort over the dead bodies.'

'It will not do — it will not do!' interrupted the generous Heyward; 'a soldier might force his way in this manner, but never with such a convoy.'

''Twould be, indeed, a bloody path for such tender feet to wade in,' returned the equally reluctant scout; 'but I thought it befitting my manhood to name it. We must, then, turn in our trail and get without the line of their lookouts, when we will bend short to the west and enter the mountains; where I can hide you, so that all the devil's hounds in Montcalm's pay would be thrown off the scent for months to come.'

'Let it be done and that instantly.'

Further words were unnecessary; for Hawkeye, merely uttering the mandate to 'follow', moved along the route by which they had just entered their present critical and even dangerous situation. Their progress was guarded and without noise; for none knew at what moment a passing patrol, or a crouching picket of the enemy, might rise upon their path.

Hawkeye soon deviated from the line of their retreat, and striking off towards the mountains which form the western boundary of the narrow plain, he led his followers, with swift steps, deep within the shadows that were cast from their high broken summits. The route was now painful; lying over ground ragged with rocks and intersected with ravines, and their progress proportionately slow. As they gradually rose from the levels of the valleys, the thick darkness which usually precedes the approach of day began to disperse, and objects were seen in the plain and palpable colours with which they had been gifted by nature. When they issued from the stunted woods which clung to the barren sides of the mountain, upon a flat and mossy rock that formed its summit, they met the morning, as it came blushing above the green pines of a hill that lay on the opposite side of the valley of the Horican.

The scout now told the sisters to dismount; and taking the bridles from the mouths and the saddles off the back of the jaded beasts, he turned them loose to glean a scanty subsistence among the shrubs and meagre herbage of that elevated region.

'Go,' he said, 'and seek your food where natur' gives it to you; and beware that you become not food to ravenous wolves yourselves among these hills.'

'Have we no further need of them!' demanded Heyward.

'See and judge with your own eyes,' said the scout advancing toward the eastern brow of the mountain, whither he beckoned for the whole party to follow; 'if it was as easy, to look into the heart of man as it is to spy out the nakedness of Montcalm's camp from this spot, hypocrites would grow scarce and the cunning of a Mingo might prove a losing game compared to the honesty of a Delaware.'

When the travellers reached the verge of the precipices, they saw at a glance the truth of the scout's declaration and the admirable fore-sight with which he had led them to their commanding station.

Directly on the shore of the lake, and nearer to its western than to its eastern margin, lay the extensive ramparts and low buildings of William Henry. Two of the sweeping bastions appeared to rest on the water which washed their bases, while a deep ditch and extensive morasses guarded its other sides and angles.

But the spectacle which most concerned the young soldier was on the western bank of the lake, though quite near to its southern termi-nation. On a strip of land, which appeared from his stand too narrow to contain such an army, but which in truth, extended many hun-dreds of yards from the shores of the Horican to the base of the mountain, were to be seen the white tents and military engines of an encampment of ten thousand men. Batteries were already thrown up in their front, and even while the spectators above them were looking down with such different emotions on a scene which lay like a map beneath their feet, the roar of artillery rose from the valley and passed off in thundering echoes along the eastern hills.

'Morning is just touching them below,' said the deliberate and musing scout, 'and the watchers have a mind to wake up the sleep-ers by the sound of cannon. We are a few hours too late! Montcalm has already filled the woods with his accursed Iroquois.'

'The place is indeed invested,' returned Duncan; 'but is there no expedient by which we may enter? Capture in the works would be far preferable to falling again into the hands of roving Indians.'

'See!' exclaimed the scout, unconsciously directing the attention of Cora to the quarters of her own father, 'how that shot has made the stones fly from the sides of the commandant's house! Ay! These Frenchers will pull it to pieces faster than it was put together, solid and thick though it be!'

'Heyward, I sicken at the sight of danger that I cannot share,' said the undaunted but anxious daughter. 'Let us go to Montcalm and demand admission; he dare not deny a child the boon.'

'You would scarce find the tent of the Frenchman with the hair on your head;' said the blunt scout. 'If I had but one of the thousand boats which lie empty along that shore, it might be done! Ha! Here will soon be an end of the firing, for yonder comes a fog that will turn day to night and make an Indian arrow more dangerous than a moulded cannon. Now, if you are equal to the work and will follow I will make a push; for I long to get down into that camp, if it be only to scatter some Mingo dogs that I see lurking in the skirts of yonder thicket of birch.'

'We are equal,' said Cora, firmly; 'on such an errand we will follow to any danger.'

The scout turned to her with a smile of honest and cordial approbation, as he answered:

'I would I had a thousand men of brawny limbs and quick eyes that feared death as little as you!'

He then waved his hand for them to follow and threw himself down the steep declivity with free but careful footsteps. Heyward assisted the sisters to descend, and in a few moments they were all far down a mountain whose sides they had climbed with so much toil and pain.

The direction taken by Hawkeye soon brought the travellers to the level of the plain, nearly opposite to a sally-port in the western curtain of the fort, which lay at the distance of about half a mile from the point where he halted to allow Duncan to come up with his charge. In their eagerness and favoured by the nature of the ground, they had anticipated the fog which was rolling heavily along the lake, and it became necessary to pause until the mists had wrapped the camp of the enemy in their fleecy mantle. The Mohicans profited by the delay to steal out of the woods, and to make a survey of surrounding objects. They were followed at a little distance by the scout, with a view to profit early by their report, and to obtain some faint knowledge for himself of the more immediate localities.

In a very few moments he returned, his face reddened with vexation, while he muttered his disappointment in words of no very gentle tone.

'Here has the cunning Frenchman been posting a picket directly in our path,' he said; 'red skins and whites; and we shall be as likely to fall into their midst as to pass them in the fog!'

'Cannot we make a circuit to avoid the danger,' asked Heyward, 'and come into our path again when it is past?'

'Who that once bends from the line of his march in a fog can tell when or how to turn to find it again! The mists of Horican are not like the curls from a peace pipe, or the smoke which settles above a mosquito fire.'

He was yet speaking, when a crashing sound was heard, and a cannon-ball entered the thicket, striking the body of a sapling and rebounding to the earth, its force being much expended by previous resistance. The Indians followed instantly like busy attendants on the terrible messenger and Uncas commenced speaking earnestly and with much action in the Delaware tongue.

Heyward perceiving that, in fact, a crisis had arrived, when acts were more required than words, placed himself between the sisters and drew them swiftly forward, keeping the dim figure of their leader in his eye. It was soon apparent that Hawkeye had not magnified the power of the fog, for before they had proceeded twenty yards, it was difficult for the different individuals of the party to distinguish each other in the vapour.

They had made their little circuit to the left and were already inclining toward the right, having, as Heyward thought, got over nearly half the distance to the friendly works, when his ears were saluted with the fierce summons, within twenty feet of them, of:

'Qui vive?'

'Push on!' whispered the scout, once more bending to the left.

'Push on!' repeated Heyward, when the summons was renewed by a dozen voices, each of which seemed charged with menace.

'C'est moi,' cried Duncan, dragging rather than leading those he supported swiftly onward.

'Bête! — qui? — moi!'

'Ami de la France.'

'Tu m'as plus l'air d'un ennemi de la France; arrête! ou pardieu je te ferai ami du diable. Non! feu, camarades, feu!'

The order was instantly obeyed and the fog was stirred by the explosion of fifty muskets. Happily, the aim was bad and the bullets cut the air in a direction a little different from that taken by the fugitives; though still so nigh them, that to the unpractised ears of David and the two females, it appeared as if they whistled within a few inches of the organs. The outcry was renewed and the order, not only to fire again, but to pursue, was plainly audible. When Heyward briefly explained the meaning of the words they heard, Hawkeye halted and spoke with quick decision and great firmness.

'Let us deliver our fire,' he said; 'they will believe it a sortie and give way, or they will wait for reinforcements.'

The scheme was well conceived, but failed in its effect. The instant the French heard the pieces, it seemed as if the plain was alive with men, muskets rattling along its whole extent, from the shores of the lake to the furthest boundary of the woods.

'We shall draw their entire army upon us and bring on a general assault,' said Duncan; 'lead on, my friend, for your own life and ours.' The scout seemed willing to comply; but, in the hurry of the moment, and in the change of position, he had lost the direction. In vain he turned either cheek toward the light air; they felt equally cool. In this dilemma, Uncas lighted on the furrow of the cannon ball, where it had cut the ground in three adjacent ant hills.

'Give me the range!' said Hawkeye, bending to catch a glimpse of the direction, and then instantly moving onward.

Cries, oaths, voices calling to each other and the reports of muskets were now quick and incessant and, apparently, on every side of them. Suddenly a strong glare of light flashed across the scene, the fog rolled upward in thick wreaths and several cannon belched across the plain and the roar was thrown heavily back from the bellowing echoes of the mountain.

''Tis from the fort!' exclaimed Hawkeye, turning short on his tracks; 'and we, like stricken fools, were rushing to the woods, under the very knives of the Maquas.'

The instant their mistake was rectified, the whole party retraced the error with the utmost diligence. Duncan willingly relinquished the support of Cora to the arm of Uncas and Cora as readily accepted the welcome assistance. Men, hot and angry in pursuit, were evidently on their footsteps, and each instant threatened their capture, if not their destruction.

'Point de quartier aux coquins!' cried an eager pursuer, who seemed to direct the operations of the enemy.

'Stand firm and be ready, my gallant 60ths!' suddenly exclaimed a voice above them; 'wait to see the enemy, fire low and sweep the glacis.'

'Father! Father!' exclaimed a piercing cry from out the mist; 'it is I! Alice! Thy own Elsie! Spare, oh! Save your daughters!'

'Hold!' shouted the former speaker, in the awful tones of parental agony, the sound reaching even to the woods and rolling back in solemn echo. ''Tis she! God has restored me my children! Throw open the sally port; to the field, 60ths, to the field; pull not a trigger, lest ye kill my lambs! Drive off these dogs of France with your steel.'

Duncan heard the grating of the rusty hinges and darting to the spot, directed by the sound, he met a long line of dark red warriors, passing swiftly toward the glacis. He knew them for his own battalion of the Royal Americans, and flying to their head, soon swept every trace of his pursuers from before the works.

For an instant, Cora and Alice had stood trembling and bewildered

by this unexpected desertion; but before either had leisure for speech, or even thought, an officer of gigantic frame, whose locks were bleached with years of service, but whose air of military grandeur had been rather softened than destroyed by time, rushed out of the body of mist and folded them to his bosom, while large scalding tears rolled down his pale and wrinkled cheeks, and he exclaimed in the peculiar accent of Scotland:

'For this I thank thee, Lord! Let danger come as it will, thy servant is now prepared!'

SINGING ARROW

Torry Gredsted

Smiling Eye

In early spring, the Dakota tribe of Chief Singing Arrow left their winter camp and set off in search of buffalo. The Indians' whole life depended on good fortune and success in hunting, as only buffalo could provide what they needed. They lived off their meat and marrow, used the skin to make their tents and clothes, fashioned tools from the bones, and made bowstrings and sewing thread from the sinews.

If a herd decided to move to better pasture and water, the Dakotas had to follow. For this reason everything was made to be easily and quickly transportable from place to place. Striking their tents was the work of a few minutes. In an instant they had turned the long tent-poles into a sort of yoke. The ends which were bound together were fastened in front of the saddle, so that the horse pulled the poles along behind it. This skid was reinforced with cross-pieces and joined together with a net, and then served to carry the whole modest belongings of the Indian family.

In the distance an Indian camp on the move looked like a huge black snake winding along the ground, a snake whose tail was constantly in motion. Only a closer inspection showed that this 'snake' was in fact made up of walking and riding men, women and children, some dressed, others almost naked, and of heavily laden horses and dogs. The broad and ever-moving 'tail' of the snake was in fact a group of horses driven along by Indian youths.

But anyone who bothered to take an even closer look at the column would see that, in spite of the apparent confusion, there was in fact a certain order and discipline about it. On either side of the caravan there were horsemen whose task it was to keep the line intact, and their orders were obeyed without question.

The sight of the Dakotas on the move was a remarkably colourful and picturesque one. Here there was a group of painted warriors with splendid head-dresses, there a wrinkled old woman whipped along her skinny horse; then a group of boys ran past with carefree shouting. Behind them a young woman could be seen, surely the

daughter of some warrior, for she was dressed in beautiful white buffalo skins adorned with fringes, and covered with shell and moose-
tooth ornaments. Next to her walked a young man whose words
seemed to interest her, for she was leaning so far out of the saddle
that her companion could see the red-painted parting which divided
her magnificent, rich black hair like a piece of string. But the young
man had picked a rather bad time to do his courting, for right next to
them a couple of dogs, which were also tied to the small skids, had
chosen that moment to begin fighting, so that others came running
along to separate the pair. Then the sound of howling rang out on all
sides as blows rained down on the pair of culprits, while the young
man hurried forward.

A long way behind the caravan, and at certain intervals, a number
of black spots could also been seen to move. They were grey bears;
they followed the Indians faithfully and perseveringly, in the hope
that where there were people, they too would find food.

A good way ahead rode Singing Arrow and the other chiefs, the
medicine-men and some of the warriors, and right behind them two
boys on horses.

One of them was fourteen, the other ten. In spite of their tender
years they were a match for the men, their naked bodies painted,
bows and decorated quivers hanging from their shoulders, and even
small tomahawks in their belts. Around their throats moose-tooth
necklaces rattled, and in their long hair, matted with earth and here
and there coloured red, strings of shells bobbed back and forth.

They were the sons of Singing Arrow, who spent as much time as
he could on their upbringing, hoping that they would soon win their
laurels as hunters and bold warriors.

The elder of the two had obviously lighter coloured skin and hair;
but even if his skin had not betrayed him, his blue eyes with their
peculiar sheen clearly marked him out from the other Indians.

If Penn Kerr's son was not a true Indian with his pale skin, he was
no different in nature. Even now he was brave and self-assured,

thirsting for glory, and had already mastered the principal attribute of a prairie son, that of self-control, so that he was able to hide from others the way his thoughts moved.

He had grown up in camp along with the other children, and since early childhood had learnt to think and feel like an Indian. If there were other features of his nature too, for the time being they remained deep in his subconscious.

Riding through the prairie as he was now, he was an Indian not only in appearance, but also in mind and soul. Like the others, he was driven on by a deep love for freedom, and was prepared to fight against everything which might threaten that freedom.

Singing Arrow was a good father to the white boy. From the very start he had seen to his upbringing himself; nor did their relationship alter even when, some years later, he married, as was the custom, his dead wife's sister, and a son of his own was born. The two boys grew up together as inseparable brothers, and the father would allow no distinction to be made between them. Whoever spoke disparagingly of Smiling Eye earned the chief's wrath to his dying day.

In the few years following the bloody morning when Penn Kerr and his wife were killed, Singing Arrow had risen in respect and honour, until at last he had become the greatest chief of the tribe and the most powerful man in the territory. It was not only because he came from a noble family, but especially because he had excelled as a hunter and warrior, and his thoughts at the council fire were among the wisest.

They all respected and honoured him, though the youngest of the braves could not understand the fierce love he felt towards his white son, who reminded them of the hated palefaces. But no one dared to speak out loud.

In those days the white settlers had again intruded into the territory set aside for the Indians, and in spite of all their solemn vows some tribes were forced to negotiate new agreements with them. But there was still enough room on the wide prairies, so Singing Arrow deliberately avoided the routes taken by the white man's wagons. His tribe had not taken part in the talks which others had been forced into, and had also rejected the proposals and the bait offered by the Indian agencies.

Year by year it grew more difficult to keep the aggressive ideas of the braves in check, for they could all see well enough that the herds of buffalo were getting smaller and smaller, and that it was the pale-faces with their rifles who had driven them away.

So far, however, Singing Arrow had managed to keep their obedience, though their discontent grew more and more apparent. The young ones in particular could not understand why he did not take the warpath against the white man.

The day was dying, and the sun close to the western horizon. The women were already so tired they could hardly put one foot in front of the other, and the beasts were panting beneath their heavy loads; but Singing Arrow still gave no signal for rest. Suddenly the leading animals of the group grew restlesss: the horses stretched out their heads and neighed, the dogs barked wildly, tugging at their leads, so that it was no easy matter to hold them back. They could smell water. Their excitement spread through the column, and both animals and men suddenly became more lively.

Singing Arrow loosened his horse's reins, and in a short while reached the crest of the hill. In front of him he saw the goal of their long trek — a broad valley, through which the River Niobrara wound. He decided to pitch camp there and then; the grass was turning a light spring green, and the willow thickets would offer good protection from the burning summer sun.

The two boys got bored during the council their father called with the elders of the tribe. Their restless blood called for action. 'Come on, Hokota,' said the older boy, turning away from the others. And right away the two of them set off in a circle on their well-trained ponies. They were playing at buffalo hunting: one of them was the prey, the other the hunter. The hunter let go of the reins, and with a cry gripped the horse between his legs, bending his bow and pursuing the buffalo in an attempt to get close to its right-hand side.

When they grew tired of this game, Smiling Eye called out: 'Catch my arrows, Hokota,' and fired into the air. Hokota rode towards him, held out his hand, and very deftly caught the arrow before it fell to the ground. They took a liking to the game, and again and again sent arrows high into the air for each other, catching them as they fell. Sometimes they missed them, and then they leaned right out of the saddle, to pick up the fallen arrow at full stretch.

Singing Arrow watched with pride as the boys practised, feeling joy in his heart for their courage, skill and horsemanship.

'Smiling Eye is a good friend and teacher for your son,' said one of the elders. 'They are both my sons, Rapid Moose,' was the chief's reply.

White Bear's Story

As soon as Singing Arrow had marked out the boundaries of the camp, the women had their work cut out. Some of them erected the long tentpoles and covered them with skins, while others brought firewood and water to start cooking supper.

The tepees were arranged in a circle, and each family had its own place. Before long, fires were glowing through the tent skins, and blue smoke began to rise through the smokeholes.

But it was not bedtime in the camp yet, and all worked hard until late evening, for the next morning they would have to send out scouts to explore the surrounding area. So the Indians had to put their weapons in order, while their horses stood tied to their tents.

The two boys lay curled up in Singing Arrow's tent, wondering in whispers what the morning would bring them on the prairie. Then, before going to sleep, they sent their wishes to Tarava — The Great Secret. Not only that, but they both made a sacrifice to him: Smiling Eye his best arrow, Hokota two splendid eagle's feathers. They begged Tarava to give them strength and courage of heart, since they were going to need it when they rode through strange country. For their father had not been able to turn down Smiling Eye's pleas to allow Hokota and himself to accompany the adults.

Suddenly, as night fell, the camp grew quiet, and sleep crept upon it. One fire after another went out, and the tents were steeped in darkness. But in White Bear's tent a fire still glowed, and muffled voices carried into the silent night. Half-naked men sat by the fireside on outstretched buffalo skins, passing a pipe from hand to hand.

The younger son of White Bear — a lad of twenty with a hard and rough face — had just explained to the gathering how all the young men of the tribe were anxious to take to the warpath. He told them of the impatience his companions felt. His bitter words ended thus:

'Instead of fighting the paleface, we choose to give up the hunting-grounds of our fathers; we choose to flee like a flock of sheep when it scents a puma on the prowl. Instead of taking our revenge and making a glorious bid for scalps, we spoil the brats of white men and give them places in our tents.'

At that moment all threw glances at the speaker, against the usual custom, which was to let him finish what he was saying. Indeed, there was normally a few moments silence after he had finished speaking, for the listeners to consider the speaker's words. But this time White Bear himself signalled that he wished to speak.

'There is much truth in what Hapadoi has said,' he began. 'But for your own sake I stopped you speaking, lest you incur the wrath of Singing Arrow. Your words were hasty. In our camp there is only one paleface, and even the women understand that they must watch their tongues when they speak of Smiling Eye, who is protected by the anger of Singing Arrow.'

White Bear was silent for a moment. 'Do you, my brothers, wish me to tell the story of Chadokah, my friend?' he asked, and looked around those present. 'Uf!' A grunt of contentment came by way of reply.

'In those days Hapadoi was still a small boy, and I had seen as many winters as he has now. My blood boiled in my veins as his does, and I burned with a desire for glory and to take to the warpath; Chadokah, my friend, felt the same as I.

'We both belonged to Singing Arrow's troop, like the others who had excelled in hunting that summer, and we were all happy about it, since Singing Arrow was the best of us.

'But an unfortunate thing happened: after a short ride we reached a tepee with thick walls, built by a paleface. His squaw was at home, and she came out, not knowing that we were hidden nearby. Chadokah was already placing an arrow in his bow, but I stayed his hand in time, for Singing Arrow had given no signal for a warcry.

'I was right, for in a while the chief said that the woman was not to be killed, but to be taken to the camp and handed over to our women.

'Chadokah was still a young man, and he was on the warpath. When the woman later cried out to alert the white man and to prevent us taking his scalp, his arrow silenced her, closing her mouth for ever, for he forgot everything in his anger.

'It was a sad day for us, for Singing Arrow took the child which lay in the house, and rode back to camp with him, and we were left without a leader. Then other palefaces came and their rifles spoke, so we had to run to our horses. Before evening we were sitting in our tents, with weak hearts and tongues tied.

'Only Flying Crane did not return. His horse ran behind ours, but the saddle had blood on it. And Flying Crane was the one with the white man's scalp on his belt.

'It was a sad day, my brothers. We were angry with Chadokah for killing the woman, for Tarava wishes us always to obey our chief; but we did not speak of it, for he was our friend and brother.

'And Chadokah sat for a long time alone in his tent, afraid of the anger of Singing Arrow. Winter and summer passed, then winter came again, and summer again, and four times it was so. We had all forgotten that day, and had made up for it many times over on the warpath against the Chipavai.

'The day Singing Arrow celebrated the birth of his son Hokota we were all merry, and Chadokah and I were among the guests. Chadokah suddenly looked at Smiling Eye, who was four years old. I tried to control him, for he was my friend and brother, but I could not stop his tongue when he began to shout that from that day on Smiling

124

Eye's place would be among the camp dogs. Nor could I stay his hand when he took the boy by the shoulders and shook him, as a dog shakes a squirrel which has been shot down from a branch.

'Suddenly Singing Arrow stood before us. He had heard Chado-kah's shouts; he came up, pulled Smiling Eye from him, and carried the boy to his tent.

'Chadokah's tongue was struck dumb, but my heart, too, was heavy, for the chief's eyes were glowing with burning anger.

'In a little while he returned from his tent, carrying a broken arrow in his hand. I saw at once that it was Chadokah's. His arrows had longer points than all the rest. The chief asked: "Is this your arrow?" — but I could see by his face that he recognised it. There was no answer, though it was clear that he had aimed his question well.

'Then we heard him call a council of the elders, and a fire was soon burning.

'We had foolishly believed that Singing Arrow had forgotten what had happened years before. Chadokah and I were the only ones who remembered, for Red Deer and Little Bee had fallen on the warpath against the Chipevai. Blue Stork had died of a wound he received fighting a bear beside the stream. You know the stream well, for now we call it Bear Stream.

'It was an unlucky day for Chadokah. The arrow was his. And what was I to do, though he was my friend and brother? For Singing Arrow was right, as always . . .

'He led us to the tent, where we sat in silence for a long while. Chadokah knew he must die, and I was convinced of the same.

'We heard the voices of the elders, and soon we were told the judgement. Chadokah's tent was torn apart, and all his property and weapons destroyed. Then the women and children drove him away from the camp, and threw stones after him. It would have been better for him never to see the light of the sun again.

'There was much that was true in your words, Hapadoi, but now I have told you what happened to Chadokah. He became my friend and brother, a good hunter and a bold warrior, but he was not able to control his thoughts, or hold his tongue.

'Singing Arrow is a mighty chief, my friends, and it is Tarava's wish that we obey him.'

The elders in the circle nodded and murmured their assent: 'A ho ho ho.' But defiance flashed in Hapadoi's eyes. He was still young, and kept all his confidence for himself; he also longed for glory gained in battle.

The men stayed sitting by the fire for a while, as its last embers died. Then they rose, and each went to his own tepee. Soon White Bear's tent was swathed in darkness like the rest.

The Buffalo Hunt

Before the first rays of the sun appeared in the east, Smiling Eye and Hokota were afoot and making ready the horses. Quite naked, they galloped to the river, where they bathed the horses and refreshed themselves, too.

Then they adorned their hair and repainted their bodies and faces. In a little while they appeared in leggings and moccasins; their weapons were already prepared. While the other scouts were still making ready, the two boys had already ridden through the camp and set off at a gallop towards the rising sun.

They wanted to make the most of their time, and what if they were the first to find the herd of buffalo, the first to return to camp with that joyful and precious news? Their father would surely by pleased, and perhaps would let them take part in the actual hunting! So they wanted to make good speed, and their small but sturdy ponies seemed to have the same idea, for without bidding they rode like the wind across the prairie.

The boys took their task seriously, and silently and intently scrutinized their surroundings as far as the horizon. They had forgotten about all the other things which usually occupied their thoughts. This morning they did not even take note of a flock of prairie chickens, which they disturbed so suddenly that they rose into the air right in front of them, causing the ponies to rear up. Soon afterwards the boys spotted a pair of eagles high in the air; at other times they would not have missed such a rare sight, but today they really had no time, wishing only to see at last the monotonous green prairie dotted with innumerable dark spots ...

When, after several hours' ride, they reached the mountain ridge the outline of which they had seen on the horizon for a long time, and from where they were hoping to get a good view, they heard a faint lowing. Slowing their horses, they listened intently.

'Do you hear, Smiling Eye?'

'Yes, they are buffalo.'

And the noise came again.

'It is only a lone animal,' said Hokota, disappointment paling in his eyes.

'But we must find it, anyway,' his brother returned. 'It may lead us to the rest. Let's go,' and he spurred his horse into a gallop again.

At top speed they reached the hill, where the lowing could be heard more and more distinctly. At the same time they heard with excitement other sounds: in a little while a single, loudly resounding howl, followed at once by a muffled, barking and whining chorus.

'Hokota, hurry up — can't you hear the bears?' said Smiling Eye, and, digging his heels into the horse's sides, charged up the long slope. 'This one has been separated from the herd, and is fighting for his life.'

He had guessed correctly. They found themselves looking down on a strange spectacle. Jumping from their horses, they tied them up, and watched with sparkling eyes a dour struggle between a buffalo and several bears.

The battle was reaching a climax. The buffalo, its huge head bent right down, was beating the ground furiously with its hooves, ready to attack its nearest adversary. But the bears were cautious. They kept a safe distance, contenting themselves with approaching now and again, whining and growling. They were only pretending to attack, and actually waiting for the animal to lose its temper and go for one of them of its own accord. Then the rest would attack from behind. Suddenly, the buffalo turned, but by then the bears were out of reach of its mortally sharp horns . . .

The boys lay in the grass, scarcely breathing with suspense. They were on the side of the lone bison, which was so bravely defending itself. It was a truly great warrior, and whenever it rushed forward, they held their breath — would it manage this time to get the scalp of one at least of its adversaries? No, the bears again jumped out of the way in a cowardly fashion, and again tried to get their victim from behind. At last! One of them did not get out of the way fast enough: the pointed horns caught it and sank into its flesh. A painful roar filled the air. The buffalo turned its head sharply and threw the bear up high. The creature's body fell to the ground with a heavy and hollow thud; there the angry bison sank its horns in yet again, and finally trampled the bear with its hooves, until its body was unrecognisable.

There was a lull in the fighting, and the bears retreated somewhat. But they soon came back with a new aggressiveness. The sun climbed higher in the sky, but no one noticed.

The huge buffalo really was a bold warrior. But weariness was taking its toll. Its movements got less and less sure, more and more hesitant, since its torn hind legs could scarcely carry its body. Though it still stamped the ground with his front legs, it was with less strength than before. Suddenly its knees gave way. It was the moment the bears had been waiting for. All at once they threw themselves on it from all sides. The creature was still trying to defend itself, and hurled its head from side to side, but that was all it could do. The bears' teeth closed on its dangling tongue, and then the hero rolled over heavily onto his side.

Smiling Eye leaped up like a cat, and his arrow flew towards that mass of heaving bodies. The bear it struck jumped up and bit its neighbour furiously in the side; at that moment they began to fight each other.

'Come on, Hokota,' said Smiling Eye. 'The battle is over. He was a great warrior, but he had too many enemies. I would like to shoot at those bears, but it would be a waste of arrows.'

Hokota suddenly stopped. 'Let us sacrifice something to his courageous death,' he said, and out of respect for the fallen warrior he tugged a string of shells from his hair.

'You are right, Hokota,' said Smiling Eye, and followed suit. He turned to the place where the bears were feasting, and laid the offering in the grass.

'Accept our honour,' said Smiling Eye gravely, 'and give us your strength when we meet our own enemies.'

It was not until late afternoon that the boys heard something like the distant roar of thunder; this time their ears did not deceive them. Soon they recognised the rumble of a buffalo herd. They were already a long way from the camp, and knew they could not return

that day if they were to continue their scouting. But what did that matter! At the first signs of that unmistakable roar they forgot all tiredness, and forced their thirsty and half-exhausted mounts into the nearest they could manage to a gallop. They were close to their goal, and could hear more and more clearly the sound of lowing mixed with the thunder of hooves. The boys' hearts started to pound with excitement; their cheeks began to burn, and their eyes glowed. By the amount of noise they judged the herd to be a huge one. Then at last they saw the long black band along the horizon.

'They are heading for the river!' shouted Smiling Eye, and turned his horse southwards. 'After them!' he went on, joyously. 'There are as many as there are leaves on the trees. Our people will be pleased when we show them the way ...'

For about an hour they lay hidden by the river and watched the enormous herd from close quarters. The bulls walked at the sides, their heads bent almost to the ground, protecting the cows, which followed with their light-brown calves.

It was only when the sun slipped behind the mountain ridge that the boys thought of their hunger and thirst. They agreed at once to spend the night where they were, and to ride to the camp as quickly as possible in the morning, carrying the joyful news.

The darkness grew blacker and blacker. The evening silence was broken by all manner of voices of animals and birds, but they did not worry the boys, for they had been accustomed to them from early childhood. They staved off hunger with dried buffalo meat, covered themselves with their saddle skins to keep out the worst of the night cold, and were soon fast asleep.

Nature ran her course — though they had supposed in the evening that they would set off early in the morning, the sun was high in the sky before they awoke. At once they saddled their horses and rode to bathe in the river.

Less than an arrow-shot away from the ford a number of Arapaho Indians were sitting round their fire. They heard someone making their way through the thicket on the far side of the river; they had reason enough for caution, since they were in strange territory.

Several years before various tribes of the Arapaho and Cheyenne had agreed at Fort Laramie to keep to the south of the River Platte and to hunt between that river and Arkansas. Some of the Dakota tribes, who had also been parties to the treaty, agreed to keep to hunting grounds to the north of the river.

With a warning wave one of the men told his companions to be silent and to make ready their horses. He himself crawled unheard in the direction of the rustling.

It was Chadokah, the outlawed Dakota, who had long wandered alone before joining the Arapaho, among whom he had earned respect as a warrior and hunter.

Cautiously, as silent as a puma, he crept among the branches and leaves to the bank of the river. There he hid in the long grass, watching to see what was happening on the other side of the river.

He started in surprise when he saw that the newcomers were not only Dakotas, but from the very tribe which had driven him from their camp in disgrace. All those old events ran through Chadokah's head anew, and his blood began to boil with hatred and a longing for revenge. He would for all the world have reached down the bow which hung on his back. The boys were watering their horses. They were standing so close that he could see their faces clearly — and again Chadokah trembled all over . . . for the pair of eyes which shone strangely from that painted face were eyes he could never forget.

Smiling Eye, said a voice inside him, and at that moment he also knew that the second boy was none other than Hokota, son of his arch-enemy Singing Arrow. Now Chadokah forgot that these were mere boys: his only thoughts were of revenge, and no matter who the victim was.

Luckily for the two boys the sun was high in the sky, which reminded them that time was precious. The moment the ponies left the water, they mounted, and with a leap disappeared beyond the tress, just as Chadokah was stringing his bow.

Beside himself with anger, he ran quickly to his companions, leaped onto his horse, and galloped a little further west, to a ford from which he could get a start on the two boys . . .

With joyful impatience to bring their news back to the camp as soon as possible, the two boys drove their horses across the prairie; then they saw a lone horseman riding to cross their path from the left.

'It will be one of our scouts on his way home,' said Smiling Eye. 'Let us turn to meet him. Perhaps he, too, has found bison — but surely not the same ones, since he is coming from the opposite direction.'

'Even if he has found them,' Hokota replied, 'the herd is surely not so large.'

Turning their horses' heads a little, they galloped to meet the rider. But in a little while Hokota caught his brother's hand and shouted:

'Wait! His horse has four white feet — none of our men rides one like that!' And they turned quickly in their original direction. Though their ponies were among the best in the camp, they were tired from the previous day's exertions.

'He's getting nearer,' Hokota said in a while, turning to look. And right away he added: 'He has a bow on his shoulders.'

'We must get away from the river,' Smiling Eye replied. 'This way we should cross the land of the prairie dogs, where horses have to go at walking pace.'

A prairie dog colony may cover several acres, and actually consists of innumerable mounds of earth, one beside the other. Beside each is the entrace to one of those animals' cleverly built lairs. These holes are so close to each other that a horse truly cannot cross such land at speed because of the danger of injury.

The boys preferred to ride along the very edge of this obstacle, so as not to lose more time than they needed to. This gave them a good start, for their pursuer sought to cut across their path again, and found himself among the mounds of sand, where his mount began to slip into the holes.

But he was soon at their heels again. He had a horse which was roughly as fast as theirs, but much fresher, for the ponies began to wheeze, and needed more and more encouragement.

When the boys were losing hope of reaching their camp in safety, and Smiling Eye was starting to consider whether it were not better to stop and speak to the stranger, a small group of riders appeared in the distance.

'Our friends!' said Smiling Eye. 'But they might also be enemies.'

The distance between them and their pursuer was getting smaller all the time. Smiling Eye reached for his bow, calling to Hokota, whose horse was lagging behind:

'Go on — ride on to our men as fast as you can! I will stop here and send my arrows against him!'

'I will stay with you,' Hokota replied, tugging his horse's rein under its bottom lip.

'No, you mustn't stop. Then we will both try to escape . . .'

Chadokah had also seen the band of riders in the distance, and was furiously spurring his horse, so that he might finally get within bow-shot before someone frustrated his efforts. And, letting go of the reins, he took down his bow.

When Smiling Eye heard the whistle of an arrow, he quickly turned his head, and saw to his horror that his brother's horse was staggering from one leg to another; then it fell to its knees, and — *how terrible*! Hokota flew over its head in a wide arc and was left lying on the ground, apparently lifeless. The other boy turned his horse so quickly, it was a wonder he did not rip its jawbone apart, though before he could get to the spot, his enemy was preparing another shot.

But Smiling Eye did not hesitate. He rushed to the spot where his brother lay, bending so that he hung from one stirrup by his horse's side, as he had long ago learned to do. At full tilt he grabbed Hokota and tried to haul him into the saddle; but he did not have the strength. Still half hanging from his horse, he held Hokota around the waist with his left hand. The only support he had was the strap which held the saddle in place.

Chadokah's arrows whistled around him, and one pierced his

pony's ear. Frenzied with fear, the animal dashed almost witlessly across the prairie towards the approaching riders.

It was Singing Arrow himself, with a few of his warriors. He had ridden out to look for the boys, worried when they did not return for so long. He had seen from afar the danger they were in. Carefully, he stopped the runaway pony, and for a while stroked his son's head, until Hokota came to.

Several of his company set off in pursuit of the hostile Indian; the others listened to what the boys had to tell them.

'You have behaved like men,' said Singing Arrow. 'This evening we shall dance the buffalo dance.' Looking at Smiling Eye, he went on: 'You have deserved great praise. I will hold a rich banquet in your honour, for you have shown the courage of a warrior. For that I will give you two eagle's feathers, which you may weave into your hair . . .'

Before they set off back again, Singing Arrow and his company went to see the spot where his white son had so courageously and skilfully saved the life of his blood son, and his sharp eyes noticed one of the arrows which had almost brought Chadokah's vengeful plans to fruition. Singing Arrow drew it from the ground, examined it carefully, and then thrust it into his quiver, muttering to himself: 'It was foolish of me to spare his life.'

In a short while all the riders set off for home.

The news of the huge buffalo herd was received with great joy at the camp, and in a while all the medicine men gathered, wearing their most precious ornaments, and with 'big medicine' hanging round their necks — various sorts of bags containing all manner of small things, such as dried beetles, herbs or coloured stones, teeth and claws which were supposed to have magic powers. The task of the medicine men was to put on a ceremony, in this case a buffalo dance, and to ask the spirits for a successful day's hunting on the morrow.

After the celebrations, when they all went their separate ways, Singing Arrow sat for a long time in front of his tent.

At last he stood up and went to fetch the broken arrow with a rusty point which he kept among his valuables. He took off the point and began to clean it.

PRAIRIE SON

Torry Gredsted

A the Great Pow-Wow

While the Civil War was raging in the south, the prairie war went on. Though the government had already set strict boundaries, confirmed by contracts, which were supposed to have the force of law for ever more, and solemnly promised the prairie Indians that no settler would cross those borders, a craving for adventure and property drove the newcomers further and further west, and all promises and written agreements went by the board.

With growing horror the Indians watched their land being whittled away year by year. With anxiety and bitterness they saw the buffalo herds get smaller and smaller, and more and more difficult to find, and indeed all animals get fewer in number. They noted with increasing fear the spread of destructive luxury and vice, brought to their tribes by the palefaces. Their magnificent, free lands, where they had until recently still been able to live the life their forefathers lived, were now crossed in all directions by long wagon trains, stagecoaches and messengers, bringing the newly-formed states news from the frontier regions, and especially by very frequent expeditions of

soldiers and engineers, preparing the way for that hugely important thing, a railway connection between east and west, which would signify the complete conquest of the prairie.

When the Civil War was over, there were many soldiers left, after four years of restless and exciting life in the field, without work, in the quiet of town or country life. Adventure had got into their bones, and where could they better satisfy their longing for new experiences than in the wild west?

There were at that time four main routes west. Southern destinations were served by the Santa Fé trail, while the route westward led along the River Kansas to Deventer, or the Oregon trail to Salt Lake. Travellers to the north-west went along the River Missouri, then in a wide arc to Montana. The lands there, famed for their mineral wealth, attracted more and more new settlers; there were more and more of them, the easier it became to get there. At that time the government decided to build a new route from Fort Laramie, north-westwards between the Rockies to the west and the Black Hills to the east. Between the two mountain ranges are two tributaries of the River Yellowstone, the Powder River and the Tongue

River. A series of small forts was built there, and the commander of the garrisons in this mountainous area was Colonel Carrington.

But there were many hard battles to be fought before the white man succeeded in imposing his will, for these lands were the pride and joy of the redskins, a splendid refuge, and their richest hunting-grounds, where there were still plenty of bears, moose, antelope and other wild animals, and where large buffalo herds still roamed.

They fought a long and bloody war for this magnificent land, and the soul of their struggle was Hokota.

Hokota was grievously wounded in a clash with a troop of cavalry led by John Elton. But the Dakotas managed to carry their young chief to safety. In vain did Jack Harrington and Willy Bell try to track him down; they returned empty-handed to their trapping.

For many days Hokota lay between the living and the dead. The young braves sat silently beside his bed, waiting anxiously to see how it would end. But finally Hokota's strong constitution and firm will to live won the day. The moment he recovered and was able to sit in the saddle, he went on the warpath again. His great, unsatiable hatred for the white man gave him no rest; it burned in his blood like a fever. Riding like the wind, he and his band went from north to south and from east to west, everywhere leaving bloody reminders of their visits.

Soon some solitary settler had to pay with his life and his scalp for his insolent intrusion into Indian territory, his barns going up in flames and his cattle being driven in all directions. Then some pony-express horse came galloping riderless into the staging-post, its saddle stained with blood, its rider lying back on the prairie, his breast pierced by an arrow. Another time the passengers of a stage-oach told the dreadful tale of how they had only just managed to escape from an ambush set for them by the redskin warriors.

All that summer Hokota made daring raids against the white settlers, destroying their property and collecting their scalps. His war party inspired fear and terror far and wide. The story of their cruel deeds spread in every direction, and no one could explain the meaning of the secret sign which they sometimes found on the left shoulder of the victims.

Of course, Hokota's band had their losses, too, but for the time being he had no plans to join one of the tribes, nor to take new men into his camp. For the moment a single thought spun around his head — vengeance, vengeance, vengeance! The palefaces had killed his father, Singing Arrow; it was the palefaces' fault that he had had to leave his native tribe in desperation. Hokota's idea of honour and duty found expression only in an effort to avenge the wrongs done to him.

It was only in late autumn that Hokota and his company withdrew to the old, hidden places in the hills to lay in a store of meat for the coming winter. Next spring he wished to continue his bloody revenge. And he would surely have gone on living that sort of life, falling victim to his burning thirst for vengeance, had not something happened wich changed his whole outlook on life and gave him a more important mission.

Early one morning, he was choosing which of his companions were to accompany him on an attack they planned on a pony-express staging-post, when he suddenly heard a faint rifle shot in the distance. He stopped, and listened carefully: in a while there came another shot, then a third. Hokota at once gave orders to take down the tents and hide them and the horses in a thicket. Then he leaped onto his horse and, taking with him a few men, went to find out where the shooting was coming from.

On the way they heard several more shots — then the firing stopped. For a while they continued in the direction they had heard the first shots coming from. Then they hid their horses and carefully crawled through the undergrowth. They reached a clearing, on the edge of which they saw the body of an Indian, in a crouching position behind a bush. Hokota took a closer look and saw that it was an Ogallala-Sioux, and when he looked around he saw another two dead Ogallala lying nearby. He would have crawled further, but at that moment a rifle bullet hit the ground right in front of his nose. Quick as a flash, he leaped back into the thicket, and stood there motionless for a moment, not knowing what was going on. But in a little while he again began crawling quietly through the thicket round the clearing, anxious to take a look behind a large tree on the far side, in the direction the bullet had come from.

He was sure it was a paleface who was doing the shooting, and his blood boiled again with desire to do battle. Thus he was amazed to find, when he reached the tree by a circuitous route, that a single Ogallala-Sioux was lying there, rifle in hand, looking cautiously around him. Hokota crawled nearer, but at that moment the man suddenly turned his face towards him and raised his rifle. Hokota saw that he had been mistaken for an enemy, that the other had failed to recognise him as a member of his own tribe.

'Let not your rifle speak, my friend,' called Hokota, but he jumped a long way to one side as he spoke, in case his words should have no effect.

When he received no answer, he made himself known, boldly stepping out of the thicket and striding right up to the Sioux brave. The latter looked at Hokota in wonder, especially at his belt, thickly hung with scalps. But he was unable to stand up. 'I cannot stand to greet you,' he said, pointing to one of his legs, which was bleeding. 'First of all, tell me who you are. You seem quite young, but your belt speaks the old tongue of war.'

'I am Hokota, and my father was Singing Arrow.'

The Sioux brave looked Hokota up and down. 'Give me your hand, friend,' he said gravely, 'and help me up! I will lean against the tree-trunk, and we will smoke a pipe together. All our warriors call you Swift-Winged Eagle, and sing your praises, though they have never seen you and do not know you.'

Hokota helped him to lean against the tree, and the wounded Sioux brave began to fill his pipe.

'Which way did your enemy go?' Hokota asked. 'Three of my friends and four horses are hidden in the bushes near here, and we can follow them.'

'I have killed all my enemies,' was the calm and assured answer, and when the Sioux saw Hokota looking around him in wonder, he continued: 'There were seven of them, and I was alone. But my rifle spoke faster than theirs.'

'These were not your friends?' asked Hokota, pointing to the dead redskins.

'If they had been my friends, I should not have killed them,' was the reply. 'But come, now we will smoke, and afterwards I will tell you of the battle.'

It was Mahpejalute — Red Cloud, later a highly renowned Indian Chief. He told Hokota how he had been tracked to this place by Buffalo Tail, also a well-known chief, who had been jealous of him, since he longed to be big chief. Buffalo Tail had had six of his followers with him, two with rifles, the others with bows and arrows. The first shot had struck Red Cloud in the right thigh, but he was in a good position behind the large tree, and had managed to pick off one after the other with his Winchester. His eyes shone and his voice trembled with pride. When he had finished speaking, he was surprised that Hokota did not say a word in praise of his shooting, his daring and his bravery.

Hokota sat silent, gazing into the distance, his brow furrowed.

Red Cloud had done a brave warrior's deed — alone against seven opponents — and Hokota's heart would have beaten faster with great joy over his victory, had those been the bodies of palefaces out in the clearing. He thought that if the white man were to attack them now, there would only be five of them, including his three companions hidden in the bushes, whereas there could have been a dozen if Red Cloud had not shot seven Ogallala. This was Hokota's first simple thought, but he suddenly remembered his own tribe, whose strength had been broken as a result of disputes and mutual rivalry between the bear and dog clans. He saw that they would never have become the white man's friend and shaken his hand if they had been united, as in the days when his father was chief.

Hokota was shaken out of his thoughts only when Red Cloud began to speak again, asking in a rather offended tone: 'It seems to me that you think it a poor warrior's deed, even though I was one against seven.'

My tongue has not spoken,' replied Hokota. 'But is not a frown the same as many words?' asked Red Cloud.

'I should like only the palefaces to be our enemies,' said Hokota. 'But now I will call my friends and we will see to your wound.' With a masterly imitation of a night-bird's cry he called his hidden companions.

Red Cloud stayed in Hokota's small camp, where they carefully tended his wound. But for the first few days there was no sign of Hokota, who in the manner of his kin stayed on his own whenever he had too much to think about and consider.

Those few days were of great importance in Hokota's life; a strange change came about in his character. From the first simple conclusion that there would be too few braves against the white man if the Indians were to kill each other, he was led to the idea that they might protect themselves from the destructive attacks of their enemies if they united in a single camp. He knew, of course, that in order to achieve this he would have to give up his way of life, and that he and his companions must join the rest. That was the first sacrifice he would be forced to make in the common interest. He would have to give up his role as leader, to obey others, which was for him indeed a great sacrifice.

When he had recovered from his wound, Red Cloud returned to his tribe with Hokota and his company. The Ogallala welcomed them with open arms. As Red Cloud had said, Hokota had a high reputation amongst his people, and he in no way disappointed their hopes. His outstanding knowledge and experience as a warrior and hunter soon won him great influence, not only among the young, but even in the ranks of the elders.

For this very reason Hokota did not lose sight of his great goal. He now saw how ambition, envy and jealousy, those very deep-rooted passions of the Indian race, stood in the way of a general alliance between all Indian tribes. And his observations gradually led him to overcome these feelings within himself. So in the following years a great change took place in Hokota's nature. He stopped pushing himself forward, and ceased to think about his own good qualities and his bravery; on the contrary, he preferred where possible to retreat into the background, so as not to arouse the envy and jealousy of others. If he had ambitious dreams, they were not for himself, nor for his own position of excellence, but related to that longed-for moment when the last stranger would be driven out of the land the Great Spirit had given the redskins. His hatred for the palefaces did not alter in the least; it was as uncompromising and as fiery as ever; its goal was no longer to accomplish his own vengeance, but the victory of the whole of his people, the assurance of the existence of his race. From being a ruthless and cruel scalp-hunter, who let himself be carried away by his own thirst for vengeance, Hokota became a freedom-fighter, a national hero, who took upon himself the task of defending his lands against the oppressor and fighting attempts to wipe his people out.

In spite of his youth, Hokota was a clear and shining example to all his tribal brothers. Though he did not have the title and rank of a chief, he had great influence, and his word carried great weight among the elders. The young braves held a deep and respectful admiration for him. Always and everywhere he tried fiercely to bring together the different tribes in one whole, and being an intelligent and eloquent speaker, he knew how to win his listeners over to his point of view.

In the early spring of 1866 the government authorities called upon the Dakotas and the northern Cheyenne tribes to gather on the great plain near Fort Laramie to negotiate agreements relating to a new route which was planned from the fort to the north-east. The government representatives took their places in the shade of the tall pine trees, at tables decorated with colourful carpets. In front of them were buffalo skins for the Indian chiefs and their splendid company — the members of their council, and the medicine men. Around the area set aside for the gathering was an arc of tents, making a very picturesque setting for the meeting.

The government commissioners had many great gifts distributed, and the gathering listened in dignity and calm to the words of the Indian envoys, who, with the florid speeches so beloved of the Indians, gave the men strings of *wampum*, praising the Great White Father in Washington, who surely loved his red children and had gathered them here to reinforce friendship with them, which would surely be to the advantage of all redskin tribes.

All the older chiefs had their say, and though their words were full of complaints and laments that the Great White Father in Washington still allowed their wigwams to be pushed further and further on, though he had often promised this would be the last time, still their speeches were not aggressive. The gathering of white men was pleased with the conciliatory mood of those present. Only one of the chiefs created quite the opposite impression. He rose occasionally from his buffalo skin and looked searchingly southwards.

It was Red Cloud. He did not share the views of the others, and was prepared to reject all talk of agreement, which meant allowing new forts to be built, and new restrictions on the Indian hunting grounds. He had not yet asked to speak, but was waiting for his faithful ally, Hokota, who was paying a long visit to the Cheyenne, to try to win them as allies in the coming war.

At last Red Cloud's brow cleared, and a contented smile played on his lips. He had seen all the young braves from the tents set aside for the Ogallala mount their horses and gallop southwards; he supposed, therefore, that one of the scouts had come to announce that Hokota was on his way back. And it was indeed the case: all the young men from his camp had set out to meet him.

Red Cloud was right. It was not long before Hokota strode with a dignified gait through the gathering to take his place alongside Red Cloud. For a long time he sat in silence and listened to the words of the current speaker — one of the older chiefs, whose complimentary words were intended to convince the government representatives that it was the firm intention and wish of himself and his whole tribe to live in peace and friendship with their white brothers. Red Cloud showed no sign of impatience or curiosity, though he was sure Hokota had brought a message of the utmost importance.

At last Hokota handed Red Cloud a bundle of red-painted sticks. 'I have been entrusted with a great message,' he said to Red Cloud in a low voice. 'These are sent by Black Cauldron. Throw away one each day, and when you have no more left, he will be ready to meet you on the western slopes of the Black Hills. His men long to do battle; they are more numerous than the bees which swarm in the trees.'

Red Cloud nodded, and hid the bundle at his breast. Suddenly, Hokota raised his head sharply, and his eyes blazed. One of the members of the government commission had just begun to speak, and the mere sound of the paleface's voice had such an effect on Hokota that he shook with anger, and it was a wonder he did not lose control of his temper. The moment the speaker had finished, Hokota leaped up from his seat and held up his hand to speak. The white men present surveyed him with wonder. They could scarcely believe their eyes. He was a mere chief's assistant, and so young at that. They did not therefore consider it likely he would be allowed to speak at the assembly. The deep throaty voices which answered Hokota's call were quite unintelligible; it was not possible to judge whether they expressed agreement or displeasure.

Hokota stood up straight, and it was a long time before he spoke, as he cast his eyes over the great assembly. Then he began his speech, in a strong, passionate voice, and with wild gestures.

He spoke in very emphatic terms for the rights of his whole race, for the land the Great Spirit gave his red children. His words were a masterly piece of Indian eloquence, and made a great impression on the listening chiefs.

Towards the end of Hokota's speech Colonel Carrington arrived, and was led into the centre of the gathering.

When Hokota saw him, his eyes blazed with anger. He called out:

'You see that my tongue speaks the truth! See, here is the white soldier chief who has come to steal our lands for his road, without waiting to see if we agree or not!'

At this Red Cloud rose from his seat, wrapped his buffalo skin around him, and without a word left the entire gathering, followed by his company.

In a little while his camp was like a busy anthill. The women quickly struck the tents and the menfolk hurried to and fro and saddled their horses, for the chief had given brief but strict orders to leave the gathering, and to take to the warpath.

The Battle of Lodge-Trail

In the mountainous part of River Plate territory, which was under the military protection of Colonel Carrington, there was only one military outpost, at Fort Reno, 160 miles to the west of Fort Laramie. Carrington received orders to march with his company to this post, move it forty miles further west, reinforce it with a certain number of men, and then proceed with the rest further into the country between the Rockies and Powder River, and set up a new fort there, which would then control that large valley. Apart from that he was to set up several more posts to act as refuges along the new route for settlers.

On May 19, 1866, the colonel set out from old Fort Kearney in Nebraska with quite a small force of 700 men, four cannon and 226 wagons, along with a few medical wagons. About 200 of his men were trained soldiers, the rest being raw recruits. They were mainly armed with old-fashioned front-loading rifles, only a few having new Spencer breech-loaders, whose range was not yet very great, but which as regards practicality and firing speed far outstripped the older type of firearm. There were also very few cavalrymen in the whole of this small company, and even fewer skilled riders.

The soldiers included all kinds of craftsmen, and the expedition took with them everything they needed to build a fort — tools, doors, window-frames, even glass, nails and bolts, stoves, iron and steel, and also all the components for a steam sawmill.

The journey was a tedious one, at slow marching pace, for the destination was a long way off. So it was not until June 28 that Carrington got close to Fort Reno. It was only there that the first skirmishes with Indians took place; they began to make persistent attempts to steal the army's horses and cattle. When the fort had been repaired and the garrison strengthened, Carrington set off, on July 9, with the remainder of his force, numbering some 500 men, into what was as yet uncharted country. In a few days he was camped beside one of the tributaries of the Powder River, about four miles from the huge Rocky Mountain ridge with its snow-covered peaks reaching skywards. Nearby they found a smallish hill, covered in grass and with all kinds of flowers growing on it, whose sides sloped steeply in all directions, making it a very suitable site for a fort. As there was plenty of space on top, Carrington decided to begin building there.

The site lay between two watercourses. On the eastern side were the high mountains, and to the west there was also a steep mountain ridge. It was an exquisite place — covered in dark green grass, with beautiful flowers growing in it. All the surrounding hills were covered in huge coniferous forests, with plentiful game in them; and there was adequate drinking water at hand. Nor did the builders of the fort have to go far for timber.

Colonel Carrington first marked out the outline of the fort, then set off on a scouting trip. He ordered the sawmill to be set up about seven miles away from the selected site, and building began.

Sentries were posted on both the mountain ridges, for these offered a fine view to the east and of the mountain range to the west. The Indians tried in vain to drive away these sentries by constant harrassment of Carrington's men. They had to be alert all the time down in the camp, and every wagon carrying timber had to be under armed guard. At first Carrington found it quite difficult to keep his soldiers within bounds and close to the camp, but the men soon learned to obey, since they discovered the unhappy consequences of disobedience and recklessness. In time they saw that those who ignored orders not to wander off disappeared without trace, or crawled back into the camp scalped and dying.

Despite all the Indian attacks, the fort grew at a satisfying pace. It was rectangular, measuring 800 by 600 feet, and was walled with thick pine trunks, eight feet high, with a loop-hole in every fourth trunk. At each corner of this massive structure was a block-house with an embrasure for a cannon, and substantial shelter for a platoon of soldiers. Apart from this there were several buildings within the walls for officers, men and horses, an open space where the cannon stood, and a parade-ground with a tall flagstaff, on which the American flag was hoisted for the first time on October 31. There was also, on the eastern side of the fort, but outside the walls, a smaller enclosure for wagons and hay supplies, which also included the workshops.

The fort was named Phil Kearney. It stood for two years only, but it can be said without exaggeration that no other fort had such a bloody history as this one. It was under continuous siege throughout those two years. In winter and summer smaller or larger groups of Indians lay hidden in the mountain passes and the surrounding forests, so that it was not possible to leave the fort at all without a substantial military escort. Those watchful redskin warriors missed nothing, lost no opportunity to attack a sentry who happened to stray away from the others. Whenever they could they stole cattle, horses and wagons. It was impossible to fell a tree or to mow a patch of grass without a strong military escort, even within a stone's throw of the fort walls. The countryside teemed with game, but the white men dared not shoot a single animal. For many of the settlers who allowed themselves to be enticed by the news from the military commission in Laramie that they had 'managed to conclude a conciliatory and friendly agreement with all the Indians of the north-west', the new route was to be a fateful one.

Red Cloud, who was chief of all the Indians here, confined himself throughout the summer and autumn to minor, though frequent incursions, while Hokota roamed the prairies, using his influence to try to form an alliance of all tribes, so that they might face the whites united. He often met with stiff opposition and unwillingness, but by and by, many Sioux tribe after tribe, joined forces with Red Cloud, and in the end there were more than three thousand of them. It was only then that Hokota was prepared to acknowledge that his place was again among the ranks of the warriors. The unfortunate whites in the besieged and entirely surrounded fort were soon to witness his deeds on the battlefield.

One evening in December, Colonel Carrington called a meeting of his officers. He knew well enough that many were dissatisfied with his leadership, which they considered too cautious, but he was sure that the circumstances now called for even greater caution, which is what he felt obliged to impress upon them on this occasion. Just as he entered the room where the officers were gathered, there was the sound of shooting from outside, and cries were heard. They all ran out, but found the parade ground around the flag calm and undisturbed. Then a sentry ran up with his report.

'Two trappers have arrived,' he announced. 'The Indians chased them right to the gate, but they made it all right.'

In a moment the two trappers, dressed in furs, were standing before the Colonel. 'What message have you brought?' Carrington asked — but then he gasped: 'Why, it's Harrington and Bell!'

The two trappers and renowned trackers were heartily welcomed by the officers. 'Well, Colonel, here we are,' replied Harrington. 'We have no message for you, but have come of our own accord. We should like to lend a hand, for we have heard something is going on here. It seems you are not exactly living in peace and contentment, eh?'

'Not at all,' the Colonel replied, grimly, 'and I have just called a meeting of the officers to consider the situation. It is more serious than it would seem. I have already asked many times for reinforcements, supplies, and above all for better and more modern weapons, but they don't believe me when I say there is a war going on here — a real war. They always tell me a peace treaty was signed at Laramie. They think we're the ones who are starting a war.'

'If you gave me eighty men, I should gladly go out and trample and shoot the Sioux to pieces,' Captain Fettermann suddenly interrupted.

'No,' replied Colonel Carrington. 'I should consider it madness; it would mean the destruction of us all. Captain Fettermann, you must admit that the main thing is for us to be cautious. The losses we have already suffered have weakened us, and as you know, we have to be extremely careful with the ammunition. We are already down to about forty rounds for each rifle. You know there are over 1500 tents at Powder River alone. You have no idea what the odds against us are.'

'But we also know that one white man, and a soldier at that, is worth any number of redskins,' said Captain Brown, who, along with Captain Fettermann, led the voices of dissent in the fort.

'Gentlemen, take it easy! I do not underestimate your personal courage and will to fight, but I should like you to keep to them.' His brow creased, the Colonel left the meeting without another word.

'What d'you say to that, Jack Harrington, you old Indian scourge?' asked Captain Fettermann, when the Colonel had left.

'What do I say? Only that Bell and me have always been ready to do what had to be done. It seemed to us that things were on the boil here, so we got hold of long-range rifles, and we're going put them to all the use we can 'gainst them red varmints!' The opportunity presented itself the very next day.

It was a very cold, but clear December day, quite without snow. At about eleven o'clock in the morning a lookout signalled from the mountains to the east that the timber wagons had been attacked, and had formed a circle about two and a half miles from the fort.

Quickly, a force was put together to go to the aid of the wagons; it consisted mainly of foot-soldiers under Captain Powell, with a few cavalrymen led by Lieutenant Grummond. Carrington himself came out to inspect the men, rejecting many of them, mainly because of their unsuitable weapons. When they were all ready to leave the gates, Captain Fettermann came forward and stood in front of his commander: 'You must allow me to lead this detachment, Colonel,' he said in a firm voice. 'No,' replied the Colonel. 'Captain Powell will lead them.'

'You cannot refuse, Colonel,' Fettermann went on. 'I am the oldest of the captains, and I must ask that to be taken into account.'

For a moment Carrington hesitated. He was well aware of Fettermann's view of the situation, and he knew that he underestimated the redskin warriors; on the other hand, he could not just thrust him aside, since he was indeed the senior officer.

'Very well, Captain Fettermann,' he said at last, making it clear that the decision was not one he made gladly. 'Take command. Relieve the wagons and drive off the Indians. But I order you not to pursue them beyond Lodge-Trail, and as soon as your mission is accomplished to return to the fort!'

Before long the detachment was on its way. It was joined by Captain Brown, Jack Harrington and Willy Bell. The force was about eighty strong, which was the number of men Captain Fettermann had asked for in order to shoot the Dakotas to pieces. As the cavalry set off, Carrington repeated his orders about pursuing the Indians to Lieutenant Grummond, and when the last rider had left the gate, hurried to the watchtower to call after the detachment that on no account was it to cross the top of Lodge-Trail Hill.

The situation of the men defending the wagons was critical, since their 'corral' was surrounded by several hundred Indian horsemen, and they could at any moment expect to defend themselves against overwhelming odds. But the whites suddenly noticed that the Indians were retreating, disappearing into the valley beyond the ridge. At first they thought this strange, but when in a little while they saw soldiers approaching from the north, along the Sullivant Hills, they supposed the Indians to have withdrawn so as not to be caught in crossfire.

But it was only the first move in Hokota's cunning tactics. He had entered the battlefield again for the first time in years, and trembled with the desire to hurl himself against his enemies. He had wanted to call upon Red Cloud to give the signal to attack the barricade of wagons, but at that moment scouts came with the news that reinforcements were on the way from the hills opposite. In an instant a new plan flashed through Hokota's head. The attack on the well-armed wagon circle would have been a bold move, but if he managed to lead the approaching reinforcements into a trap, there was a prospect of destroying the enemy altogether. At his suggestion Red Cloud assembled his foot-warriors in the valley, hiding them in a masterly fashion in suitable cover. He and his horsemen were to be the 'bait'.

Hokota's clever ruse was all too successful. Captain Fettermann saw the Indians waiting in the valley, and by their challenging gestures and mocking calls he supposed that they were ready to fight.

'What do you think, Harrington?' he asked, excitedly. 'You have fought enough battles with the redskins! Is this not a good opportunity to teach them a proper lesson? To my mind it is not a chance to be missed. These fellows seem anxious to cross swords with us, though I swear they'll regret it!'

'Hmm. Your old man back at the fort doesn't want you to cross Lodge-Trail,' Harrington replied.

'The devil take it. The old man has no idea of the situation here. We have relieved the wagons without a struggle, and I think it's time these cheeky fellows got what's coming to them. The more careful we are, the more impudent and the more daring they get!'

And he gave Lieutenant Grummond orders to ride round the Indians with his thirty cavalrymen, and to attack them from behind when a suitable opportunity presented itself.

The Indians soon saw what the cavalrymen were up to. Red Cloud, out of an old fear of being caught in crossfire, wanted to retreat, but Hokota persuaded him otherwise.

'I think this time the redskins are really going to fall into the trap,' said Jack Harrington merrily, spoiling for a fight. 'We can go now — the cavalry will have got far enough.'

Captain Fettermann set off with his men marching in long lines, but the Indians began to retreat at the same pace, so that the distance between them was always the same. In their enthusiasm, the soldiers began to run, which made the group led by Red Cloud break into a run, too. But then the Indians suddenly stopped, and a huge warcry from many hundreds of throats cut through the air far and wide.

'Halt!' ordered Fettermann. 'And now . . .' but the words froze on his lips. His eyes were presented with a fearful sight which sent a shiver up his spine — and also that of every man present. The whole valley had suddenly come to life. From behind every stone, every bush and every clump of grass of any size an Indian had suddenly leapt, and from all sides poured wildly whooping, bloodthirsty redskin braves.

Utter panic broke out among Fettermann's soldiers. 'Get back, get back!' they called. Fettermann and Brown tried in vain to stop them. First of all they hurled insults at them, but it was no use; then they begged the corporals to re-form ranks, but to no avail: these terrified men had no thought but to escape across the gentle slope which was still open in front of them, and to reach the protective walls of the fort. In the end the two officers tried in desperation to force individuals at least to stay, but they could not even manage that, for the men were wild with fear, and dragged their officers along with them. When the two officers managed at last to free themselves from their own soldiers, they stood back to back and began to fire at the Indians, so that their way opened up for a moment and they were able to see better. But they witnessed horrifying scenes being acted out only a few paces away. The redskins rushed in from all sides, engulfing their soldiers like an avalanche. There was only an occasional rifle shot to be heard, while the hatchets just flew up and down. Before long the victorious Indians had closed an impenetrable circle around the unfortunate white men, and a bloody scuffle ensued. For a little while the soldiers fought a last desperate battle for their lives with rifle, sabre and bayonet, but they were hopelessly outnumbered, and their fate was sealed.

'We've had it,' gasped the two officers, almost with one breath. For a while they went on shooting at the enemy like mad.

'Brown!'

'I'm ready.'

'Do you remember what we promised?'

'Promised? Yes, I know: we vowed to kill ourselves rather than fall into the hands of the Sioux. I'm ready! Do you hear?'

They held their fire, and the Indians rushed towards them.

'Come on, then, you stupid good-for-nothings,' muttered Fettermann bitterly. 'Quickly, Brown — I'll count to three.' And they both put their revolvers to their heads.

'One, two, three...' The two shots rang out simultaneously, and the two officers who had ordered their men to their deaths fell to the ground. The Indians let out high-pitched shrieks when they saw that the scalps they had longed for had been denied them. Indians never scalp an enemy who has taken his own life. It is 'bad medicine'.

The two experienced hunters, Jack Harrington and Willy Bell, saw to their horror the panic-stricken, mindless flight of the soldiers. Their long years' experience told them that retreat in such circumstances meant total defeat and annihilation. So, as soon as they saw they were

surrounded, they hid behind the nearest substantial heap of stones, resolving to sit it out there. And indeed, at first the fleeing soldiers occupied the entire attention of the Indians, and so the trappers were able to spend a little while behind the stones unobserved.

'If only one of them at least could get back to the fort, then ...'

'No chance,' Harrington interrupted his friend in a decisive voice. 'Not Fettermann, or Brown, or anyone else. They'll be cut down to a man. If only we could go to meet the cavalry.'

He had scarcely said this when they both saw the cavalry detachment under Lieutenant Grummond approaching at full tilt the thicket in which they lay hidden. Grummond also saw that he had fallen into a trap; it became clear to him only when he saw his enemies rising up in front of him as if they had suddenly emerged from the ground. Now he was in retreat, with redskin braves on small, fast horses hard on his heels. He rushed to the place where he expected to find Fettermann.

'Here they are! Here they are!' called Willy Bell.

'They're retreating, too,' muttered Jack Harrington. For Christ's sake, had these people no idea of the rudimentary rules of battle? Did they not see that to retreat was to choose certain death?

Leaping out onto the heap of stones, he started to wave his fur cap wildly, calling out at the top of his voice: 'Over here, over here! Wait, for God's sake!'

Lieutenant Grummond saw him and waved to him, but at the same moment the Indians gathered round him with wild cries.

The massacre of Fettermann's foot troop was complete, and the Indians, drunk with success, began to hurl themselves on Grummond's cavalry in their hordes.

'Stop! Stop!' Harrington cried again, while his comrade kept the nearest Indians at a respectful distance with his fire. 'Come here, and get off your horses, quickly!'

Only Grummond and a few of the older soldiers listened to his plea, while the others dashed off in the direction Fettermann's men had also taken in the belief that they would escape.

'Shoot your horses,' called Harrington. 'Take cover behind them.

Fire!' And he himself jumped onto the pile of stones and began to shoot at the onrushing Indians again.

'W-what about Fettermann, Brown and the others?' stuttered Lieutenant Grummond, immediately taking Harrington's advice. He placed his revolver against his horse's ear.

'Cut down to a man — they tried to run away,' came the cold reply.

'Fettermann ran away?' Grummond almost shouted, for he knew the captain's prodigious courage.

'It wasn't his fault, or Brown's; they did what they could, but the others carried them along. Look over there — and over there — ugh! Not one of the poor fellows came back.'

The retreating cavalrymen disappeared in the chaos of battle, and the small group, cut off and surrounded by bloodthirsty enemies, defended itself desperately. Lieutenant Grummond was paralysed with fear. Whenever he heard the wild warcries of the blood-drunk victors, he realised that another dead white man had fallen to the frozen ground, scalped and mutilated.

'The same thing happened to the infantry,' Harrington commented, quietly.

The redskins moved in closer and closer to the small, weak group of defenders, whose only faint hope was that perhaps new reinforcements might arrive from the fort before they fired their last shot.

Soon after Captain Fettermann left the fort, Colonel Carrington recalled that he had not assigned a doctor to the relief force, and sent doctor Hines after them with a small escort. The doctor soon returned with the news that the wagons were on their way, but that there was no sign of Fettermann's force, while Indians were swarming all over Lodge-Trail Hill.

The news was received at the fort with considerable dismay, which further increased when the sound of heavy rifle fire was heard coming from Lodge-Trail. At once Carrington sent the whole of the remaining garrison to the combatants' aid, under Captain Eyck. The captain had strict orders to join Fettermann's detachment, and after fighting off the Indians to return to the fort at once.

The Colonel himself then went to the watchtower, from where he stared into the distance in the direction of the gunfire, with grim thoughts and a premonition of misfortune. His anxiety was soon increased by a new and unfavourable report.

A messenger came from Captain Eyck with the news that the valley on the other side of Lodge-Trail was teeming with Indians, but that not one of Fettermann's force was to be seen.

The gunfire died away, and Carrington was now sure that the great catastrophe he had feared had come to pass.

Before Captain Ted Eyck had time to reach the battlefield below Lodge-Trail, the Colonel heard new, occasional gunshots. It was Jack Harrington and Willy Bell firing off their last rounds.

Lieutenant Grummond and his few faithful soldiers were lying dead at their feet. All around there were also mounds of red bodies, for the two hunters were excellent shots and they made every bullet count. But their position was hopeless.

'I've only two shots left, Jack,' said Willy.

'Me too,' his companion replied, quite calmly, although he was at the brink of death. 'But we'll fight to the last breath, and won't die any other way than white men should. I haven't time to shake your hand, Willy, but thanks for being my friend all these years. I think we've both kept our oaths.'

At that the redskins rushed in from all sides. The two trappers fired their last rounds and jumped up to use the last weapons they had, the butts of their rifles. A hail of arrows engulfed them, and Willy Bell fell to the ground with a deep sigh.

Jack Harrington, a sworn enemy of the Indians, stood quite alone. One arrow hit him in the left shoulder, but he quickly pulled it out and raised his rifle again, ready to strike out in all directions.

At that moment there was a loud, piercing shout, and a rider tore his way through the throng as swift as an arrow, straight to the condemned white man. It was Hokota.

Hokota's sharp eyes had recognised the man who killed his father the moment Jack Harrington leaped up for his last desperate attempt to defend himself. At that moment he forgot all that was going on

164

around him. Digging his heels into his horse's side, he rode towards Harrington. No one must beat him to it, for he had resolved to avenge his father himself.

With a blow of his axe he smashed the butt of Harrington's rifle and knocked it out of his hand. He jumped from his horse, and before his enemy could reach for Bell's rifle, his tomahawk whistled once more through the air, cutting off Jack Harrington's head.

With wild, shrill cries, all the redskins rushed to the place where this bloody scene had been played out. Hokota stood there motionless. First he carefully surveyed his fallen enemy, then he bent over him, tore the fur coat from his left shoulder, and with his knife cut deep into the flesh the slaver's mark of Thomas Garland.

Then he leaped up, threw his head back proudly, and looked around him with a clear gaze, sparkling with contentment, and a satiated longing for revenge.

'It was the paleface who killed my father, Singing Arrow.'

THE LAST
OF THE CHIEFS

Joseph Altsheller

The Indian Village

When Dick came round, he could see up above him the steeply sloping ceiling of their hut in the valley. His gaze wandered down the walls, to the floor, which was covered in reed mats. It was on one of these that Dick lay, and a few paces away, beside the door, sat two Sioux, cleaning their rifles.

To his surprise, Dick was not afraid of the two warpainted Indians; instead, he admired the strength of their arms, the beauty of their bronzed bodies.

Then he remembered Albert. He looked round again, but his brother was nowhere to be seen. He raised himself slightly on his elbows, but before he managed to turn on his side to relieve the pain in his back — apparently the result of a blow from a rifle butt — a tall, dignified figure stepped out of the shadows to his right. His expression was more one of curiosity than of anger, and he asked: 'Why did you come here?'

Dick had to laugh at the question. Even though his head ached, and he was well aware that he was a prisoner of Indians about whom he had heard the most fearful tales.

'I didn't come. I was brought.'

'That is so,' the chief replied in the precise English used by educated persons. 'You were brought here, and it was my braves who brought you. But what were you doing in our hills?'

'It would be nearest the truth to say that I don't know myself,' Dick replied without hesitation and truthfully. 'My brother and I got lost on the prairie, and I ended up here. I've no idea where I am.'

'You are in the village of the Mdewakanton Sioux, the family of Queyatoto-we,' the chief explained gravely. 'I, too, am a member of that family and that tribe. The Mdewakanton are one of the foremost tribes in the great nation of Sioux of the Seven Fireplaces. But all the tribes are large — the Mdewakanton, the Wahpeton, the Sisseton, the Yankton, the Teton, the Ogallala and the Hunckpapa — all of them, down to the smallest troop of each tribe.'

168

Bright Sun declaimed all this in a ceremonious, monotonous tone, filled with pride. All that was left in him of the white man's civilisation was his slow, precise English, with faultless pronunciation. In all else he was an Indian, the proud chief of a proud tribe.

'What about this hut?' Dick asked.

'This is the house of the Akitcita, the tepee of our boldest braves, men aged between twenty and forty. They live here together, and neither woman nor child may enter. I have read in your books how the youths of Sparta lived together under one roof as soldiers, eating simple food and performing difficult tasks. And now the whole of your world admires their deeds. Well, the Sioux, who had never heard of any Spartans, have been doing the same since long, long ago, since before anyone can remember.'

Dick looked with renewed interest at this tall, proud man, about whom he had heard and read so much. Perhaps this great Sioux chief really believed himself not only equal to white men, but better than them. Better, braver and wiser than other men — except for those of his tribe.

It was such a surprising idea that for a moment Dick forgot all about the most important thing he wanted to ask the chief, which was where his brother Al was.

'I've always heard folk speak well of you. They say the Sioux nation is courageous, wise and strong!'

'We are the nation of the Seven Fireplaces. What the Six Nations once were in the east, we are today in the west. Except that we are much more numerous and stronger, and we will never allow a dispute to arise among us. We have leaders who know the truth, and know what to do.'

There was defiance as well as pride in his voice. The defiance of the entire Indian race, cruelly and unfairly cheated and persecuted by white settlers and colonisers.

Dick understood the chief, understood his defiance — but that did nothing to alleviate the situation. He was a prisoner, and had nothing to look forward to. Neither had his brother Al.

'Where is my brother Albert, whom you captured with me?' he

170

asked in a voice shaking with apprehension. 'You haven't killed him, have you?'

'No, we have neither killed him nor injured him, even though we have taken to the warpath against your people. Your brother is here, and for the time being he is in no danger, any more than you are. True, some of my warriors wanted to kill you, but I studied at your schools. Why should we dispose too soon of that which may be of use to us? We shall keep you and your brother as hostages.'

Dick gave a sigh of relief. He was sure that Bright Sun was speaking the truth, that Al really was all right, and that the Indian chief was not a bloodthirsty Sioux, as he had heard at home, but a wise and honourable man, who knew the weight of his own words.

Then he asked about something which had been weighing on his mind for some time. Now was his chance...

'Bright Sun, was it you who led the wagon train into an ambush in the pass, where they were all killed?'

Bright Sun shrugged his shoulders, but his eyes flashed.

'Why do you ask? According to your moral code it was an act of treachery and cunning. But those who are small and few in number must use cunning as a justified weapon — sometimes it is the only one they have. Especially when they are on the defensive!

'If a small man is to resist a big man, he must make use of every advantage he has. The Sioux are the last stronghold of the Indian race, and therefore every means is justified.'

For a while both were silent; then the Indian asked:

'You and your brother ran away. That was nearly two years ago. But you did not return to your own people — where have you been?'

Dick thought quickly. The Indian was straightforward with him — Dick could not be so frank in return, but he did not wish to lie, either. So he was silent.

'Will you not tell me where you were those two years, what you did, and what happened to you?' the chief asked again.

This time he could not remain silent.

'I won't. We've not harmed you, nor anyone else. It's our secret.'

'Who taught you that the greatest of virtues is to be silent?' Bright

Sun enquired with a smile. 'For the time being you shall keep your secret. But give me your word you will not try to escape. That will make life much easier for you in our village. In any case, we should soon catch you. If you wish later to try to escape, you only have to say that you take back your word.'

Dick laughed merrily.

'That's what I call fair dealing! Because — so you say — there is no chance of my escaping, I can easily promise not to run away. All right — I promise not to try to escape.'

The chief nodded gravely.

'Soon they will bring your brother — you will be together again. He promised not to escape provided you promised the same.'

'Then it's clear. For the moment I won't run away,' Dick closed the conversation.

Bright Sun bowed his head and left the hut.

Dick watched him through the open door, until the Indian's tall, erect figure disappeared among the neighbouring tents. Then he began to look round the inside of the hut. It really did seem more like a barracks than a civil building, but everything was simpler, indeed more Spartan than the military buildings of the white man. Only he had a mat to sleep on; the other two were used for laying weapons on, as Dick was soon to see for himself. For a number of braves entered the hut, all tall, well-built, athletic figures. Some of them wore European-style clothes — shirts and trousers — but most had only blankets, leather leggings and moccasins, with eagle's feathers in their hair. All were armed with rifles, and some also had revolvers in their belts. They were the Akitcita, the chosen warriors: in this village of around two hundred tepees there were sixty of them.

The Indians took no notice of Dick, behaving as if he had not been there. They sat on the rough wooden benches, cleaning and polishing their weapons, smoking pipes, chatting. They did not even take any notice when a second paleface, Albert, entered the hut. He stopped in the doorway, looking around the large hut for a while in bewilderment; but as soon as he caught sight of Dick, he ran joyfully towards him. He embraced his brother and sat down next to him on the mat.

'It's a beautiful village!' Albert began, enthusiastically. It was his way — he always succumbed to first impressions.

'And Bright Sun is treating us well, so far. We can move freely around the village if we promise not to try to escape.'

'I spoke to him, too,' Dick confirmed. 'And I promised the same as you.'

'That's good. We can go and take a look round the village. If you're strong enough to walk, that is.'

'Wait a minute — I'll see if I get dizzy,' Dick said, standing up gingerly.

There was a humming in his head, and the inside of the hut spun like a merry-go-round, but it only lasted a few moments. Dick took a deep breath and exercised his arms and legs. His limbs were in order — he must have received only a blow on the head. But Albert put an arm round his waist just the same; he was glad to be able to support his older brother again. Physically and figuratively. Dick soon noticed how content Albert was in his solicitude, so he leaned his whole weight on his brother. But after a few steps he extricated himself and continued on his own. Sleep and a hearty meal had restored his strength.

The warriors, of whom there were now about a dozen in the hut, continued to take no notice of the white boys, apparently on the orders of Bright Sun. Dick and Al passed by them like a breeze.

As soon as they were outside, Dick took a deep breath. The fresh air carried the scents of the awakening spring. Dick soon forgot he had ever had a headache. He looked around him curiously. He had already seen the valley by moonlight, but now, in broad daylight, it did not seem so mysterious and beautiful, though he could now see clearly what had in the dark been a matter of surmise.

The village comprised some two hundred huts made of thin trunks and bark. The good-living enjoyed by the braves of Bright Sun was apparent from the amount of buffalo, moose and deer meat which hung drying on the branches of trees or on low benches made of poles. Among the huts Indian children played with dogs or practised shooting with small bows. In the shade of one of the larger buildings sat six women. The boys stopped for a moment and watched them.

The Indians love games of chance — like the white man — and these wrinkled old women were playing with such excitement that they did not notice they were being watched. The game was one of dice, called *Woscate Tampan* by the Sioux. Three women sat on either side. The game was played with a *tampan*, or basket, *kansu*, or dice, and sticks used as counters, which the Indians call *kaniy wawa*. The *tampan*, woven from willow branches, had a bottom some two and a half inches across, and was a little wider at the top. A player placed the *kansu*, consisting of six plum stones, some of which were carved, in the basket. Then he covered the top of it with his hand, shook the dice several times, and then threw the *kansu* on the ground. The score was calculated according to the type and carving of the dice. The wagers, the *kaniy wawa* or counters, lay on the ground between the seated women. They were small, round sticks, about the size of a pencil, and represented a value which had been agreed before-hand. It was known that old Sioux women were capable of playing *Woscate Tampan* two days and nights without a break.

Among the Indians, playing with dice was not the privilege of old women. A number of braves were sitting on the grass, also playing with dice. The boys went up to them and watched for a while.

As in the house of the Akitcita, here, too, no one took any notice of them. But Dick had an unpleasant feeling that their every step was being watched. And by more than one pair of eyes. The whole village was surreptitiously watching them. Some out of curiosity, some because the chief or somebody else had told them to.

He told his brother of his suspicions.

'But I shouldn't try to escape just now. Not even if we hadn't promised Bright Sun, I mean.'

'Nor should I,' Albert agreed. 'We wouldn't get ten yards before all these Indians were on our heels. There's nothing for it but to pretend we're satisfied, Dick.'

Dick silently nodded his agreement, and once more began to look around him. The village was built in a very favourable spot. On one side it was protected by the river, which, though narrow, was quite

fast-flowing and deep. On the other side was a broad open space without a single bush or tree. No enemy would have been able to approach the village without the Indians seeing him. Beyond that was the edge of the deep forest.

When the boys had seen enough of the gamblers, they headed for the northern end of the village. There a large number of Indian mustangs were grazing, at least seven hundred horses. Indian boys were guarding them.

'Dick, if we had a dozen of those horses, we could go back to the mountains and take all the skins to town.'

'That's right,' Dick agreed. 'If we had horses, if we knew where we were, if we were free to leave the village, and if we could find our way back to that valley of ours — then we could really do as you suggest.'

'You're right — it's all ifs,' laughed Albert. 'That's why I don't believe we can. Not yet, anyway. The only thing left for us is to get used to what's happened to us, and for the time being to put up with it.'

And he led the way back to the centre of the village, Dick following hesitantly.

The Gathering of the Sioux

Dick and Albert had lived in the large hut of the Akitcita for nearly a fortnight, and felt more like guests than prisoners. They were treated well and courteously — if anyone noticed them at all.

The boys, on the other hand, followed every movement the young Indians made. The Akitcita seemed more and more like a company of Spartans about whose deeds they had read. Each of the braves had a mat to sleep on — Dick had been wrong about this — and a place for his weapons, which was the only private property the young Indians had. Simple food, water and wood were brought to them every day by the women, and the whole tribe made each of them a gift of tobacco every week; it was the only luxury the Indian Spartans enjoyed. The members of the Akitcita lived together in complete harmony; they did not speak unnecessarily, and their chief virtues were humility, reserve, discipline and courage.

The brothers could see this for themselves. But there were many other things which they did not see, but which interested them no less. So they always asked chief Bright Sun, who willingly explained everything to them. The life of the Sioux was basically governed by ancient rules and regulations, though these seemed surprisingly modern and just.

The office of chief was not hereditary, for instance, but could only be won by strength, valour and merit.

Bright Sun himself was a living example of this principle. He had won his position of privilege among his people on the basis of his knowledge, his wisdom and his courage.

None the less, he had acquired these qualities to a large degree at schools founded and run by white men! He had chosen the best of their teaching, combining knowledge with the courage, valour and natural honour of his kin. It was this combination which made him a man of such excellent and exceptional qualities as Dick and Al had never seen before. None of this altered the fact that Bright Sun did not like the white man, did not trust him, and condemned him. In his eyes the Howard brothers were an honourable exception.

After ten days in the Akitcita the chief ordered the prisoners to be transferred to his own hut. The boys welcomed the change. At least they would have peace and quiet, and could think about the future. They did not intend to spend the rest of their lives among Indians, after all.

In any case, it seemed that the latter would themselves bring matters to a head before long. Life in the village changed suddenly. They no longer saw the old women playing *Woscate Tampan* so often; the menfolk gave up their usual pastimes entirely, and behind the mask of calm they maintained the boys could sense excitement and anxiety. At night-time they were kept awake by war-drums and the cries of medicine-men, as they prepared their medicine bags in their tents.

This change in the behaviour of the Sioux worried and frightened Dick. He shared his fears with Albert:

'It's as though they had changed. They're getting ready for something. I'm afraid it might be a final blow to end the war with us. And our people don't know it!'

Albert smiled bitterly.

'You'd like to warn them, wouldn't you? But you mustn't forget the promise we made Bright Sun. Apart from that we haven't a chance of getting away. There must be at least a hundred pairs of eyes watching us.'

'It seems to me that there are two hundred, a thousand,' Dick added, grimly. 'You're right, Albert, it's no use thinking about escaping.'

And on the fifth day after the white brothers moved to their own tepee, the excitement of the inhabitants reached a climax. The village burst into shouting and yelling like dry wood catching fire; women, children and dogs rushed to the northern end of the village, with the men following at a slower pace, holding themselves back. With them went Dick and Albert.

Those whom the whole village had been waiting for impatiently had arrived. They walked in a long line; there were at least four hundred of them, tall men, their hair decorated with eagle's feathers, their bodies draped with gaudy blankets. They were armed with rifles and revolvers.

The boys recognised which tribes they belonged to by the cries of welcome the women and children let out.

'Sisseton! Wahpeton! Ogallala! Yankton! Hunckpapa!'

The newcomers, among whom there were many chiefs, acknowledged the greetings with dignified nods of their heads, and walked silently through the crowd, which opened up before them like the surface of a lake beneath the prow of a swift-moving boat.

'The nation of the Seven Fireplaces is going to hold a big pow-wow in the house of the Akitcita,' said Dick in a half-whisper.

'A pow-wow of the cream of the cream,' added Albert, who knew the Sioux well enough to make out the names the rejoicing crowds called out.

And they were names whose English translations were already well

known, such as Sitting Bull, Man In A Storm, Little Giant and many others.

And it was these men whom Bright Sun led straight into the tepee of the Akitcita, while the other warriors went to the tepees of their friends among the Mdewakanton to accept the hospitality which befitted such a rare visit.

Dick was right; the nation of the Seven Fireplaces, or the most important part of it, had gathered for a great council. The pow-wow which took place in the tepee of the Akitcita lasted all day, and had not finished even when evening fell. The excitement which reigned throughout the village had its effect on Dick and Albert, too, though the boys still had no idea what all the fuss was about. That evening they could not sleep: the monotonous chanting of the medicine-men carried through the night, and occasionally also the quiet conversation from the tepee of the Akitcita.

When the boys had not fallen asleep even at midnight, they decided to test their luck. They crept out of the low tepee, but soon saw that to pass unseen that night of all nights was impossible. The village was full of people; not only the menfolk were awake, but the women and children, too. On the other hand, precisely because it was a night without sleep, no one took any notice of the boys, and they passed safely through the middle of the village to the tepee of the Akitcita, where the great pow-wow was being held. They even reached the open door.

The pale moonlight and the fact that the boys' imagination had been stirred made the tepee of the Akitcita suddenly take on immense, ghostly proportions. Inside sat at least a thousand painted chiefs, with Bright Sun at their head, undoubtedly in charge of the whole meeting.

The graveness of the occasion extended beyond the door of the tepee, where the braves who acted as bodyguards to the visiting chiefs stood motionless.

Though they had no idea what was going on inside, Dick and Albert stood as if enchanted, looking at what they could not see and listening to what they could not hear.

At last the meeting ended, and one by one the Indians went out-side — the guests to get a breath of fresh air before going back into the Akitcita to sleep, the villagers to make their way home. The last to leave was Bright Sun. He was the only one who noticed the white prisoners, and he made straight for them.

'I am sure you would like to know what we spoke about,' he said to Dick.

'We ask no questions,' Dick replied gravely. 'But I am sure that whatever happens will happen by your will and according to your wishes.'

Bright Sun smiled.

'You have learned to flatter, I see.'

'I didn't mean it as flattery,' Dick objected. 'But that's not the point. I'd like to say something else: we want to take back our promise not to try to escape. I'm sure you remember our agreement — that we could end our promise whenever we wanted.'

'That is so,' Bright Sun agreed. 'Do you think the time has come for you to leave?'

'Yes, we will leave if we can,' Dick proclaimed, staunchly. 'Just as you say — if we can. And our agreement was also precise: from now on our promise doesn't count any more.'

'You must do as you see fit. But I can assure you that you will not escape. We need you both as hostages, and in addition I can tell you that tomorrow we shall be leaving this valley. A great march will begin.'

'Just as I thought,' said Dick.

And with that their conversation with Bright Sun ended.

When they had lain down on the mat in their small hut, Albert asked his brother:

'What do you think about it?'

'It's what I expected. The Sioux have reached an agreement at last and are going to make a last attack against the white man. Tonight they agreed, and tomorrow they are going to set out to attack. If only we could manage to get away in time!'

Albert crept over to the doorway of the hut and looked out. A number of Indians were walking through the centre of the village, a few yards apart.

'They've put a guard inside the village as well as round it,' he announced in a whisper, when he returned to his bed.

'As I expected,' Dick replied. 'But now go to sleep, Al. It's the most sensible thing we can do tonight.'

It was a good while before they fell asleep, and with the first light of dawn they were awake again.

The moment they went outside, they saw Bright Sun had spoken the truth. Most of the lighter tents had been folded, only the huts and large tents remaining; the Indians had breakfasted, and were ready to move. All the horses which had been in the camp were going with them; two, without reins or saddles, were given to Dick and Albert.

This did little to enhance their hopes of escaping. They were unarmed, and without reins they would scarcely be able to persuade the horses to leave their four-legged companions. In addition, they rode in the middle of the ranks, surrounded by braves.

They left the valley and headed due north. Their route took them between hills which were ever lower and longer, to a river; on the other side of the river the hills and forest soon gave way again to the undulating, endless prairie. By the position of the sun the boys could tell which direction they were travelling in, but otherwise they knew nothing at all of the countryside they were passing through. Two or three times they tried to strike up a conversation with one of the braves, in the hope that he might understand English, but it was no use.

That night they camped on the open prairie. Dick and Albert, wrapped in warm blankets, slept in the middle of a ring of Indians; there were several such circles. The Sioux always slept in families, and each family played host to a number of guests, who were given the best places to sleep.

The brothers were surprised that the Indians did not light fires that evening; instead, well into the night, they scrutinised the long line of the horizon. These two circumstances — a blackout in camp and unusual wariness, could mean only one thing: there were white men not far away, most probably the army. If that was so, then let's hope there are plenty of them, thought Dick, and with this wish he fell asleep.

He was awakened by voices and the neighing of horses. Dick raised himself on his elbows and was able to make out a group of about two hundred riders entering the camp.

As Dick found out the next morning, the newcomers in the night were also Sioux, bringing the number of warriors up to nearly seven hundred. But that was not the last of them. The next day another size-able group joined them, and it was the same the next day, and the next, and all that week. The arrivals were greeted with mere nods of the head, without words or shouting.

It must all have been arranged beforehand in great detail, so that there was no reason for unnecessary words or displays of feelings.

All that time Dick and Albert saw Bright Sun only three times; the Sioux chief did not stop to speak to them, however, or even notice them. The rest of the Indians, too, were veiled in silence, so that the boys had to try to work out for themselves what might be going on, at the risk of being far from the truth.

Then at last the prairie gave way again to more varied countryside, at first two or three small hills, then shrubs, and finally forest.

'I think we're going to stop soon. The Indians seem to be getting ready to take a rest,' Dick said.

And as if to confirm his words, a large group of horsemen rode out of the forest and galloped to meet the newcomers. All their horses were quite fresh, indicating that there was a village close at hand.

Bright Sun's people greeted this group more heartily than they had the others. Dick and Albert were soon to find out why.

The column rode through the forest, and came to two smallish hills; when they reached a third, the tallest of the three, the boys held their breath at the sight which met their eyes down below.

Beneath them was a long valley, about a mile across, with a shallow river flowing through it, lined with shrubs and trees. On the left bank of the river an Indian village, or rather an Indian town, stretched as far as the eye could see.

The tepees, of which there were hundreds, perhaps thousands, had clearly been erected a short time before, and were densely populated: there were fires everywhere, and women and children were moving back and forth.

'I should never have believed we'd find such a large Indian village so far west,' said Albert.

'I'll bet it hasn't been here long. Not as big as this, anyway. They've made it the meeting-place of the Sioux tribes — before the great battle!' said Dick.

Albert pointed silently in front of them. Chief Bright Sun had left the column and was heading for the ranks where Dick and Albert were riding. They could see he was going towards them — he waved to them from afar. When his horse reached them, he turned in the direction the Howard brothers had been looking.

'Do you see how many of us there are?' he asked, pointing into the valley. 'The Sioux nation has many warriors; it is a strong and powerful nation!'

'There really are a lot of you,' Dick admitted. 'More than I expected. But what is that compared with us? There are more white men than there are leaves on the trees! Hundreds and thousands of them fly away, fall to the ground; but before the last of them have fallen, new ones have grown. And there are countless trees!'

Bright Sun smiled.

'Indeed, you are as numerous as the trees in the forest — as sand in the river. But you are not all here, and that is what matters. The white man is held back by mountains, prairies, deserts — these are our allies.'

Dick felt like declaring that the Indian was wrong, that it only took time to overcome the mountains and the prairies, that there were soldiers enough in the white man's army, ready to fight the devil himself if necessary; but in the end he said nothing. He respected the Sioux chief, and did not want to cause him grief. What was more, it was only thanks to him that they were still alive.

Meanwhile, Bright Sun continued his explanation.

'The river you see in front of you is called the Little Bighorn. And in the village, which stretches for five miles on either bank, you will see the Seven Fireplaces of the Sioux nation. All the tribes of the Sioux have gathered here.'

The Indian spurred his horse on and returned to the head of the column. The ranks set off again, beginning the descent into the valley.

On the bank of the river they first rode along a narrow path among the bushes; then the path widened, and the bushes gave way to sand. The Indians at once turned sharply away from the river towards the forest.

'Shifting sands,' Dick explained to his brother. 'It's just as dangerous as a swamp — it'll swallow horses, riders, everything.'

They turned again and continued along the river, but now keeping a respectable distance between themselves and the perilous sands. Soon they passed through the first dwellings, forming up a sort of suburb of the Indian town. Then there were more and more tepees, and more and more of the inhabitants of this strange town, mainly women and children. It seemed to Albert that there must be not ten, but a hundred thousand people living here.

'How many warriors do you suppose they have here?' Al asked his brother.

'Maybe five thousand, maybe more. That's going by the groups that joined us on the way. What do you think of the valley? Isn't it like ours?'

'No, it's not!' gulped Albert. The comparison was an odious one to him. 'And I'm regretting more and more that we ever left our valley. It's the most beautiful place in the world!'

The group in which the brothers were travelling continued along the riverside path for another two miles or so, halting at a place where the valley and the village were at their widest.

A young Sioux told them in broken English to dismount. Then he led them into a low hut, which, he told them, was to be their new home.

Inside the boys found two rough mats, two clay bowls and a drinking bowl. It wasn't much, but it was just what they wanted at that moment. They stretched themselves out comfortably on the mats and rubbed their saddle-weary limbs. When they had rested a while, they grew hungry and thirsty.

'I hope they aren't going to starve us to death,' said Albert, grimly.

The answer came not from Dick, but from two old Indian women, who slipped inside the hut like a pair of grey mice. They brought the boys food: a few pieces of game, and the popular Sioux food called *wan-sa.* This was a sausage made of buffalo meat and strawberries. Dried buffalo meat and dried strawberries were ground up finely, and the mixture was stuffed into pieces of intestine. The sausages were then boiled or roasted.

When the Indian women left the hut, the two boys followed them. But the moment they crossed the threshold, a young Sioux stepped out to meet them.

'I am Lone Wolf, and my friend is called Tall Fir Tree,' he said, pointing behind him. 'You may move freely about the village, but we will go everywhere with you. Chief Bright Sun has made us your personal guards!'

'OK, Lone Wolf,' said Dick, cheerfully. 'Four men; that's just the right number to have a good time. Two is not enough. We're real glad you and your friend Tall Fir Tree are going to keep us company on our wanderings. I don't think we could find better companions in the whole of this town.'

Though Dick's words were spoken in jest, it soon proved that the young Sioux had been chosen wisely.

They truly allowed their prisoners freedom, and willingly answered all their questions; they even explained from time to time of their own accord what they considered important or interesting.

So the boys learned that the Sioux village was indeed the largest in the Far West, and that all the tribes of the Sioux nation had gathered there, even those which lived in reservations.

The Indians also admitted that a great war was being prepared. They did not exactly know the purpose of the war, or did not want to say. But of one thing they were certain — they were going to win it.

Dick did not argue with his guards on this point. If only because he had received no news of what was going on in the world for two years, and he did not know what forces his people intended to throw into battle, whether they intended to parley, and so on. He was convinced the white man would win in the end, for he held all the trumps: a solid base, superiority of numbers and military techniques, while the Indians had only justice on their side, a value which unfortunately had little currency in the present circumstances. But all these thoughts were too general for expression, so Dick declined to speak further on the subject.

They had been in the Indian village for three days, and no one had yet told them what the Indians proposed to do with them — whether they wanted to go on keeping them hostage, or whether they intended to kill them before the battle began.

It was on the evening of the third day that their guards led them to one of the large tepees in the middle of the village which served as the home of the Akitcita.

'Bright Sun wishes to speak to you,' said Lone Wolf, and motioned to the boys to step inside.

The two young Sioux remained outside.

Dick and Albert went in, but it took them a while to get used to the dim light inside the tepee. When their eyes had grown accustomed to it, they were able to make out twelve men, the twelve great chiefs. In the middle stood Bright Sun.

They stood as motionless as statues, stern, grave, cold, enough to send a shiver down anyone's spine. The flower of wisdom and strength of the greatest of Indian nations!

They were dressed in the manner of their race, rejecting all that was reminiscent of the white man. The only thing of his they had

192

retained was his weapons of death — repeating rifles and revolvers.

Bright Sun motioned to the boys with his hand, and began to introduce the chiefs, one by one.

'I would like you to meet the greatest of Sioux chiefs,' he said.

'This is Horse Breaker.'

He pointed to a tall, slim young Indian.

'And these are *Ite-o-magazu*, Rain-in-the-Face, *Pizi*, Bile, and *Pej*, Blade Of Grass.'

In this way Bright Sun introduced all the chiefs. Of the most important ones only one was missing — *Tatanka Yotanka*, the renowned Sitting Bull, who at that moment was preparing his medicine bag.

'And now,' Bright Sun continued, 'now that you know all those who lead the great Sioux nation, I will ask you before all of them what I have already asked you. Whether or not you saw the white soldiers before I took you prisoner.'

'I haven't seen a white man for at least two years!' Dick answered, truthfully. 'Nor has my brother. We told you when you captured us — and we were not lying!'

Bright Sun was silent. Only his black eyes looked steadily at Dick, as if he wanted to penetrate to the bottom of his heart, to the bottom of his soul, to find the truth. Nor did the gaze of the other chiefs leave Dick's face. But he did not bow his head, did not avoid their gaze. He was telling the plain truth!

'I ask you for the last time,' Bright Sun continued in an urgent voice. 'Where were you all that time?'

'We can't tell you that,' Dick replied staunchly. 'It's a secret we want to keep to ourselves. That place is a long way from here, and in the two years we lived there, no human being set foot there. That is all I can tell you.'

The chief they called Rain-in-the-Face shook his head with dissatisfaction, then spoke a number of quick sentences in an angry voice. It occurred to Dick that the impetuous young Sioux could only be suggesting one thing — torture. So he was most relieved when Bright Sun shook his head.

'Up there in the mountains there really is a place where humans set foot only once in a lifetime,' he said. 'Perhaps the white boy is speaking the truth.'

'I am, I am,' Dick confirmed, quickly. 'I can swear it!' added Albert.

'Then why do you not wish to tell us where it was?' Bright Sun asked again.

'I've told you — we want to keep the place for ourselves!' Dick repeated.

Bright Sun smiled.

'Wherever the place is, it belongs to us alone,' he said quietly. 'But I believe that you are speaking the truth, and that you speak honestly. Therefore I will tell you openly why we ask you. There is a great battle before us, and we want to know all that may help us. The soldiers of your nation are already marching against us, led by Generals Custer, Terry, Gibbon and others. It is a strong force, but the Sioux are much stronger, and what is more they are braver. And they are fighting in a just cause. So they must win!'

Dick was silent. He knew nothing of what was happening in the world of the white man, so he could not deny Bright Sun's words.

The chief looked at Dick and said:

'You may go.' And with a smile he added: 'No harm will come to you!' It was as if he had read in their faces what both brothers were thinking with all their hearts.

The boys left the tepee of the Akitcita; outside their two guards, Lone Wolf and Tall Fir Tree, were waiting for them.

The Great Dance of the Sun

The next day Dick and Albert were shut up in their tepee; only in the afternoon were they permitted a brief stroll around the camp, again with Lone Wolf and Tall Fir Tree as their escorts.

The boys were surprised to see the feverish activity which surrounded them the moment they left their tepee. The Indian village was apparently preparing for some exceptional event.

All the hustle and bustle was concentrated around one spot:

a broad stretch of grass beside the river. Lone Wolf and Tall Fir Tree took the two brothers there, too, and Dick and Albert witnessed a spectacle few palefaces had ever seen.

They became unwilling spectators at the ceremony of the Great Dance of the Sun.

They arrived just in time to see the beginning. First of all the Indian women made a circle about fifty yards across out of short posts which they drove into the soft earth; this formed a space similar to a circus ring. For a while the medicine-men prayed over it, then they placed a slender tree in the middle, which had to be cut down by a young maiden. They stripped it of branches, and the medicine-men gathered round. It rose up like a thin stalk, a good six metres tall. A large number of long thongs were attached to the top of it, reaching down almost to the ground.

Then the ranks of spectators around the magic ring parted, and a group of young men entered it with a dignified step.

They wore short aprons decorated with beads and coloured with animal hairs and eagle feathers, with a horse's tail attached to the back. Their faces and bodies were painted the most fantastic colours the human imagination can contrive. Even their nails were painted! But what was even more remarkable was the small wooden sticks which were thrust under their skin on either side of their chests; to these was tied a belt, forming a loop about a foot long.

'Heavens, what are those wooden sticks for?' Albert asked in sincere wonder.

Before his brother could answer, Lone Wolf informed them:

'Dance of the Sun. Many young men become braves today.'

Though this did not answer his question, the brothers knew at least the name of what they were in a few moments to witness with their own eyes, and understood at least roughly what it was all about.

The novices — for that is what the Indians called them — had reached the centre of the circle. They lifted the ends of the long straps hanging from the top of the pole, and tied them to the loops which hung from the sticks on their breasts. Then they formed a circle, similarly to the way white nations dance around a maypole.

Around this inner circle braves who had already been through the Dance of the Sun formed a second ring.

Then one of the medicine-men began to whistle on a small pipe cut from the wing feather of an eagle, the sacred bird of the Sioux. At the call of the pipe the ring of novices began to move, and the young men began to dance in time with the piercing, monotonous music.

It was a simple dance, but fascinating in its rapid tempo and convulsive movements. The main aim was to pull the wooden sticks out of one's body; to suffer any pain with calm and resolution, and thus prove one's worthiness to become a great warrior.

Dick and Albert felt like turning round and running back to their tepee, or even further, out of the Indian village, where they so stupidly tortured young men. But the eyes of all the Sioux were watching them surreptitiously, and the brothers knew that they would be considered cowards if they could not even look on at the pain which was being suffered patiently and manfully by boys not much their elders.

None of them gave up, even though many fainted after tearing themselves away. They were carried away to recover their senses somewhere in peace. But even these, like all the others, were not permitted to touch food or water for three days and nights. And as soon as they came to, they had to join the outer circle of braves, and for three days and nights dance around the novices, whose places around the pole were constantly filled by newcomers.

The second group of novices was prepared a little differently to the first. The wooden pegs were driven into the upper part of the shoulders instead of under the skin of the chest, and a buffalo head swung on the loop hanging from the pegs. They danced until the weight of the buffalo head pulled the pegs from their shoulders. As soon as this happened, they moved out of the centre and joined the dancers in the outer circle.

The ranks of the novices were constantly swelled; one group took over from another, and the circle around the fenced area grew denser. By now there were hundreds, perhaps a thousand dancers leaping around the clearing to the piercing sound of the pipe. Beneath their feet a fine, invisible dust began to rise. It filled the air, got into the eyes and throats of the dancers, inflamed their brains, so that they saw the world around them in a ruddy haze. Every so often one of the dancers collapsed. His place was always taken by another, and the crazy dance, like the antics of huge, coloured mayflies, went on.

Everywhere, as far as the white brothers' eyes could see, a sea of waving heads and brown bodies shining with sweat ebbed and flowed, rose and fell. And the whole huge sea was ruled and goaded by a single, devilish bone pipe. Its sound could be heard above the stamping of dancers, and its single piercing tone, similar to the monotonous tune of an Indian snake charmer's pipe, reached every corner.

In the end it began to affect even Dick and Albert. Especially when the dark, crimson sun fell behind the hill, and a twilight which seemed splashed with freshly-shed blood crept across the valley.

The dance did not end even after sunset — did not even lose any of its vigour. But it took on a new appearance, more oppressive than ever. The darkness behind them was almost impenetrable, and the light of red torches on the dancing ground contrasted weirdly with this blackness. In the yellowish light the dancers turned into shadows, into monsters of the magician's night.

The Howard brothers were snapped out of the trance they were beginning to fall into by the one person who at least partly under-

stood what was going on in their minds, Chief Bright Sun. He came up to them, sweating and breathless from the rapid dance, and without hesitation said to them:

'You are surprised that I, too, joined in the dance. You seem to think our dance is barbaric and superstitious. But I can assure you that you are wrong. It is a custom which my people has had for long ages, and it has gone deep into our bones, into our blood. It is therefore a useful custom, which can encourage and strengthen us for the great time and the great deeds which lie before us.'

Dick and Albert did not reply. They knew that words would be wasted. The chief, at other times calm and collected, had, like the others fallen under the spell of the eagle pipe, and there was no point in trying to argue with him.

When Bright Sun saw that the boys had no answer for him, he left without a word, and again mixed with the dancing Sioux.

The words of the great Indian chief awakened the boys from their enchantment. They shook off the magic under whose spell they had fallen, and asked their guards in a calm voice to allow them to return to their tepee. Lone Wolf and Tall Fir Tree had no objection. The boys suspected they agreed to their wishes so that they might join the dance themselves. So far they had fulfilled their task as sentries, keeping at bay all the charms of the pipe.

'Now it just seems like a dreadful nightmare,' said Dick, when at last they had crossed the threshold of their hut.

But the moan of the eagle pipe reached their ears even there, and it was a long time before the boys fell asleep. They woke up several more times in the night, and it was the same story for two more nights.

But then, at the precisely ordained moment, the dance suddenly came to a halt, although they were all prepared to go on dancing for several more days. The result was that every one of them wanted to go into battle at that very moment, against a thousand enemies if need be — as if they had all drunk some strong draft which stupefied their senses.

DAKOTA ON FIRE

Georg Goll

Bloody Sunday

Like a huge, scaly prehistoric monster, the Cavalry under General George Armstrong Custer headed westwards along the old Indian track through the paling night. Twelve full companies of horse from the most famous frontier regiment of the day, with fourteen officers and a hundred and eighty mules carrying food, ammunition and all the other requisites of an army on the move. Because of the difficult terrain of the Indian track they could not use wagons. The mules were protected from possible attack by a selected troop under Captain MacDougall, for to lose their baggage would mean the doom of the whole expedition.

As usual, the Americans covered themselves constantly by means of a large group of scouts, mostly Crow and Shosho Indians, who spied out the direction of march in wide circles, suspecting every bush and boulder. The whole expedition rode, walked and trotted on and on through the wilderness from the River Rosebud to the River Little Bighorn, under the mistaken impression that they had escaped the attention of hostile eyes.

General Custer rode in front, surrounded by his officers and entirely preoccupied with thoughts of the coming clash with chief Sitting Bull.

The night was cold. Warmer weather comes late to the region around the snow-covered Dakota mountains. The pale forelight of the coming dawn was already visible in the sky.

Unvoiced misgivings lay heavy on the general's mind. Should he not have reported to his superior, General Sheridan, that the expedition's battle plans had been stolen? That would, of course, have put his carrier on the line. But what if the papers really had in some way or other got into the enemy's hands? The consequences were unthinkable ... But Custer knew nothing of General Crook's defeat on the upper reaches of the Rosebud. He could not wait to face the Indians and get this uncertainty over.

Just then his scouts announced that his favourite tracker, Curley, trapper Gabriel Dumont and 'the Black Cloak' had returned from their hiding-places in the rocks. In a few minutes they were recounting their adventures of the night.

And Custer? It was as if the light of a fever lit his eyes when he heard in turn the reports of the scout and the trapper, tugging impatiently at his blond moustache as he listened.

Suddenly, he began to laugh so loudly that his black horse threw back its head with a start.

'Excellent! All respect for your experience, Mr. Dumont, but what can you have heard and seen in those mountains? Do you really think a few hundred savages can set a trap for a whole regiment of cavalry, or even surround them? I should like to see Tatanka Yotanka do that. And anyway, Mr. Noname, or whatever they call you in that black cloak, it seems to me that you wanted to hand that red Napoleon over to me in chains, eh?'

The nameless one shrugged his shoulders.

'That will have to wait for now, general,' he muttered.

Custer grinned mockingly, and turned to the trapper again.

'I think, Dumont, you dreamed of ghosts all night...'

The Canadian paled with anger, and told the general coldly:

'You may soon change your tone, general! But now, allow us to follow the Seventh Cavalry, for nothing awaits you but an Indian death!' The nameless one joined him, while Curley was ordered by the general to bring Colonel Reno from the middle of their column.

'Anyone who wants to outmanoeuvre fate is out of his mind,' grunted Dumont, as he rode away, and that was the last warning Custer was to receive.

As dawn slowly broke, other scouts announced the exciting news that from some hill or other up front they could see a large Indian camp in the valley of the Little Bighorn, bigger than they had ever seen before. At least fifteen hundred people must live there.

'Forward, forward!' cried Custer, when he heard this. He was like a man transformed, and with a grin he went on: 'A few Indian hovels! What are they to the Seventh Cavalry!'

And he spurred his horse on. In a little while they stopped beneath a few scattered trees. What the sharp eyes of the Indian scouts had made out unaided, Custer discerned through his eyeglass: in the distance streaks of smoke rising from conical tepees wound into the morning fog. Beyond the silver mists and the shining creeks of the Sweet Grass River there was indeed a huge Indian camp — for General Custer the most beautiful sight of his entire army career. He had his long-sought enemy at his feet.

For endless minutes the general stared at the camp through his eyeglass. The rising sun lit the tips of the tepees. Smoke was coming from their grey-white cones. A few riders drove their horses, whose muscles had stiffened up in the night, among the tents. What the general saw was a picture of the everyday life of an Indian village. There was no doubt about it — his sudden route-march had taken the Sioux completely by surprise...

In the meantime Colonel Reno, the archetypal cavalry officer, had arrived. His face was shaded by one of the large stetsons soldiers, too, used to wear in those days.

'Give me the maps!' ordered Custer, urgently. The officers gathered round, and the general explained in a steady voice:

'General Terry's orders are: to attack the enemy wherever their numbers permit. Otherwise, to wait for the northern column to arrive. But our regiment is strong enough. We will attack the enemy at once, in case he should retreat... And now we will split up. Colonel Reno, you and your three companies shall proceed several miles upstream along the right bank, until you reach this wide ford. But you

207

must stay hidden! The ford lies on our route. From there you will attack the camp from behind at once! Do you understand?'

'Yes, General! How many Indians are there in the camp?'

'According to the scouts' reports, around two thousand, but a thousand warriors at the most. If we take into account the element of surprise, you will have an easy time of it with your hundred and fifty horses. Only you must cross the river unnoticed! I shall take five companies along our bank and we will hide also. We will cross the river somewhere below the camp where the bank is not too steep. In that way the enemy will be caught in crossfire. When Colonel Benton arrives with the third company, he will prepare to attack, and so will Captain MacDougall with the force that is guarding the mules. But that may not be necessary. By the time Terry and Gibbon arrive, there won't be many of the enemy left. Is that clear to all of you? Or have you any questions?'

'No, General!'

'Dismiss, gentlemen! See you after the battle!'

Custer briefly took his leave, and, spurring on his horse, rode at

a gallop to the top of the hill to take his place at the head of the two hundred and seventy horsemen who were waiting for him. Pointing the tip of his sabre in the direction they were to ride, he turned once more and waved his hat to Colonel Reno and his men. No one had any idea that the general was parting with them for ever...

Reno watched the departing horsemen for a while. Then he gave orders to his three companies.

'Careful, boys! Everything must go smoothly! Officers, to me! Scouts on the wings, and outriders are to be sent out. If you see anything suspicious, give the alarm. Otherwise keep as quiet as possible. Understand? Ready, forward!'

The cavalry stood four abreast. Now they set off. They were able to ride through that open country at a gallop. In a little while they wheeled left and, under cover of the long hill, continued their ride upstream along the Little Bighorn. The sun was high in the sky now. A new day had begun; it was Sunday, June 25, 1876.

Colonel Reno's cavalry stuck sprigs of fir in their hats. Their hands were still a little numb from their cold night ride. Now and again one of them put a water-bottle to his lips to take a long draught.

Now they rode at a steady pace up the last hill. Beyond the river lay the calm, undefended, unsuspecting village. Now the companies began to descend the other side of the hill towards the river, increasing their pace. The horsemen's hearts began to beat faster... and now they were at the ford. They hurried through the shallow water, which splashed beneath their horses' hooves, still quietly, still unseen... Colonel Reno pulled his hat down more firmly on his head, and was the first to leap ashore on the opposite bank, with a shout of 'hurrah!'

At this cry, which rang out terribly loud in the morning silence, a few startled Indians, who had gone for water and almost walked in front of the horses' hooves, began to run. Yelling, they vanished in the thickets along the bank.

'At a canter!' Reno called. The riders bent nearer their horses' necks and prepared their weapons. It seemed to the colonel that they were still moving too slowly.

'At a gallop!' came the new order. Snorting, the horses flew on. They sensed the imminence of battle. The closed ranks of the riders spread out in the open space, and they rode like the wind towards the tents, whose shining whiteness was almost dazzling. The first soldiers were already there. Shouting, they poured among the tents like a flood, firing without orders in all directions. They hacked at tent walls with their sabres and pushed aside the covers at the entrances. But at once they pulled up, as if stopped by a huge fist.

'Treachery, Colonel! There's no one here!' And they turned their horses as if on pivots.

The enemy was behind them, as if he had dropped from the sky! Even after the battle, no one knew where the Indians had come from so suddenly. But there they were. The prairie teemed with hundreds and hundreds of redskin warriors, appearing from all sides like ants crawling from a demolished anthill: from the bushes, from the camp, from the trees they hurled themselves upon their white enemy with furious whoops that frightened the horses and pierced men to the marrow. At the same time the soldiers were attacked by a pack of dogs, half wolf, half wolfhound, such as only the Dakotas knew how to breed. In an instant Reno understood what had happened: they were in a trap!

'Fire!' he thundered, but his order was superfluous. All rifles were already spitting death at the attackers. But where a dozen redskins fell, hundreds took their places. In the middle of the throng a number of chiefs on agile horses could be seen riding among the braves and encouraging them to greater efforts. And though the plain could scarcely hold extra men, more and more Indians came running from the wooded slopes. Suddenly, the cavalrymen came to a complete halt, faced with a living wall of redskins.

'We must go back, Colonel!' blurted one of the junior officers in the front row. As he spoke, he wound a scarf round his head; at once it turned bright red.

'That would be the end of us!' Reno shouted above the din. He could see in front of him an undefended, open space. Then he called out at the top of his voice:

'Into the wood! We must hold on until reinforcements arrive. Follow me!'

And, firing his revolver in all directions, he dug in his spurs. Followed by his men, he set off for the spot in question. There they all leaped down from the saddle and lay behind their horses' bodies ...

It had all happened so quickly, like a bad dream: the attack on the village, the ambush, the break for the wood. And that path of death was littered with bodies ... But the tide of Indians, accompanied by the frenzied dogs, poured towards the cavalry's position yet again. At their head came a line of black and crimson-painted braves. They were selected warriors from the Hunckpapa tribe, lead by chief Rain-in-the-Face, who had already reached the first rank of soldiers, sowing death with huge blows from his obsidian war-axe.

'Shoot that devil!' cried the colonel. The grimacing chief was at once the target of several dozen rifles. Strange to relate, he was not even scratched. Before the soldiers could shoot another round, the Indians were upon them, throwing themselves at them like wolves at a flock of sheep. Whenever a redskin fell, three took his place, and the wall of attackers closed in on the cavalrymen ever tighter. With gritted teeth Reno thought of his reinforcements, riding towards them in close-knit ranks, almost as if on a parade-ground. 'This is the work of the Red Napoleon, whom Custer has so underestimated,' he thought. 'We can't hold out much longer ...'

Around the wood a bloody sea seethed. The red hordes threw themselves on the white men with greater tenacity than ever before. The number of enemies increased by the minute. Soon the moment must come when that handful of cavalrymen would, despite the most heroic of resistance, literally be torn to pieces.

The colonel had no choice. He had, with a heavy heart, to try to withdraw to the river, onto the sloping bank from which his troop had ridden to the camp earlier that morning; there he would have to hang on and wait for reinforcements. He gave the orders to mount ...

Breaking through the ranks of the attackers was a hazardous affair. It was a great disadvantage to the soldiers that the Indian ponies were faster in such terrain than their heavy cavalry horses. Apart from that there were enemies behind every tree, bush and boulder. And so the cavalrymen fell from their horses like dummies on a rifle range. Sometimes five or six Indians would throw themselves at one soldier; the retreat soon turned into a wild flight. It was a race against death, who would reach the ford first; the Dakotas fell, too, but there were always more and more of them.

Yet another unpleasant surprise awaited the soldiers — the ford, too, was held by Indians!

'At a gallop!' Reno ordered. 'Attack!'

Their onrush was so sudden that the redskins blocking their route to the water were literally thrust into the sands by their heavy horses. For a while the scene at the ford resembled a tangled ball of wool. The water reddened with blood. Then the remnants of the cavalry troop took the opposite bank, still under heavy fire from the Indians. But the ford was too small for so many horsemen, and Reno lost more men there than anywhere. The horses reared up in the commotion; many of them fell along with their riders. Mortally wounded soldiers were at once carried off by the water. As soon as the first line of cavalrymen reached the opposite bank, they flung themselves to the ground and put up rapid rifle fire to cover those who were still crossing.

At last help came. The rearguard, three companies under Colonel Benteen, had just arrived, and without more ado they gave battle. Large numbers of Indians had swum across the river above and below the ford, and were trying to take the soldiers' new position in a single attack. Once again they were led by the frowning Rain-in-the-Face. But under fire from the fresh reinforcements their attack collapsed, and Colonel Reno and his men were able to breathe a brief sigh of relief.

Contact Custer! That was his first thought now. But where *was* Custer? They could hear the distant rattle of rifle fire. The firing grew heavier, then weaker, until it died away altogether. The platoon Reno sent along the ridge returned empty-handed; they were almost cut off from the force above the ford by a much larger force of Ogallalas.

An hour of horror passed. The sun beat down without mercy, and

214

another hour went by. Both seemed endless. There was no sign of
Custer. But there was no new Indian attack either. It occurred to the
colonel that most of them might be engaged with the main cavalry
force. Custer would never come to their aid! He was also fighting for
his life, as they had been two hours earlier. But the colonel did not
lose heart, even while he was thinking about how he might get to the
general with all the survivors of his command. But what about the
wounded? Every step along the ridge would have to be paid for in
blood. To take the wounded along with them would be impossible.

But then the unbelievable happened. The force commanded by
Captain MacDougall, which was guarding the mules, reached Reno
without meeting any Indians! The Colonel therefore decided to set
up a defensive position, as far as it was at all possible on the slope.
The ground was dry, and as hard as rock, and death threatened from
all sides as they worked. With exhausting labour they managed to dig
some sort of trenches at least, and to raise low protective mounds in
front of them.

The horses and the wounded were placed in a depression on the
side away from the river. There they were at least partly protected
from fire, and there was shade. But there was a shortage of water. The
wounded were thirsty, and groaned in fever. One of the troop's
doctors had already been killed, and all the work had to be done by
the one surviving medical man, Dr. Porter.

No sooner had they finished the main work on the trenches, after
a desperate retreat beyond the ford, than whole hordes of Sioux on
fresh horses rode up and began again to surround the ridge, in ever
closing circles. Anxiously, the cavalrymen watched these red warrior
hosts. The remainder of the wine, which had been found in one of the
field bottles, was fraternally handed round. Right after that the storm
broke loose again.

Once more at the head of the attackers, again apparently invulner-
able, like some god, his face freshly masked with warpaint, came chief
Rain-in-the-Face — Ite-o-magazu. The cavalrymen had already shot
two horses from under him, but he was mounted on a third. Drunk
with the fever of battle and a desire for victory, the Hunckpapas

hurled themselves, screaming warcries, right at the defenders' trenches. A hand-to-hand struggle began. Dozens of Indians fell in a hail of bullets. But the attack was so fierce and so tenacious that for a few minutes the fate of the besieged hung on a thread. Then the more prudent, disciplined army tactics began to tell. The Indians wavered. One last time they threw themselves forward with deafening warcries, attacking the defenders with rifles they had taken from fallen cavalrymen, pieces of branches, and even stones. When their tomahawks disintegrated in their hands and their bowstrings snapped, they attacked with tooth and nail, like men possessed. But Reno's men were fighting for their lives; their resistance was so resolute that in the end the Indians had to withdraw. The last to retreat was Ite-o-magazu, tears of frustrated anger shining in his eyes.

When the uneven struggle was over, the bloody and dirt-blackened defenders of the trenches looked at each other as if seeing a vision from another world. They did not know whether to laugh or cry.

'Where is Custer?' was the colonel's first thought when the Indian attack subsided. 'Where is he?'

*　　*　　*

Early in the morning of that bloody Sunday Tatanka Yotanka, Sitting Bull, rode with his aides to the heights above the camp, where he got a good view if the whole of the coming battlefield, as if from a high watchtower. From there the Red Napoleon directed the Battle of Little Bighorn, a battle that was written in bloody letters into the history of the United States as one of the few wars in the west that the Indians won. In it, so-called savages defeated and almost annihilated a whole regiment of trained cavalry, whose members were all experienced frontier-fighters, not raw recruits sent out fresh from basic training against a dogged and highly resolute enemy.

At first Tatanka Yotanka did nothing to calm his allies' anxieties. It was only when, just after sunrise, a message began to flash from the distant fir trees, that he took a mirror from his belt and replied to it. On these golden rays, reflected by ordinary bits of glass, the fate of

216

a whole cavalry regiment hung that day. Tiny flashes were exchanged between the two positions more and more often — the Dakotas were experts in heliography. The intervals between messages got shorter and shorter, until suddenly the golden arrow stopped at the feet of the big chief, drawing rapid circles on the ground. That was the most important signal which had been arranged.

'They're here!' the chief said tersely. And he began to conduct the battle. From his belt he drew a map, captured on some raid or other, of the Little Bighorn Valley, and spread it on the ground in front of him. Then a spyglass appeared in his hand; the others could scarcely contain their wonder! The chief extended the spyglass, and began to observe the countryside closely.

From the opposite slope the mirror began signalling again, quickly and jerkily. The news seemed to be very important. Tatanka Yotanka, spyglass in his left hand, used his right hand to give constant signals to his scouts in the distance. With great pleasure he noted from their

signals that Custer and his five companies had just separated from the colonel. At that moment the fate of the Seventh Cavalry was sealed. By entering the enclosed creeks of the upper Little Bighorn, Custer was signing his death warrant...

Tatanka Yotanka folded his spyglass, and put away the map.

'The moment for action has come. Pizi's wish to fight Chief Yellow Hair will soon be fulfilled. If he and his tribe set off at once, they will reach the White Birch heights opposite before the sun moves a palm's breadth. That is where Yellow Hair is heading. Let Pizi lead his people into battle!'

Pizi's eyes lit up with battle fever, but inborn Indian caution led him to ask one more question:

'And if Pahin-zi (Yellow Hair, the Indians' name for General Custer) gets reinforcements?'

'Pizi is not going into battle alone. From Wolf Gulley the mighty chief Mehpeja Luta, Red Cloud, will attack the enemy with his three hundred braves, and his son with another hundred. And Ishay Nishus, chief of the northern Cheyenne, and his brave men. As soon as Yellow Hair and his men enter the lowlands Pizi can see from here, we will begin the attack. Pizi is responsible for it!'

These words flattered the pride of the hot-tempered chief. With a brief gesture he took his leave and rode to his braves, who were hidden beyond the hills. There, too, stood hastily erected tents for the women and children. With Pizi rode the others whom Tatanka Yotanka had appointed to make the first attack on the enemy.

Now Chief Rain-in-the-Face stepped up to Sitting Bull, and asked gruffly:

'And Ite-o-magazu? I have taken the oath of the stout heart! I smell the smoke of dust, and my tomahawk scents blood. Tatanka Yotanka promised I should be able to make Yellow Hair...'

'The tomahawk of Ite-o-magazu will drink the blood of Yellow Hair. But first it must destroy the chief Reno, who will ride across the upper ford and attack the camp. Ite-o-magazu will let him get right up to the tents, and then will tear him apart as the falcon tears apart a feeble sparrow. For this he will win the greatest honour of the day, for he will be the first to fight the enemy. Let his braves start the battle with great resolve. If they do not manage to destroy the enemy between the ford and the forest, they shall try to make them retreat over the river onto the heights, and there Ite-o-magazu must hold them fast. There he must also surround and enclose any reinforcements which may come ... Go, friend! Fight for Dakota!'

A smile of reconciliation crossed Rain-in-the-Face's dark face.

More such orders were given, one by one, and the circle of chiefs grew smaller. The Red Napoleon sent them out to their appointed places like chessmen being moved across the board. Eventually, Tatanka Yotanka was left on the heights alone. The battle began. The raucous shouts of Reno's cavalrymen rent the air as they charged into the camp. The face of the big chief lightened.

'We shall be victorious!'

* * *

When General Custer had taken leave of the colonel's group, he did all he could to reach the camp as quickly as possible. He was still afraid the enemy would disappear, and was only reassured when he learned that groups of Indians were still riding heedlessly around in the vicinity of the camp. Little did he know that almost at his feet, in what he thought was the unguarded valley of the Little Bighorn, hundreds of his bitterest enemies lay in wait.

In the group of officers surrounding Custer was the war correspondent of the New York Herald, Mr. Kellogs, an old friend of the general's. He looked preoccupied, which was unusual for someone of his cheerful nature.

'I don't like those heliographs, General,' said Lieutenant Sturgis. 'I've heard that the Dakotas can send very complex messages over long distances that way.'

The General just waved his hand, as if throwing away something of no importance.

'Don't worry, my friend!' he said. 'It's just a childish imitation of our army heliographists. Sitting Bull isn't capable of more than that, even if they do tell whole legends about him. His whole strategy is that he wants to have it out with us here, in open country, instead of occupying the passes.'

'It certainly doesn't seem as though the Sioux want to withdraw,' observed Lieutenant Calhoun.

'Not any more. In a while that Red Napoleon and his thousand men will be in a trap ... But what's going on? Aren't the redskins starting to leave their village?'

The general's fears were well-founded. The whole plain was astir. Clouds of smoke rose everywhere, obscuring the movements of the Indian warriors. It seemed as if the whole camp had suddenly decided to retreat. And a shout went up from the soldiers: 'They' re retreating — they're running!'

Their shouts made him unsure of himself. He rode along the ridge of a knoll, heedless of the fact that he and his horse must be clearly visible from the valley against the clear blue sky. None of the white men were surprised that the sharp-sighted Indians below did not acknowledge him with loud shouts.

'Men!' called Custer to his regiment, which was still hidden behind the ridge. 'Down there in the valley there is another ford. We will cross over and attack the enemy from the flank. Companies, left — turn! Ready to open fire! Forward!'

Custer drew his sabre and, at the head of his two hundred and seventy trusty cavalrymen, rode down through a gully. The thunder of their hooves was ear-splitting: one could no longer speak of a concealed approach. The time for decision had come, and no one considered the fact that their flanks were quite unguarded.

'Victory is ours!' the general cried jubilantly, as he rode out into the open. 'Upon them, men! We have them!'

But something quite different happened ... Again a few signals flashed over the landscape. This time they were for the hosts of Indians hidden in the 'valley of death'. As silent as a cloud of ghosts, these warriors left their hiding places and galloped after the cavalry. They rode at the same speed, spread out like a flood along the slope on either side of Custer's horsemen, and had them in their jaws before the ambushed white men, who were staring fixedly ahead at the village, knew what was going on around them.

When Custer turned in the saddle, he thought his eyes were playing tricks on him. As far as he could see, there was head upon head, horse beside horse, a brown wall enclosing his cavalry: thousands of painted Indian braves, as if conjured up from the ground.

'Treachery!... Halt!'

One of the officers shouted this order with the utmost urgency. It was not Custer, who sat like a statue on his horse as his companies drew up. He was as pale as death, and held his hand to his throat as if he was choking.

'George!' Captain Tom Custer called to him. 'For God's sake! What are you staring at? Let's get back, or it'll be the end of us!'

This shout seemed to put an end to the general's paralysis. The blood came back to his face. He shook himself, and was the old Custer again. He, the pride of West Point, had fought often with Indians outnumbering him five, even eight to one. And good fortune had never deserted him. So this highly courageous man did not consider even this danger extreme.

He first thought, 'Fire off a few salvos, then cut our way out with sabres!' At that moment the dull thudding of hundreds of axes could be heard. The white men looked at each other, and understood. The Dakotas were chopping down trees as fast as they could to cut off their retreat into the gully. The way back now presented obstacles horses could not cope with.

Now Custer knew that there was only one way to save themselves. To occupy the hill they had just ridden round ...

He shouted orders, and the soldiers had no sooner heard his voice than they began to form up and, surrounded by enemies, rode slowly up the hill. But they had not gone far when all hell got loose. Across the slope flew something as fearful as when a freezing northern storm wipes out a fine day in June; the whole hill was suddenly veiled in white smoke; there was a banging and cracking, a whistling and whizzing on all sides. Indian bullets rained down on the serried ranks of the white men like a hailstorm which flattens a grainfield. Mortally wounded horses whinnied with pain. Wild warcries rang out, frightening the beasts even more. Custer's black charger was bleeding from several wounds, and began to limp.

When the smoke cleared a little, there were many blue patches on the green of the hillside. Custer saw it, and bit his lip in anger.

'Forward, men!'

Under the hail of the Indians' second salvo the cavalry reached the nearest depression on the slope, and were covered for a moment at least. The hill was also shrouded in dust, so that the two sides could no longer see each other.

'Dismount!' ordered the general. In a while the horses were under the shelter of a ravine, and the wounds at least superficially treated. Then a bugle called the officers together.

'We must try to get Colonel Reno and his three companies here,' the general began, but one of the sergeants interrupted him:

'Colonel Reno is fighting, too — listen!'

And indeed the sound of rifle fire could be heard in the distance; in a while it subsided. Reno had just been through the cruel test of his confused retreat across the ford.

Custer could only shrug his shoulders.

The clouds dispersed, and what the cavalrymen saw on the plain in front of them was enough to inspire even the most courageous of them with abject terror.

As far as they could see over the hills and ridges, there were teeming hordes of Indians, on horseback and on foot. The valley was literally covered in them. And they were preparing to attack.

Before the onslaught came, General Custer did try to make contact with the colonel. But his scout soon returned, saying that there was an impenetrable wall of enemies on that side, and that fresh reinforcements were arriving all the time. The general began to see the light. It was the work of Sitting Bull...

But the urgent voice of one of his officers interrupted his thoughts:

'Look out! They're coming!'

'Keep calm, men!' Custer reminded them. 'Don't shoot until you are sure of your targets!'

They came ... Like a red sea, the hordes of Indians rushed towards the cavalrymen's position. In front were the Stouthearts of the sacred tribe of the Ometepe, denoted by a black eagle on their naked breasts. They were competing for the honour of starting the battle ... Beside them and behind them were the other Teton tribes, parties of Hunck-papas, northern Cheyenne with their bold chief Two Moons, then the Ogallalas, behind them Mehpeja Luta and his aides with their men, both the Tashonka Cocipaps, father and son; behind them the Dakota tribe of Sichangu under Chief Spotted Tail, the Arapaha, and many, many more. Who can recount the names of all the tribes and clans who took part in the battle with the 'long knives' that scorching June day in 1876?

Amidst the throng waved the threatening owl-wings of the Dakotas, woven into their tall black coiffures, and eagle-feather head-dresses which barely stayed on their wearers' heads as they rushed forward. Perpendicular feathers showed where the Arapahas were. Others had the heads of foxes and wolves. Colourfully embroidered clothes marked out some tribes — the yellow and red of the Cheyenne, the bright blue and white of the Dakotas, the dull black and red of the Ogallalas, and the hard, dark brown of the Siseton tribe.

In dense ranks they rushed straight up the hill. It had once been their way to ride round their enemies at a distance, but now they were rushing into the arms of death, towards the barrels of the rifles. The first salvo, fired at a bare fifty paces, cut great swathes through the red wall, but every gap was at once filled with more warriors. A second salvo was even more damaging. Again, whole groups fell, but the Indians did not waver. Even the older and more experienced officers, who had clashed with the Indians many a time, looked on in horror. The bitter struggle for the hill had begun: the day of disaster, the day of vengeance, wrath and retaliation had come. It was descending on the Americans, who for decades had robbed and deceived the Indians, and driven them from pillar to post, until at last the pot of anger boiled over ... Each of those under arms today was full of that bitterness which is the inevitable fruit of inhuman oppression. The flower of the Indian nation had gathered today to do battle together in such numbers and with such a unity of purpose as had not been seen since the time of Pontiac or Tekumseh. There were hosts of handpicked warriors here, sent by every tribe who came.

Among the fighters, there were boys, armed with bows and arrows, who were still half children. As a historian has noted, there were certainly among the men, women and girls on fast ponies. Everyone who lived in Dakota and had Indian blood in his veins came rushing into that life-and-death struggle against the white foe.

Soon the scene on the hill resembled the fires of hell. Shots sounded incessantly on all sides. The cavalrymen fired one round after another, until their rifle barrels scorched their hands. Mingling with the rifle fire came the sharp cracks of the officers' revolvers. It was fortunate for the cavalrymen that they had taken along so much ammunition. After a fierce battle, lasting around an hour, they finally managed to fight off the first attack.

General Custer was still in the front ranks. His men, now dust-blackened and unrecognisable, greeted him raucously.

When a lull came in the fighting, the general went to the centre of the line of defence, wiping the sweat from his brow and the stinging smoke from his eyes. He found there his brother Tom, who had also been up front a moment ago, Lieutenant Calhoun, and Kellogs, the reporter from the *New York Herald*. The last had just completed a rough sketch of the battlefield. He was one of the bravest of correspondents, and had already covered the Civil War, which is where he met Custer.

'There we are,' he said, writing the caption to his drawing, 'I'll put this sketch at the end of the first report of the battle. I think, General, we may rightly describe this little outing that way.'

Custer just nodded. But his nephew Reed, who was experiencing his first battle with Indians today, looked at the reporter rather glumly, and said with a forced smile: 'Do you think you will get the chance to take that notebook back to New York?'

'My dear friend, I am a soldier in the face of the enemy, and if I do not take my report to my paper myself, someone else will do it for me. But I am afraid . . .'

At that moment the general leaned towards him.

'What are you afraid of, Kellogs?'

But the reporter read in Custer's grey eyes the same dreaded question he had seen in Reed's a moment before, and he changed the subject.

'I am afraid, General, that it will be very difficult to make contact with the colonel. Listen — they are shooting only occasionally now.'

'Yes,' replied Custer, 'I think they have been surrounded just like us. We must hold out, my friends! What do you think, Tom? And what about you, Calhoun?'

He suddenly noticed a thin trickle of blood running across his nephew's right wrist.

'Reed, you're not wounded, are you?'

The soft, almost girlish face of the young man darkened.

'It's only a scratch, Uncle. And, anyway, you haven't yet dictated to me anything for the report on the victorious campaign!'

The general's thick eyebrows creased with annoyance.

'The time will come, lad. Your uncle has always done as he promised.'

He seemed to want to add something, but it was lost in the hubbub of battle, for at that instant the Indians launched another attack.

Now something happened which was reminiscent of the ancient days when warrior captains challenged each other to single combat before the ranks of their armies. A proud rider in the dress of a chief, riding a tall horse, thrust his way through to the front of the Indian hosts. His resolute face was framed with eagle feathers. When he got within a hundred paces of the soldiers, he pulled up his horse and shouted, cupping his hands to his mouth:

'Which of the palefaces dares come out into the open to fight Nishus, chief of the Cetistash?'

The response was such a burst of rifle fire that the Indian attack halted almost before it had begun. Some groups of attackers wavered. At this Chief Two Moons quickly took his rifle down from his shoulder and fired. Up on the hill one of the officers, shot through the head, fell at the feet of his companions. Then Nishus sat up proudly in the saddle so that all could see him well, and called out to his hesitant men:

'After me, braves! Or you have seen your war chief for the last time today!'

As soon as he had said this, he loaded his rifle and charged straight towards the soldiers' position. They began to fire at him, but by some miracle he was left unscathed. Behind him came a savage flood of Indians, and the air quivered with their shouts. Following their leader's example, they were at the top of the hill on their swift horses before the soldiers knew what was happening.

But they soon recovered themselves, and their rifles spat death at the attackers. A fearful hand-to-hand combat ensued ... Tomahawk against rifle, buffalo-skin shield against Colt revolver, fist against fist. When rifles jammed, the defenders struck at the enemy with their butts. With scalping knives, half-smashed shields, the splintered remnants of lances, and in the end with bare fists, the red warriors set about the palefaces.

At the height of the struggle Tom Custer and his horseless cavalrymen made a sudden counter-attack. Caught off guard by their boldness, the Indians fell back a little. The cavalry immediately took advantage of this, and with a resolute attack forced a full retreat.

Custer's Doom

The battle entered a new phase. Hailed loudly from all sides, Pizi now led his warriors into battle. They were the reserves, the main body of the Hunckpapas, prepared for the hardest of battles. With wild cries, these warriors whipped their ponies mercilessly, and rushed up the hill, thirsting for blood. Their onslaught was so forceful that the soldiers were pushed back from their position to the nearest mound on the hillside, where they just managed to hold their line.

But a counter-attack came just as quickly and unexpectedly.

General Custer himself led about fifty of his best riders, who had quickly mounted their horses, striking the ranks of the resting

Hunckpapas with a counter-thrust which took them by surprise. The heavier horses of the cavalry, riding downhill, had the advantage of the small ponies. A mad tumult broke loose. The soldiers, who had so far been tied down in defence, made the most of the opportunity and attacked the redskins mercilessly. A number of troops on horse came riding up from the sides to compound the Indians' distress. The fact that the Indians would be driven back to the soldiers' previous position was in no doubt. It almost seemed as if the strength of the two sides had balanced out.

But as Chief Two Moons had before, now Pizi rode out in front of his faltering ranks ... Once more the ridge seethed with picturesque lines of Indian horsemen, and again the charge was broken by the incisive fire of the defenders. But this time the attackers only halted; they did not give an inch. They were not fighting for a hill; they were fighting for Dakota. That fearful day the freedom of the red nation was at stake. Where dozens of dead were already covered in dirt, where frightened, riderless horses ran in their droves from the decimated ranks, three new warriors replaced every one that fell, filling all the gaps. Again and again that wild tide surged into the attack, rushing up the hill to the sound of wild warcries.

Custer's men went on firing while there was still anything to fire. The hill above the river turned into a fire-disgorging throat, from which constant flashes came. The wounded feverishly reloaded the weapons of their unhurt comrades, passing them back into hands blackened with dirt. Here and there hoarse cries they did not understand rose above the din of battle. Sweat poured in rivulets from their tired bodies, yet there was no sign of an end to the tide of attackers. Wave upon wave of horses brought the Indians fresh reserves. The front line of attackers melted in the blast of rifle fire at the brow of the hill. But those who fell were replaced by hundreds more. This was the moment the Dakotas had held off their attacks on Reno's position above the river to throw all they had at Custer.

At the head of the attack on Custer's position came Ite-o-magazu, Rain-in-the-Face, who had sworn to destroy the Custer brothers. His black, white and red head-dress of eagle feathers bordered his frown-

228

ing face like a gleaming sun. A good-luck charm of white weasel tails fluttered around his neck in the wind; the chief firmly believed it would protect him from all wounds. Now he approached the enemy proudly erect. His warriors' onslaught was so fierce that the desperate defenders of the hill were driven about forty metres higher, almost to the very top.

At the moment the attack began to run out of steam, Ite-o-magazu dug his moccasins into his horse's sides and drove it forward, right into a group of riflemen around the banner of the fourth company, which was blackened and shot to ribbons. Like a demon, Ite-o-magazu hurled himself at the dismayed standard-bearer, tearing away the banner in a single movement. At the same instant his horse collapsed beneath him, riddled with bullets. But the chief must have been on his feet again in a fraction of a second. His left arm waved the captured banner, while his right, armed with his stone axe, cleft the standard-bearer's head in two. His dead body fell at his comrades' feet. Ite-o-magazu ran back to his men, threw them the captured banner, and leaped onto an abandoned cavalry horse. Once more he headed for the ranks of the defenders; again his horse was shot from under him, and again he jumped onto another, this time an Indian pony. The chief constantly urged his men to attack. He always rode far out in front of them with his tomahawk held up high, and it was only many years after the battle that he admitted that it had surely been the war songs and the scent of dust that had aroused in him such untold heroism.

Again he drove his fainting horse forward, seeking out his next victim. It was to be the officer at the head of a group of retreating soldiers, riding a dark horse with white feet. His name was Captain French, and when Rain-in-the-Face rode into the attack he showed no inclination to withdraw any faster than before.

But suddenly, before the pair clashed, the Indian's pony began to show signs of panic. It reared and kicked in all directions, throwing up a cloud of dust. French gaped in surprise, not suspecting it to be a trick. Then the axe whistled, and when the dust-cloud cleared, the heroic captain lay on the ground with his skull smashed open.

Things looked grim around where the General was standing. The defences had weakened visibly, and ammunition was getting low. In front of the line of defence lay the bodies of dozens of cavalrymen, whom the Indians had scalped remarkably quickly, right in front of the barrels of the rifles. The best of the officers had fallen. Even his favourite, Lieutenant Sturgis, was dead. The courageous newspaperman, Kellogs, stood in the ranks of the defenders, bleeding from a number of wounds. There was no one left unscathed.

'I don't suppose we'll ever get out of this hell,' young Reed said to the reporter.

'You're right,' was the calm reply.

'Then why are you still taking notes? Who knows which medicine-man will use them to light his fire ... I've already torn up my "Report on a victorious campaign" and thrown it away.'

At these words the young man smiled with a deep bitterness. But he had scarcely finished speaking when he threw up his arms, croaked, fell to the ground, and lay motionless.

'Lucky lad; you've got it over with, and we've still got it coming,' muttered Kellogs. The general's face reddened with grief and fury. Raising his heavy cavalry sabre, he leapt over the saddles and dead, and with a single blow cut down the Indian who had just fired a fatal shot at Reed from such close quarters. Three more redskins fell to the general's sword before the arrival of reinforcements forced him to withdraw to the protection of their last position.

Suddenly there came from the top of the hill, where the last of the cavalry horses stood with their sentries, an infernal din, a shouting and whooping, mingled with a deafening neighing and stamping of hooves. Behind the backs of the defenders something had taken place which took away their last hope. The Indians, led by Ite-o-magazu, had attacked their horses! With a few shots they had disposed of the sentries, and now burning bundles of brushwood fell among the animals. Scared out of their wits, the horses rushed from the hollow. To prevent them from running off in all directions, the Indians drove them to the nearest fold in the hillside.

'That's it!' murmured Kellogs, sadly, and he snapped his pencil in half. Then, tearing his notebook to pieces, he threw its remnants in the face of the nearest attacker. Then he grabbed a revolver and began to shoot like a seasoned frontiersman, until a tomahawk suddenly flew through the air, tearing his throat open...

Yes, the end was near. The end of the Seventh Cavalry. They could all feel it clearly. The men's knees were collapsing with exhaustion. Red circles spun before their eyes. All sense of time and space was lost. Their lips were dry and cracked with thirst. The scorching June sun, now slowly dropping westwards behind the ridge, had beaten down all day on the living and the dead. Those who survived waited in vain for a miracle.

It was then that many of them began to think of their far-off homes, fathers, mothers, the family house, different parts of Europe they had left for America, years ago...

But there was no time for day-dreaming. The final battle was raging. Their ranks had long since lost all semblance of order. There were no more commands. In small groups and in ones and twos, the remnants of a renowned cavalry regiment made their bloody last stand against an underestimated and disdained enemy that was all the more merciless for that. The soldiers saw the last rays of hope fade, and were now trying to make their final rounds of ammunition tell, before death caught up with them in the form of an arrow or a tomahawk.

It was a group of young Hunckpapas who finally put an end to it all. Galloping up, the reins of their wild horses released, the bold youths charged among the soldiers, thrusting lances into their breasts at full tilt. Then, with whoops of victory, they rode on...

The men of the second company held out longest of all; they were the only ones whose line had remained intact, resisting all attempts to break through it. Pace by pace, the exhausted soldiers withdrew to the top of the hill, where they were cut down in a straight line when they no longer had anything to shoot.

In the meantime, Custer surveyed the scene of horror which surrounded him. At his feet lay the body of poor Reed; beside him was his brother-in-law, Calhoun, a little way off Captain Tom Custer, beyond him Captains Yates, Miles, Koegh and Boston Custer, and beyond them Lieutenants MacIntosh, Riley and Crittenden. The standard-bearers, too, had fallen to a man.

And in the mind of this proud man, who had been quite sure he would put down the Indian rising with an iron hand, and thus restore his dented reputation, there appeared faded pictures of the past: in his imagination he saw the West Point military academy, with the grey walls of the fort and the silver mists over the smooth-flowing Hudson River ... he saw himself at the head of a company in the Civil War, and lived through again his day of glory at Appomatox, when the southerners had surrendered.

In the thunder of hooves of the last charge, the whole world collapsed around Custer.

The curtain of dust and smoke in front of the general opened. They were riding at him on foaming chargers, over the bodies of men and animals, with a shrieking that tore at a man's nerves. Savage Indians trod on the dead, wounded and dying, raining down on them a new cloud of arrows and bullets. These were not men, but devils incarnate, hurtling onward on crazed horses! They flew past the general. Some figure or other, radiating terror, rose before him in the saddle.

'Chief Yellow Hair! I fulfil my oath!' came a roar like the clarion of doom. 'Stand and defend yourself!'

And as if he had grown out of the ground, the impassioned Ite-o-magazu rose four paces away from the general. Custer had two rounds left in his revolver. When fighting Indians, officers always kept the last bullet for themselves. He aimed at the Indian with his left hand, and pulled the trigger. At that distance the powder charge should have burned the victim's face, but Ite-o-magazu stood like a treetrunk.

'You are mine, Chief Yellow Hair, as was your brother, who I have already killed.'

And he raised his terrible obsidian axe to such height that it seemed as if he were about to fell an oak tree ... Custer summoned his strength for a last defence. With an effort he raised his broad and

heavy sabre, but the Indian's tomahawk was faster. It fell like light-
ning on the general's head. Almost the last to fall at the Battle of
Little Bighorn, on Sunday, June 25, 1876, was the commander of the
Seventh Cavalry, General George Armstrong Custer.

The passing day's sun lit up, with its dying rays from behind the
Dakota and Montana hills, a dismal scene: the dead lay scattered
across the open prairie, and the light of sunset was reflected in the
sheen of their blood. And it was only when the last afterglow died
away, and the purple shades of the approaching night covered the
battlefield, that nature finally took its leave of that bloody day, no
longer gazing into the glazed eyes of all those dead.

* * *

With an emphatic and heavy step, like the figure of the avenger
from the days of ancient legends, late that evening, when the cloud of
dust had already settled, Chief Ite-o-magazu strode across the silent
battlefield. His shadow — that of a figure with a huge tomahawk on
his shoulder — stood out sharply against the dull red evening sky.
Whenever he came across a scalped soldier whose mouth had stayed
open in his last mortal struggle, he stopped, dug up a piece of earth
with his axe, and filled the mouth of the dead man, so that the white
robbers might after death at least be satiated with the earth they so
coveted when they were alive ... Thus had King Tomysir of the Mas-
sageths once done to the head of the fallen Cyrus; thus had the great
Tekumseh done seventy years before the Battle of Little Bighorn;
and thus did Ite-o-magazu, a Dakota, at this bloody hour.

THE GHOST
OF THE LLANO ESTACADO

Karl May

The Scout

Towards noon farmer Helmers was sitting at the table in front of the farmhouse with Juggle Fred and Hobble Frank. Bob was absent. He was chatting in the stable with the farmer's black servant.

The men spoke of the previous day's events, of the fight between Bloody Fox and the stranger, and of the stranger's death. Little wonder, then, that their conversation also turned to various circumstances connected with these things, and eventually to ghosts.

But they soon fell silent as they saw a uniformed rider approach. The markings on his uniform showed him to be an officer, and before long he called out: 'Is this Helmers' farm?'

'What else?' replied Helmers. 'And you are looking right at the owner.'

'Oh yeah? That's great, 'cause I have something to ask you ...'

'Go ahead — at your service.'

'It's not that easy. Let me sit down for a while!'

He jumped down from his horse and took a seat, making himself comfortable in an empty chair. They surveyed him closely, but the soldier did not seem to notice. He was a strong, broad-shouldered fellow with a piercing gaze and a huge moustache which covered his lips.

'I'm out here scouting,' he said courteously. 'We're at Fort Sill, and we have to go to the Llano.'

'Why's that?' asked Helmers.

'There're some bandits giving trouble there, and two whole companies have orders to go and sort them out. They sent me out in front to get to know the country and to meet the inhabitants. I hope you'll back us up.'

'You can rely on me, sir.'

The farmer had faith in the officer from the first sight. He told him everything he had heard of the Llano Estacado recently, and of yesterday's fight and the stranger's death.

The officer listened very closely. He was impassive, only his eyes twinkled. Helmers supposed his guest to be interested in the fight, but a more observant onlooker would have noted that the twinkling of the man's eyes was in fact a sign of irritation. But the man otherwise behaved very calmly, betraying nothing but the interest one would expect the narrative to arouse in any other listener.

When Helmers had finished, he asked the officer if the Llano was safe, adding that it would be almost impossible for two whole companies to cross it. A lack of water and fodder would be the doom of any large expedition ...

'I daresay you are right,' said the officer, thoughtfully. 'But you should tell me about the legend of the ghost of the Llano. I have often heard tell of this mysterious creature, but I have yet to hear anything definite.'

'Then you are like all the rest of us. Everyone has heard all sorts of things about the ghost, but they are probably just tales. I can tell you what I know in a few words. The ghost of the Llano is a mysterious rider to whom no one has ever been close. All those who went too near paid for it with their lives, since they got shot in the head. The strange thing is they were all suspicious characters *I* would never have gone into the Llano with. The ghost seems to me to be some sort of just avenger ...'

'A man, then?'

'Of course!'

'But how come he's everywhere, but can't be seen? He must eat and drink, and so must his horse. Where does he get his food?'

'That's what no one can understand.'

'And how does he manage not to meet anyone?'

'Hmm, you are really asking too much of me, sir. They have seen him from a long way off, riding like the devil. They say sparks fly around him and behind him. I know a man who saw him at night. He'll swear to you that the rider's head, shoulders, rifle and even his horse's muzzle, ears and tail were alight with small flames.'

'That's nonsense!'

'Seems so. But my friend's a truthful fellow, and not one given to telling tall tales.'

Now Frank entered the conversation.

'There you are!' he cried. 'No one wants to believe in the natural-ness of unnatural events. I say the ghost of the Llano is not a man, but a ghostly creature left over from the Greek Furies, and that he moved into the lonely Llano like a pensioner into the attic. I believe he gives off sparks. We blow out tobacco smoke when we're smoking: so why can't a spirit breath fire?'

'But can a spirit shoot with a rifle?' asked the officer.

'Why not? Years ago at a Christmas fair I saw a chicken shoot from a little cannon. There was a hare that could do the same. And what a chicken or a hare can do, a ghost can't find difficult!'

'The reasons you give are hardly plausible, sir. Very shrewd, cer-tainly, but they will scarcely convince me . . .'

Frank took offence at these words. He retorted sharply:

'You have your reasons for speaking as you do. I know my re-sponse is far-fetched, but I am saying something that is out of your reach. Your face and your uniform suggest you would understand nothing a schoolboy wouldn't.'

'Sir!' the officer burst out. 'You offend a captain of the United States Cavalry!'

'Just don't lose your temper, now. I don't care if you are a captain or a lamplighter. You insulted me, so you got what you deserved. And if you don't like it, we can fight over it. Your rank doesn't mean a thing here!'

The officer was clearly striving to overcome his anger, for he repli-ed quite calmly:

'I should be sorry if you were to be killed in a duel. In any case, it would not be fair on the farmer here if I were to kill you. I should like to stay here until the army arrives, and I should like peace and quiet in the house.'

'I'm grateful to you for that, sir,' said Helmers. 'We'll get you a room ready and see to your horse.'

'Fine. Where is your stable?'

'I'll take you there, and then we'll go and meet my wife.'

The two of them stood up and walked the horse towards the stable. After a while the farmer came back on his own, and told his two guests that the officer was staying in his room to rest. Frank started to shake his head, saying:

'There's something I don't like about the fellow. Something funny about his face. And those eyes — like two fatty blobs in a lean soup! They have a sharp look about them, but there's nothing wise in them.'

Frank was quite upset, and would have gone on. But at that moment Helmers pointed to the north, and when his two companions looked that way they saw three riders. Hobble Frank gave a cry of joy and stood up.

'Do you know them?' asked Fred.

'Do I know them?' the small fellow replied. 'It's — well, I won't tell you their names for the moment, but I'll wait to see how you take to 'em.'

The first rider was small and fat, the second tall and thin. The third had a normal sort of figure and was riding a beautiful horse. Juggle Fred shaded his eyes with his hand, scrutinising them carefully, then cried out:

'Frank, you want to surprise us. But I shouldn't be a frontiersman if I couldn't guess right off who that was.'

'Who is it, then?'

'If the first man is fat and the second remarkable thin, the small one on a tall trotter and the tall on a measly mule, then it can't be none other'n Tall Davy and Fat Jemmy. I suppose the third one'll be Old Shatterhand.'

'How did you know?'

'Didn't I say he'd come with Jemmy? Doesn't Old Shatterhand ride a black horse, as anyone who has heard of him knows?'

'Yeah, you're right. That's them. They're here a deal sooner than I expected. I trust you'll greet them with due respect.'

The three riders drew nearer, then stopped and dismounted. All eyes were on Old Shatterhand. He went up to Helmers, put out his hand, and said warmly:

'I hope you were expecting us, Mr. Helmers, and that we're not going to be in the way.'

Shaking his hand, the farmer replied:

'Frank here told me you were coming, and I'm mighty pleased. My house is at your service.'

'Won't be staying long. We want to cross the old Llano, to meet someone on the other side.'

'Winnetou?'

'That's right. Frank told you that, too?'

'He mentioned it. But first of all, sir, how do you know me? You addressed me by name.'

'Out west it's best to know someone before you meet him. D'you mind if I ask who that other guy is?'

'They call me Juggle Fred,' the erstwhile juggler required. 'But I don't suppose you've ever heard of me.'

'Why not? Anyone who who's been wandering the West as long as I have has heard enough about Juggle Fred. You're an excellent tracker, and, what's more, a just man. I'm sure we'll be good friends.'

Though all trappers in the far West were equal, special honour was usually paid to the outstanding ones. Fred's face lit up with happiness and pride. He gripped the proffered hand heartily:

'It's a great honour for you to talk of friendship. I should like to ride along with you long enough to learn something. I'm going across the Llano Estacado, too. D'you mind if I ride along?'

'Sure. It's best not to ride through the Llano Estacado on your own. But I hope neither of us is going to have to wait for the other. When do you intend to set off?'

'I've been hired by a trading company. Their folk are supposed to come today.'

'Suits me; have to leave tomorrow. Traders, you say; are they going to Arizona?'

'That's right, sir.'

'Then you'll meet Winnetou, as well. Now let me introduce my two companions, so's you can get to know them.'

'Sure, but there's no need. Frank has told us enough about them ...'

Meanwhile, Helmers had welcomed Jemmy and Davy, too. Bob the negro came running up to see to the horses, and then they all sat down, and the farmer went inside for refreshments.

The officer had said he wanted to rest, but the moment he got to his room, he behaved quite differently. He shot the bolt, and began to walk up and down, thoughtfully. The room was on the northern side of the building, so he, too, noted the arrival of the three riders. Stepping over to the window, he watched them closely.

'Who are they, and where are they heading?' he wondered. 'They must want to cross the Llano. Hm. That is a bold intention. One of them has an exceptionally good horse. If these people were to get on the track of the settlers, they might spoil everything. Anyway, even that juggler is causing me bother. Luckily, the diamond dealers will never reach Helmers's farm. Let Fred go on waiting for them until it was all over ... I ought to try to keep the other three here until we've finished, too ...'

He waited just a little longer, then went outside to join the group of men.

This false officer was none other than Stewart, who had the day before ambushed two Comanches, pursued them, and come across the Sharpnose Brothers. His hare lip was hidden under the thick moustache.

Before he got downstairs, Old Shatterhand had heard of his visit. When the farmer saw him coming, he called out:

'Here comes Señor the captain now. He can tell you himself why he is here. Another knife and fork for the captain!'

The last words were addressed to his wife, who had just appeared at the window to look at her guests. She brought a plate, and the officer sat down to eat. There was nothing in the world which was less to his taste than the presence of Old Shatterhand. He looked him over carefully, and the hunter was not slow to notice. But he pretended to pay only passing attention to the officer.

During the meal the captain merely repeated what he had said before. When he had finished, the hunter asked casually:

'And where is your company, sir?'

'Up at Fort Sill.'

'And you have scouted out the area around it?'

'Of course!'

'So you know it pretty well round there?'

'Sure do!'

'I was there years ago, when Colonel Olmers was in charge of the fort. Who's in command there now?'

'Colonel Blaine . . .'

'Don't know him. And your cavalry are coming here? A pity they won't be here by tomorrow; we could've ridden across the Llano with them, safe as houses!'

'Then wait here for them . . .'

'I'm afraid I have neither the time nor the inclination for that.'

'You can surely wait one more day. Think of the advantage of having a military escort.'

'One day, you say?'

'That's right — two at the most.'

'Then I must disagree with you.'

'What do you mean?'

'I'm sure your cavalry will never arrive.'

'What are you talking about?'

'I know one thing: that there's no company of soldiers outside or inside Fort Sill waiting to set out for the Llano.'

'Are you suggesting I'm lying?' laughed the officer.

'Yes! I declare that you are a liar,' said Old Shatterhand, as calmly as if he had been paying a compliment.

'By all...!' That's an insult, I'm not...'

'Yes, of course. We should fight, if you were a real army officer. But you aren't...'

'You have the cheek to say that to my face?' cried Stewart, getting up from the table. 'I give my word that I am an officer of the United States: my uniform is proof of that anyway. And if you do not believe me, I challenge you to draw!'

Old Shatterhand looked him in the face with a smile and replied:

'Take it easy. If you heard my name, you must know that I am not at all easy to fool. I don't fight rogues, but if I did I should deal with you with my bare hands.'

'Insolent fellow!' shouted Stewart, drawing his gun. 'I'll shoot you like a mole!'

The threat had scarcely left his lips when the gun flew from his hand. At the same time Old Shatterhand said in a completely changed voice:

'You're crazy. Anyone who draws on me is usually done for. I let you off lightly, because I have no proof. I simply wanted to say that I have just ridden from Fort Sill, and I know the commander well. The one before was called Blaine, but three weeks ago Major Owen took over, though you probably don't know it. You say you left the fort about a week ago; if that were so you would surely know Major Owen. So your stories about cavalry and an expedition to the Llano are nothing but lies!'

But Stewart showed no sign of hesitation, as one might expect. He said quite calmly:

'All right; I admit that my company is not at Fort Sill. But that doesn't make me a liar and a trickster. As a scout I have to be careful. I just didn't want to give the game away...'

'Nonsense!' The hunter interrupted. 'I might believe you if I had never seen you before, but I have. Didn't you stand trial in Los Animas for train robbery? You managed to get away with it that time, but you were guilty, all the same. You got off in court, but you only just managed to avoid getting lynched. Don't deny it. You were called Stuart in those days, or something like it. I don't care what they call you now. Just lift up that moustache of yours. I think we'll find a hare lip underneath.'

'Who gave you the right to question me like this?' cried Stewart, but there was fear in his voice now.

'I have the right, since I know what I'm talking about. Here's your gun — be off with you! But don't cross my path again, or you'll regret it!'

And he threw the pistol at the officer's feet. Stewart picked it up, put it in his holster, and said:

'The whole thing is ridiculous. You are making a mistake. But I have papers upstairs; I'll bring them down.'

'Don't bother. They are stolen, I daresay. But you can show them to the others if you want. I don't need to see them.'

Stewart left.

'This is terrible,' gasped Helmers. 'Are you quite sure?'

'Quite sure,' replied Shatterhand, and Hobble Frank added:

'I thought so right away. I said to him straight out, but the rascal fooled me with his oversincere words. Wasn't I in Arcadia, too, and didn't I ride on the Hippocrates, so as to have a poetic knowledge of human nature and ...'

'Hippogryph, hippogryph, not Hippocrates!' cried Jemmy.

'Ah, there you are, you fat old hippodrome! Only just arrived, and have to argue with me! You can't stand my being cleverer than you. You know all words starting with 'hippo' come from Sanskrit, and that I'm far better than you are at Sanskrit.'

'Perhaps you are, but it's a Greek word ...'

'Greek? Understand Greek, do you? I'll bet you don't even know what Alexander the Great's horse was called.'

'What was it called, then?'

'Minotaur, of course.'

'Really? I thought it was Bucephalos.'

'Thought it was, did you? Bucephalos was a euphemistic conjugation of Olympic games with Carthaginian justice. He was a factory owner in Carthage whose treasurer made off with the fireproof safe. And he had paid millions for it! Alexander's white horse was called Minotaur. It was the same horse that the groom Froben got shot on soon afterwards at the Battle of Cannes.'

'But Frank, that was the Battle of Fehrbellina!'

'Nonsense! At the Battle of Fehrbellina Andrew Hofer defeated the Western Goths. And if you don't wish to believe my superior intelligence, ask Old Shatterhand. He is well up on all the arts and sciences — let him decide who is right.'

'Just don't drag me into learned disputes,' the hunter smiled. 'We have other problems just now.'

This shifted the conversation in another direction. Old Shatterhand asked in detail what had happened, and he seemed most interested in Bloody Fox, who had won this strange nickname as an eight-year-old, when they found him after an Indian raid with his head cut open. He also asked about the diamond merchants, and then the conversation turned to the Llano in general. Everyone knew something or other about the desert, and their talk dragged on, until black Bob interrupted:

'Massa Helmers, where shall I put all the horses when they come?'

'What horses?' asked the farmer.

'The cavalry horses that the officers spoke of. He has just gone to look for them.'

'So the officer's ridden off, has he?'

'Yessir, he's gone. But he says he will bring plenty of horsemen.'

'Which way did he ride?'

'He rode round the stable and go thataway.' The negro pointed northwards.

'That's strange. He said they were sure to come, that he was to wait here for them, and now he rides to meet them. I've a mind to follow him and ask him about it.'

'If you did,' Old Shatterhand said with a smile, 'you wouldn't ride north for very long.'

'How come?'

'Because he only rode that way to fool us. He's no officer, even if he does wear a uniform. He's up to no good, and since we saw through him, he thought he'd better make tracks. But he went a different direction to the one he's really heading.'

'Where would he go? The Llano is to the west and south-west; he came from the south, and there's nothing for him to the east, so that only leaves the north ...'

'Mr. Helmers, I reckon you're wrong. I guess he did just the opposite of what he said. He came from the south, and he headed north; if we tracked him, we'd soon find he changed direction. What he said about the army was a lie.'

'Then why did you let him go?'

'Because right now he can't do anything worse than tell lies.'

'Why did he come, then?'

'How should I know? I can't tell you anything for certain, but I have the feeling he came to ask about something and to find something out. What might that be? For lots of folk your house is the starting-point for a trip across the Llano. I reckon he's interested in those sort of folk. He must expect some profit from them ...'

'Hm,' grunted Helmers. 'D'you reckon he's one of the vultures — the stakemen?'

Old Shatterhand just nodded.

'Then we shouldn't have let him go. But we had no proof, of course. He found out that Fred was expecting diamond merchants, and maybe he's gone to make his plans with someone.'

'That's as good as for sure. That guy is not alone. But there was nothing we could prove. Let him go! At least I'll be sure whether he was right or not, and I'll track him. When did he leave?'

'It was more than an hour ago,' the negro answered.

'We'll have to hurry. Is anyone coming along?'

They all offered, and Shatterhand chose Juggle Fred — apparently to get to know him better. But Frank was upset at this decision.

'If you take along anyone else but me, you could scarcely call it a compliment. Do you reckon I can't help? If I was allowed to go, it would give me a special geographical pleasure.'

Old Shatterhand smiled.

'And what have you done to deserve it?'

'In the first place, there is my terrestrial existence in general; then it is a natural consequence of my being no less inquisitive than anyone else. And thirdly, I might learn a lot on a trip like that.'

'Such modesty deserves a reward, to be sure! You'll go with us then, Frank.'

'Excellent!' cried the little trapper. 'I express to you my most indulgent gratitude, monsignor. In my humility I have also offered the other gentlemen an example to be followed, good Edward demonstrandus!'

And he went to get the horses from the stable. Helmers had offered to lend them undemanding mounts with plenty of stamina, an offer Shatterhand was glad to accept. Soon the trio of riders was making for the horizon.

The tracks led northwards, but only for a while. After that they

turned through east to the south, finally adopting a south-westerly direction. Stewart had traced almost three-quarters of a circle, and what was strange was that it was a circle with quite a small diameter.

Old Shatterhand rode out front, leaning from his saddle to keep his eyes on the tracks. When, after a while, he was sure they were maintaining the same direction, he pulled up his horse and asked:

'Mister Fred, what do you think? Can we believe these tracks?'

'Sure thing, sir,' Fred replied. 'From here on the guy shows his true colours. He was heading straight for the Llano, and . . .'

'Yeah?'

'He seems to have been in a hurry. The arc he rode round Helmers's farm is a small one; he don't seem to have had time to make a bigger detour. And he was riding at a gallop. Reckon there was something driving him on.'

'What could that have been?'

'Couldn't rightly say. Reckon you might guess better.'

'I wouldn't like to guess. I'd rather be sure. We've plenty of time, and a few hours won't make any difference. Let's ride on!'

They spurred their horses to a gallop, which was no problem, since the tracks were quite clear.

They could soon see that Helmers's farm really did lie on the very edge of inhabited country. The landscape soon changed.

To the north the lowlands were still bordered by forest. To the south they could see nothing but solitary trees, and even these had soon disappeared. The shrubs and the buffalo grass, too, soon grew sparser. Instead they saw bear-berry — a sure sign that the soil was becoming barren. After that there were more and more bare patches of sand, and the undulating countryside gave way to an endless plain.

In a while even the bear-berry disappeared, its place being taken by spiky cactus and long, snake-like creepers of the Cereus genus. Stewart had prudently skirted such places, where his horse might have been injured. Now and then he had given the animal a few minutes' rest, but then again spurred it into a gallop, as the deep hoofmarks showed.

On and on he had ridden. It was now two hours since the riders had left the farm. They had ridden at least fifteen miles, and still there was no sign of the man they were following.

Suddenly they spotted a dark line running into the desert to their left. It was a hill overgrown with bushes, and the tracks headed in that direction. Old Shatterhand pulled up suddenly; he pointed forward and said:

'Careful, now. I reckon there are people beyond those bushes. Did you see anything?'

'Nothing at all,' replied Fred, surprised.

'I thought I saw something moving. Let's ride to the left.'

So they made a detour, as quickly as possible, so as to get off the plain, where they were easy to see. When they reached the bushes, Old Shatterhand jumped down from the saddle.

'Stay here and hold my horse,' he said softly. 'I'll take a look myself. But load your guns, and be ready. If I shoot, come quickly!'

He bent over, stepped into the bushes, and disappeared. Within three minutes he was back again, a satisfied smile on his lips.

'The officer isn't here,' he said. 'Nor are his companions. But I think we are going to meet some interesting people. Fred, have you ever heard of the Sharpnose brothers?'

'You bet I have.'

'Then come with me! I haven't had the pleasure myself, but I guess from their noses that's who they are.'

'What are they wearing?'

'Woollen trousers and shirts, laced shoes and felt hats, rattlesnake skin belts and blankets for cloaks.'

'That's them! Did you see their horses?'

'They're not horses, they're mules.'

'Then there's no doubt about it: that's Jim and Tim with Polly and Molly.'

'Quiet, for Christ's sake!' Old Shatterhand warned them. 'They're not alone. There's a young Indian with them.'

'No matter, sir. Anyone who's with the Sharpnoses is no danger to us. I spent a month or two hunting beavers with them in the Black Hills. And we agreed a signal so that we can recognise each other from a long way off. You'll se. What are they doing now?'

'Sitting in the shade and resting.'

'And their mules?'

'They're nibbling leaves.'

'Are they tied up?'

'No.'

'Then you'll see that Polly and Molly are just as clever as their masters. I bet you the mules are here as quick as Jim and Tim. Watch this!'

He stuck his fingers in his mouth and gave a long, warbling whistle. There was no reply.

'They're surprised,' Fred supposed. 'I'll try again.'

He whistled again, and no sooner had he finished than they heard the mules coming. There was a rustling in the bushes, and a voice could be heard over the pounding of hooves:

250

'Hey there! What's going on? What's the meaning of this, out here in the desert? It can't be Fred . . . Juggle Fred?'

'None other!' came another voice. 'Go on — the mules wouldn't run to anyone else like that!'

There was more rustling in the bushes, and the Sharpnose brothers appeared — first Jim, then Tim. When they saw Fred, they rushed up to him like a whirlwind and embraced him.

'Hang on, boys, you're going to crush me,' the ex-juggler protested.

'Don't worry!' Jim told him. 'But Juggle Fred! This *is* a pleasant surprise. But how come you whistled? Did you know we were lying in the bushes?'

'Fine backwoodsmen you are! A herd of buffalo could go past, and you wouldn't know it. I guess you're surprised to see me here . . .'

'A little bit, Fred. But we knew about you.'

'Who from?'

'Do you know six men whose leader is called Gibson — a lawyer?'

'Sure do. I'm waiting at Helmers's farm for them, to take them across the Llano. Have you met them?'

'That's right. And they told us about you.'

'Where are they? And what are you doing in the bushes?'

'More about that later. First of all, we'd like to know who these gentlemen are you've got with you.'

'I'll tell you right away. This famous fellow with an Amazon hat on his head is called Hobble Frank, and he's . . .'

'Hobble Frank? Not the famous scholar who once rode about Yellowstone Park with Winnetou and Shatterhand?' Tim interrupted. 'That was his name, wasn't it?'

Tim spoke the words 'famous scholar' ironically, but Frank took them very seriously, and said:

'Yessir, I'm Hobble Frank. Where do you know me from?'

'We heard about you on the Blackbird River, and we were amazed at your exploits, sir. And who is the other one, Fred?'

All eyes fell on Old Shatterhand.

'Him?' Fred retorted. 'Take a good look at him. Who d'you think it might be?'

They didn't have to guess for long, since an explanation was forthcoming from another quarter. The young Comanche, Iron Heart, had just come out of the bushes. The moment he saw Old Shatterhand, he called out:

'Nina-nonton — the Hand that Shatters! Shiba-big is too young to look such a famous warrior in the face!'

And he stepped to one side, as Indian modesty demanded. But Old Shatterhand placed a hand on his shoulder and said:

'I know you, though it is many suns since we met. You have grown since then. What of your father, Tevna-shohe, Big Chief of the Comanches, with whom I smoked the pipe of peace? Where is his camp?'

'His spirit is journeying to the Happy Hunting Ground ... but it can reach it only when I get the scalps of his murderers.'

'What's this? Fiery Star is dead? And who killed him?' cried Old Shatterhand. 'Tell me who!'

'Shiba-big will not speak of it. Let my white brother ask friends who saw the chief dead, and buried him with me this morning!'

And he turned away again. When Old Shatterhand looked round, he saw that the eyes of both the Sharpnoses were fixed on him. He held out his hand, saying:

'It seems you have something important to tell us. Fiery Star was my friend: I have to know what happened to him. But the sun is too hot out here. Let's go in the shade. Then you can tell me what's been going on.'

Jim and Tim walked straight through the bushes. The other three led their horses along the edge of the thicket. The young Comanche was already sitting in the shade. The white men sat down and Jim began to tell of the previous day's events.

First he told them how they had met five men led by Stewart, who had driven them off at gunpoint. Then they had met Iron Heart, who led them to the grave of his father Fiery Star, murdered by six white men on his way from Austin.

It was lucky that Jim spoke English. If he had used Frank's native tongue, the little scholar would surely have tried to put in comments

of his own whenever the opportunity presented itself. When he had told of the meeting with the young Indian, Jim went on:

'As soon as the sun rose, we buried the chief; just for the time being, till his braves come to build his last wigwam. Then we'll go after his murderers.'

'I thought you were heading for Helmers's farm,' said Shatterhand.

'We did intend to. But we've made friends with Iron Hand, and got involved. He wanted us to track the killers, so here we are.'

'Did you manage to find their tracks?'

'It was difficult. The men rode south, to a place where they split up to make a string of sentries. They were watching some sort of camp there.'

'Whose camp was it?'

'Who knows. Settlers, I guess. We saw the tracks of ox-wagons and horses; we reckon about fifty people spent the night there.'

'And now they've gone? Which way did they head?'

'South-west.'

'For the Llano, then? With wagons? Hm. Either they have a very good guide, or someone wants to lead them into a terrible ambush. What do you think, Jim?'

'The second.'

'Why?'

'Because Fiery Star's killers have a hand in this. The diamond dealers joined the wagon train, too. According to the tracks it set off soon after midnight. That's suspicious. As if someone wanted them to get away from the farm as soon as possible.'

'Did you follow the wagon train?'

'No. We're only after the chief's killers. The tracks show they didn't

join the wagon train, but rode westwards. And we saw the tracks of a rider who joined the wagon train in the evening.'

'Yeah? In the evening? Could it have been the Mormon missionary, Tobias? What about your tracks, Jim?'

'Those guys rode very fast. Then one of them left the group. His tracks headed due north. We rode after him a while to make sure.'

'I guess that was the officer.'

'Which officer?' asked Jim. 'There wasn't one with them.'

'That's as maybe, but one of them became an officer. We'll soon see. Did you speak to those guys? Was one of them a long-legged fellow with a dark beard?'

'That might be their leader.'

'He had a moustache hanging right down over his lips. Do you know why?'

'He had a hare lip. We saw it clear enough.'

'That's him! He rode to the farm to make sure there was no danger from that direction. What then?'

'I'd rather not tell any more. It ain't pleasant when a man got to admit to being stupid. You'd better tell them, Tim.'

'Thanks a lot!' Tim said. 'As you make your bed, so you must lie on it! Why should I start just at the point we made a mess of it?'

'Because you know how to make something foolish sound better. But since you're my brother, I'll try. The truth of the matter is that we lost the track, and haven't been able to find it again.'

'You can't have!' cried Old Shatterhand.

'"fraid we did . . .'

'The Sharpnose brothers lose a track! If anyone else told me that, I wouldn't believe them.'

'Thanks, but it was Tim Sharpnose himself told you.'

'How did it happen?'

'The easiest way in the world. Out there in front there's stony ground that stretches several miles east and south. You'd have to go there to understand how we lost the trail.'

'I know a place like that. The Mexicans of that region call it the Devil's Plain.'

'That's it! Have you been there?'

'Twice.'

'Then you won't wonder the trail got lost before our eyes, as if the wind had carried it off.'

'Hm! But the wind can't carry off four riders!'

'You're right, but even our Comanche couldn't find anything.'

'I'd like to know if the same thing'll happen to me.'

'You and Winnetou'll find the track even if those guys did get lost in the wind! And I should think that's what happened. Believe me, there isn't a stone out of place, not a scratch from a hoof on the rock. We did what any good tracker would have done in our place. We rode along the stony ground to find the spot those guys rode out onto the sand. It took so long we haven't finished yet. But when we got here we saw a rider galloping southwards. And he stopped in these bushes.'

Old Shatterhand became alert. For a moment he thought, then he got up, examined the various hoofmarks which were left around the bushes, and then walked a little way away from the rest. Suddenly they heard him say:

'Jim, have you or your brother been over here?'

'No, sir,' Jim replied.

'Come here, all of you!'

When they reached the place, the trapper pointed to the bushes.

'Here you can see where someone went into the thicket — look at the broken twigs. Now follow me, gentlemen!'

He went deeper and deeper into the bushes, until he reached a patch of sand. It was several paces square, with nothing growing on it. Old Shatterhand knelt down and seemed to be examining every grain of sand. At last he stood up, a smile on his lips, and looked at the surrounding bushes. Then, pointing to one place, he said:

'Here someone reached a hiding-place, and I'll swear he got off his horse outside the thicket, on stony ground. Tell me two things, Tim. Was it south of here that the rider parted from his four companions?'

'South-west, sir.'

'Ah! And did he have a uniform on?'

'No, sir.'

'Then it's quite clear. When he left his companions, the leader of the five rode here to put on his uniform, and went on to Helmers's place as an officer. On his way back he stopped here again, and did the same thing the other way round.'

'What do you mean? D'you suppose there's some sort of cloakroom here?'

'Yes, or at least some sort of cache, like the pits beaver hunters use to hide their furs in. Let's have a look around; it seems to me this sand is heaped up just a little too carefully.'

The Sharpnose brothers looked at him in amazement. Frank, on the other hand, flung himself to the ground and began digging as fiercely as if the sand had concealed all the treasure in the world. The rest followed suit.

Sand flew in all directions, and Frank had got no further than ten inches deep, when he shouted:

'Got it! I've got something hard!'

'Just carry on,' Jim encouraged him. 'If it's hard, it may be a rock.'

'Carry on? I'm digging like a mole or a ground-squirrel. And it ain't a rock, but wood. Thin little sticks.'

'Some sort of switches,' Old Shatterhand said. 'They're bound together to make a cover for the hiding-place.'

Once again Shatterhand was right. Sticks as straight as rulers were tied together with baste to make a cover for a deep, square hole. It was about two yards by two, and filled to the brim with various objects.

The first thing the trappers saw was a sabre and a uniform, with a piece of folded newspaper lying on it.

'The officer's uniform and sabre the gang's leader wore!' cried Frank. Then he drew the blade from its sheath and waved it around. 'If only the rogue were here now — I'd stroke his head for him. I'd give him a croisé ...'

'You'd give him a what?' asked Juggle Fred.

'A croisé, ignoramus! Don't you know the language we fencers use? Why, when I was just a little lad I used to carve all sorts of swords and sabres out of wood, and later on I learned the proper words, or as the Latin scholars say, the 'thermopylus polytechnicus', and I can still remember them. A blow from above is a croisé. As 'tempus passatus' of the forest, that's something I should know, my friend —'

'Frank, hand me that piece of paper!' Old Shatterhand interrupted.

'Here you are. I can educate Frank when we get this den of thieves sorted out.'

And he handed Old Shatterhand the newspaper. The latter unwrapped it, and took out a slip of paper with a message pencilled on it. He read it out:

Venid pronto en nuestro escondite! Precaucion! Old Shatterhand está en casa de Helmers.

'What does it mean?' Fred asked. 'Frank, you're the expert in languages!'

'Naturally!' Frank replied. 'It's about Old Shatterhand and Helmers. But this Hebrew is so mixed up with Indian endings and so infested with Indogermanic bugs that my stomach turned over at the very first word. So I'll wash my hands of it and give that uniform a look over.'

And he began to go through the pockets. Meanwhile, Old Shatterhand translated the Spanish message:

'Come quickly to our hideout! Careful! Old Shatterhand is at Helmers's house.'

For the moment they had no inclination to think about the meaning of this message, since they were more interested in the contents of the pit. These included well-worn, but still usable items of clothing of all sorts, colours and sizes, rifles, pistols, knives, lead, tin boxes of matches, and even a cask half-filled with gunpowder. The pockets of all the clothes were empty. They found some Indian ornaments, too.

'We'll burn the clothes,' said Old Shatterhand. 'It's a pity to waste the rest; you'd better help yourselves to what you fancy. We'll take the rest back to Helmers's place. I'm sure the bandits have several of these hiding-places that they use to keep their booty. The uniform must have belonged to an officer; these ornaments were taken from Indians they ambushed. But for me the most important thing is this piece of paper. What do you think of the message, Jim?'

'Two things,' Jim replied. 'First of all, the guy was afraid of you. I reckon he would have stayed longer at Helmers's place if he hadn't met you there. I don't know what happened there, but I can guess.'

'And the second thing?'

'The second thing is that he has some helpers he wants to warn. They are heading for the Llano Estacado, too, and they are going to open the pit. The message tells them to go to the spot they call the hideout. That seems to be some place they meet.'

'I agree. So you can see that you don't have to give up looking for your lost tracks. That guy will join his four companions again. If you want to find them, all you have to do is to come with us. Their tracks will be clear enough from here, and they'll lead to the hideout the message refers to. And guess why he wants them to go there.'

'Of course! They're going to ambush the wagon-train!'

'That's what I think. And he wants to do it as soon as possible. He's afraid we've cottoned on to his plan, and that we might foil it. So he's in a hurry.'

'Then we'd better move fast as well! I hope you'll help us ...'

'Sure I will. First of all I'd like to have a word with those guys about the murder of the chief, and secondly we ought to prevent any other misfortunes before they happen. So what shall we do?'

'You want Sharpnose to make a suggestion? What an idea! We'll do as Old Shatterhand thinks fit, eh, Tim lad?'

'Sure thing,' his brother agreed. 'I guess Old Shatterhand has decided already, whereas we should just beat about the bush. Or do you want to suggest something, Fred?'

'Sure don't,' the trapper replied. 'Ain't the right man to do so. But I'll tell you my opinion: Wouldn't it be better to set off after that fellow right away? He's the leader and the brains of the gang. If we find him, the rest'll give up their plans.'

'I don't think so!' said Old Shatterhand. 'He may have been the spokesman of the five, but whether he's the leader of all the bandits or not, that's another thing. By getting rid of him we won't draw the fangs of the others. Anyway, I don't reckon we'd catch up with him now. The sun's starting to set, and we're not likely to find him at night. Let's call it a day; we'll pick up the trail tomorrow. You camp here, and see to the ones the message was intended for. Meanwhile I'll take three horses back to the farm and bring Jemmy, Dave and Bob the negro to reinforce us. We'll set off at dawn and hope we'll be in luck. If there are nine of us we needn't be afraid of bandits.'

They all liked the idea. Each took the guns and ammunition he wanted from the cache. They took the clothes out into the open and burned them. When Old Shatterhand swung into the saddle, the pile was still smouldering. He promised to bring food and water; then he pointed westwards, saying:

'I reckon there's something on the way from there. Must be a storm, I guess.'

Then he set off northwards with the three horses. The others watched the western sky, where a light greyish-red cloud had appeared over the setting sun. It formed a circle in the centre of which the sun's rays met. It did not look dangerous, so they did not attach any great importance to Shatterhand's words. Only the Comanche stared upwards, whispering:

'Temb metan — the mouth of the lightning!'

The Hour of the Spirits

After Old Shatterhand left, the others sat down and told the Sharp-noses about the events at the farm. Their accounts were long and drawn-out. Time passed quickly, and no one noticed that the sky had changed colour dramatically. Only the young Comanche, sitting silently to one side, kept looking at the western horizon.

The circle of cloud opened at the bottom, taking on the shape of a horseshoe, the ends of which became elongated to form two narrow strips. In between, clear sky could be seen. The nearer of the two strips bent to colour the southern horizon with yellowish-red dust. A storm seemed to be in progress.

To the east it grew dark, though no clouds were visible there. The Comanche suddenly leaped up and cried out, pointing to the east:

'Maho-timb-yuavah — the spirit of the prairie!'

They all stood up. Only now did they notice the change which had taken place in the sky, and alarm leapt into their eyes as they looked in the direction the Indian was pointing.

It looked as if a rider was galloping across the sky a few metres over the horizon. The dark silhouette stood out against the lighter

background, which moved along with it. But the horse and its rider were of huge size, and each of its legs could clearly be seen. The rider was holding the reins in his right hand; his head was framed with long hair, and he wore Indian ornaments in it. The rifle on his back jumped up and down in time with the rhythm of his ride. The mane and tail of the horse trailed in the strong wind. The awesome creature was riding as if the very devil were after it!

And all that in broad daylight, a full hour before sunset! The on-lookers were filled with awe, and not a word was spoken.

The black wall to the south broke open, almost in an instant, and from top to bottom. That was the spot the rider was making for. It got closer and closer: ten more leaps, five more, three more — one more, and the animal leapt into the emptiness to disappear along with its rider.

The trappers stood there in silence. They looked backwards and forwards, from the place they had last seen the apparition to each other's faces. At last Jim shook himself out of his trance and said:

'For Chrissake! If that wasn't the ghost of the Llano, my name's not Sharpnose! I used to think it was just a tale, but now I don't doubt it's true. My heart's still cold. What about you, Tim lad?'

'I feel like an empty nugget bag without so much as a speck of gold left in it. But look how fast the sky's changing! I've never seen any-thing like it!'

The top edge of the black wall was now crimson; the red colour jumped back and forth. The part of the horseshoe which had re-mained quite high in the sky sank to the ground. The lower it came, the wider and darker it got. To the south a sea of dust and smoke was twisting around, driven by a gale. The sun was hidden behind a thick veil, getting denser and taller every second. It seemed that the dark band of cloud was falling from the sky to the ground. Suddenly they all felt very cold. A piercing roar could be heard in the distance.

'To the horses!' cried Fred. 'Get them down! Hold them tight — lie down with them!'

All five men rushed to their horses, which were fretfully snorting, and offered no resistance when they were dragged to the ground.

They lay close to the bushes, their heads among the branches. Then it came: a whistling, groaning, howling, rustling, crackling and roaring which is hard to describe. And men and horses were pressed to the ground with such force that they could not have stood up, even if they had tried. An icy cold cut them to the bone. Their eyes, noses, mouths and ears seemed to be filled with freezing water. Then they suddenly felt a warm breath on them again, and the din of the Llano Estacado receded in the distance. Ice-cold night was replaced by clear sunshine and reviving warmth. They all breathed a sigh of relief. The men got up, wiped the dust from their eyes, and looked around them.

Yes, it had been a tornado, that central American storm of such huge force that the devastation it causes is so fearful as to be almost incredible. Wind speeds reach hundreds of kilometres an hour, and are often accompanied by electrical phenomena, which usually last long after the storm has passed. Not even the *samum* of the African desert is as savage; only the sandstorms and blizzards of the Gobi desert can be compared with a tornado.

The trappers shook the sand from their clothes. The bushes had saved them: in front of the thicket was a new sand dune almost one metre deep.

'Phew! We were lucky!' said Jim. 'Anyone who's caught in that out in the open has had it!'

'Don't reckon so,' Fred disagreed. 'Usually these twisters are less than half a mile across, even if they're mighty powerful. We only caught the edge of it. If we'd have been in the middle, it would have carried us and our horses to who knows where.'

'Quite right,' Tim confirmed. 'I once saw the mess a tornado made in the forest. There were huge trees, some of them six feet across, uprooted and lying there like matchwood. But the clearing it cut was so sharply bordered that the trees on both sides were practically untouched. The Yankees call these storms hurricanes, like the clearings they fell in the forests.'

'It was bad enough!' commented Frank. 'I couldn't breathe, and I was blowing my whistle on the last hole. And to make it worse, your asses kicked me so bad I was half dead from it ...'

'They're not asses, they're mules,' Jim interrupted.

'Oh no they're not: if they kick like that they're the biggest asses under the sun. They trampled the whole artistic structure of my Gothic figure. I should really take you to court for inflicting grievous bodily harm through negligent care of animals, but no one would give a fig for someone as alone in the wide world as I am. So I'll take the course of mercy rather than that of law, but in future you'd better see to it that there's no more donkey business of that sort. Fixi et salvavi animal!'

'It's dixi and animam!' Fred cried.

'Quiet! As far as Latin is concerned, I'm not interested in your opinion!' Frank shouted him down. 'That's all I need, for some two-bit juggler to tell me what to do. Learn something, and then you'll

know it. I wanted us to be friends, but if you're going to get on my nerves like that, I'll lose my temper and throw you into space, where you'll fly around under the stars till eternity like a dreadnought. Fixi, and three times fixi, which means: I said it, I, Hobble Frank! Remember that!'

Then he slung his rifle across his shoulder and set off, like Achilles insulted. The others looked on with a smile, but no one said anything to calm him down. They knew the little fellow would soon be back.

The sun was shining again, but its rays were almost saffron-coloured now, like the sky.

The animals were still restless, and had to be tied up securely.

The Comanche spread his blanket on the sand and sat on it. Even now, after the storm had passed, he kept the silence which was usual for Indians. The other three sat down close by, and Jim asked:

'Has my young Indian brother been in such a storm before?'

'Many times,' came the reply. 'Once such a storm even buried Iron Hand in the sand, but the Comanches found him.'

'But you've never seen that apparition before?'

'Yes, I have seen it once when I rode through the Llano with my father. We heard a shot, and then saw a spirit on a black mustang. Some way off there was a white man with a bloody wound in his head. My father knew the dead man, and said he was an evil man, and much feared.'

'What did the spirit look like?'

'It had the head and body of a white buffalo, with a bushy mane around its neck. It was a fearful sight. But it is a good spirit, or it would not have the form of a sacred animal. The Comanches know well that it slays only evil men, but helps the good. Two of our men once got lost in the Llano, and were in danger of death. The spirit came to them, gave them food and water, and showed them the way.'

'Did it speak to them?'

'Yes. It spoke their own language. Good spirits speak all languages...'

He turned away, thus indicating that he did not wish to speak any more.

Meanwhile, Frank had appeared a little way off. He could never keep up his anger for long, and so he came up to Fred and said:

'I've given you time to repent. I daresay you've realised how you insulted the scientific authority of my pomological methods. Do you admit it?'

'Yes,' said Fred, with a straight face. 'I admit that none of us can match you.'

'Well, watch out in future, and don't get carried away by your hemispherical nature. I'll let you off this time; after all we've just been through together, I'm willing to make peace. If a man sees a real ghost in broad daylight, then his neck and his skin are at stake. My goosepimples came up like balloons.'

And he sat down next to Fred. But the latter said with a smile:

'You mustn't wonder too much. What we saw can be explained quite naturally...'

'No way. That was a real ghost. It rode across the sky, and it was neither air, nor mist, but a material figure of a real and supernatural being. How else could you explain it?'

'Hm! How many fake ghosts have I played myself...'

'Best not speak of that; that's no more than a trick. How did you do it?'

'Either with a sheet of glass at an angle, or a camera obscura — a darkroom.'

'I can do that too. I once made a camera obscuriosa. I should have succeeded, too, only I forgot to make the little hole for the lentils. But there weren't any of those anyway, so I had to put it away for the time being.'

At that moment Fred and the Sharpnoses burst out laughing so loud that the Comanche turned and looked at them in surprise. Frank called out:

'Salicium! Quiet! if you don't stop laughing I'll make you a blood-bath like Mohammed the Second made for the Carthaginians! I say to you that your so-called philosophy is full of holes and your wisdom smells of castor oil. You'd laugh at my camera procura, would you? It was quite correctly conceded, only I didn't have enough time as a lumber jack to find lentils and grow them. I've long ago seen through you, you illiterate lot, but I tolerated your lack of frequency with magnanimity, hoping that something could still be made of you. But now I'm coming to the conclusion that you are lost both for science and for art.'

Large in his anger, he knocked the dust off his shoes, blurted out the last words with a gesture of rage, and went to hide in the bushes, thus punishing mockery with disdain.

After he had gone, the laughter subsided, and Fred said jokingly:

'I never thought he'd lose his temper like that. We'll have to calm him down — he's a good fellow, and his infamous intellectual pretensions won't do anyone any harm.'

He told the Sharpnoses everything he knew about Frank, arousing their interest in the strange little fellow. Then they spoke about the tornado, and finally went on to discuss the ghost. They agreed that it must be some optical illusion, though they were unable to explain it more exactly.

The day was at an end, and night fell. When it got dark, Frank appeared again, not wanting to be on his own. For the time being he did not sit with others, but stayed a little way off, though listening to their conversation intently.

The air had cleared now, and a south-westerly breeze fanned them pleasantly after the heat of the day. A few stars twinkled in the sky, their lack of motion seemed to remind them of the passing of time.

They tried to sleep; only the Comanche stared up at the sky, even though he had not slept a wink the night before. His father's violent death would allow him no rest.

The night gradually passed. But suddenly the Indian cried out loud. The sleepy trappers sat up.

'Mava tuhshta — look over there!' the redskin said, pointing southwards.

At the point where the sky touched the horizon, there was a clear spot in the shape of a segment of a circle, which attracted the attention of them all.

'Hm!' grunted Jim. 'If it were in the east I should think it was the dawn coming...'

'No,' said Tim. 'The dawn looks different. That light is too clear.'

'Because it's a dark night.'

'That's just why it can't be the dawn — anyway, it's the wrong way.'

'Could it be a fire, then?'

'On the Llano, where there's not a splinter of wood to be found? Someone would have to be burning sand.'

'Then I don't know what it is, but the bright spot's getting larger. And the wind's changing. It was blowing from the south-west, and now its getting colder. What can that mean?'

'It's not the northern lights,' said Fred, 'and I've never heard of any southern ones.'

Frank had remained silent, but he could contain himself no longer.

'That bright spot on the horizon means something,' he said. 'It must be connected with the ghost. It was riding southwards. Maybe it lives there, and it's lit a fire.'

The others would have burst out laughing, but they contained themselves. Then Fred said:

'Do you think the ghost camps by a fire?'

'Why not? With such a cold wind blowing.'

The wind was bitter. And the bright spot in the south was getting higher and higher above the horizon. It seemed like some very large star, or even the moon. It almost formed a semi-circle now, with a blood-red core.

It was a little frightening, but a beautiful sight. None of the five men made a sound.

The wind was blowing from the north. Within a quarter of an hour it had turned 180 degrees, and was now blowing towards the place where the magnificent spectacle was unfolding.

'Old Shatterhand should see this!' said Juggle Fred. 'A pity he can't get back yet, 'cause it's only midnight.'

And Frank said at once:

'Midnight! The witching hour! Something fearful's bound to happen at that fire!'

'What do you suppose might happen, if, as you say, it's burning already?'

'Don't ask silly questions. At midnight hell opens up, and ghosts come out. Just like every country and every nation is different, the ghosts of different countries are different. In one place they wring your neck, in another they haunt crossroads. Who knows what these ones do? Maybe they're the worst and most dangerous of all. Let's watch out and — look, look . . . it's coming!'

It has been said that the strange light in the southern sky formed a large semicircle. At the point where it touched the horizon to the left, they suddenly saw a huge rider. The horse was black, the rider white. He had two horns on his head; the typical hump and body of a buffalo could be seen, merging at the back with the body of the horse.

He rode like the wind, but did not move in a straight line — that is across the diameter of the semicircle. Instead he rode upwards, galloping along its circumference.

In this manner he reached the highest point, and then rode down the right-hand half of the gleaming semicircle; at the bottom he vanished as suddenly as he had appeared.

They stood there a little longer to see if the scene would be repeated, but in vain. The semicircle shone for a few moments with the same intensity, but was then gradually swallowed in the darkness.

At that moment the dull sound of hooves could be heard in the sand. A group of riders approached, halted, and dismounted. The first of them was Old Shatterhand.

'I'm glad to see you alive!' he called, still some way off. 'We thought we would have to dig you out of the sand!'

'It wasn't so bad,' Fred replied. 'I see you wasted no time. We didn't expect you back so soon.'

'Well, we raced back, 'cause we were afraid for you. As you can see, Mr. Helmers is here with his men. We watched the tornado from his farm, and didn't give you much chance of surviving.'

With him were Jemmy, Davy, Bob and Helmers, with several farmhands. They greeted each other, and then Fred told them of the strange apparition. Jemmy and Davy shook their heads in disbelief, but Helmers was the first to voice their doubts.

'What you're telling us must have happened, since five pairs of eyes saw it. But I can't understand the whole thing; I know well enough that there's no man on earth that can prove that ghosts exist just like real creatures do.'

'Oh, but such a man has been walking the world for some time, and that's me,' Frank piped up. 'There can be no question of any Coptic disillusion, since we saw it all in complete dexterity. The spirit is a supernatural being that can fly through the air, the Yankees call it the ghostly hour, a circumstance which conspires to explain the whole phenomenon, and is indisputable proof of the fact that it is a ghost from the next world. I don't think there's anyone here who would deny that.'

He was wrong, for Old Shatterhand himself answered:

'And what if someone did have a different opinion?'

'Hm! That depends who it was. If you yourself should wish to take issue, I should be exceptionally willing to instruct you.'

'Thanks for your kindness. But the first time the spirit appeared was in broad daylight, which suggests it is not from the next world, as you suppose ...'

'Then what ...' Frank began to ask, but he got no answer, since something quite different happened.

As they had spoken, the light in the south had continued to sink and fade. It seemed it would disappear altogether, but suddenly it burst into a fiery sea which flowed over half the sky.

Frank cried out: 'The performance is beginning again! I've never seen such an hour of the spirits before. That fire is of supernatural origin, 'cause ...'

'No sir,' Old Shatterhand interrupted him. 'The images you saw were caused by the air acting as a mirror — in a number of hot and cold streams — from the fire, for instance. So those flames are ...'

His attention was suddenly attracted to the fire which blazed dark red in the west, covering the clouds. But up above the clouds, in front of the fire, there appeared in the sky an inverted picture of flat, red-

dily illuminated countryside, in which they saw again the rider with the buffalo horns, this time upside down.

'. . . just a reflection of what's going on somewhere near here, like the picture you see now,' Old Shatterhand finally finished what he had been saying.

But before he had even finished speaking, a second rider appeared, galloping after the first.

'Gracious!' cried Frank. 'It's the spirit we saw in the afternoon before the tornado!'

'Really?' asked Old Shatterhand. 'Then you must admit I'm right, that they're two different things. And over there are some more of them!'

Behind the figure of the second rider there now appeared a further five or six figures on horses, all of them upside down.

Frank just shook himself.

'A fine witching hour this is! I've heard of ghosts going about with their heads under their arms, but I've never heard of them riding upside down!'

'Don't worry. The pictures you saw before were reflected several times, but this one only once. But we'll soon meet those ghosts. On your horses, gentlemen! That first rider, the one you call the ghost of the Llano Estacado, is being chased. Let's give him a little help . . .'

'Are you crazy?' asked Frank. 'Do you want to leave the land of the living?'

But no one was listening, and the others quickly prepared to leave.

'Should we take the pack-horses with us?' Helmers asked.

'Sure. I don't think we'll be coming back here. Are you going to ride along?'

'Sure would like to. I'd like to speak to the spirit, too.'

The horses Helmers had brought to take the things away from the hiding-place were being looked after by his men. Frank, too, swung himself into the saddle, since it was his habit of opposition rather than fear which made him reluctant.

The riders had scarcely set off when the whole scene, except for the blazing flames, disappeared from view.

Shatterhand rode out in front, followed by the Sharpnose brothers. Their mules rode like the wind after the black horse, heading for the northern end of the glow.

Within ten minutes the group had ridden a good three miles, but no one was aware of them getting any nearer to the real fire.

Another ten minutes passed. Suddenly Old Shatterhand called out loudly and pointed to the north.

Two blobs were approaching from that direction: the first was light-coloured, the second dark. Beyond them more dark spots appeared, apparently trying to catch up with the ones in front. These were surely the riders they had seen.

The fire illuminated them from behind, so that in a few moments they could clearly see the bony figure of the first of the riders. Old Shatterhand pulled up his horse and dismounted.

'Halt!' he called. 'Get down! We're coming out of the dark, so they haven't seen us yet. Get the horses to lie down.'

The trapper wisely selected a slight depression in the shade, and when the horses lay down and their riders crouched beside them, no one looking into the light would easily be able to make them out.

But they had a good view of the plain in front of them. The first rider was approaching rapidly, with the others close at his heels.

'What now?' asked Helmers. 'Are we going to shoot?'

'No. They haven't done us any harm, and I don't want to shed blood if it can be helped. But I should like to speak to the first one. Leave it to me. Don't do anything, only keep the other six from getting too near to us.'

Untying the lasso which he carried wound around his waist, he tied the end with a ring on it to the saddle of his lying horse. At the end with a loop he made a noose big enough to go round a human body, and hung the rest of the rope between his thumb and forefinger.

All this happened so quickly that he was ready before the first rider drew near, heading straight for the depression where they were.

The sound of his horse's hooves could be heard. It was a powerfully-built black stallion. The rider's face was hidden by a buffalo skull, so that it was not possible to recognise him.

When the rider was about ten strides from the depression, Old Shatterhand stood up. The rider saw him at once, but was unable to stop his horse until he was just a few paces away.

'Who are you?' called the famous hunter.

'The spirit of the Llano,' came a sinister voice from under the skull. 'Who are you?'

'Old Shatterhand. Get down from you horse, and don't worry. We'll protect you.'

'This is my home, I don't need your protection. Out of my way!'

At these last words the stranger spurred his horse on again. The conversation had lasted only a few moments, but another rider had almost reached them. Now Old Shatterhand stood astride his horse's body, lasso at the ready. He clicked his tongue, and the black stallion stood up suddenly, as if it had grown out of the ground.

The rider started, but he, too, was unable to stop his horse as quickly as he would have wished.

And again the hunter called: 'Who are you?'

'Go to hell!' came the reply, and the rider dug in his spurs.

'I want you to stop,' ordered the hunter. 'I only want to see your face . . .'

'Later — there's no time now.'

And with these words he hurled his horse into the darkness. But Shatterhand was at his heels.

The young Comanche had now stood up, too.

'I know that voice. I, too, will speak to this man!'

He raised his rifle and took aim, but then let it drop again, saying:

'Old Shatterhand has him!'

The fugitive had not got far, when the hunter whirled his lasso four or five times round his head and threw it at him. The noose landed round the fugitive's neck. Old Shatterhand stopped at once, but since the lasso was fastened to his saddle, it pulled the other man to the ground. Old Shatterhand jumped down and ran up to him.

In the meantime, something else had happened. The other six riders had reached the hollow, where their progress was barred by Shatterhand's companions. These stood up as if on a command, swung into the saddle, and rushed out to meet the newcomers. At that moment, the six saw their leader lying on the ground hogtied with a lasso, and rode off in all directions. No one pursued them. Shatterhand stood over his prisoner, and said:

'You'd better do as I tell you. It would pay you not to oppose me. Who are you, anyway?'

The prisoner made no reply.

'Then let's have a look at your face!'

Taking hold of him, he stood the man up with his face to the light.

'Well, well!' cried Helmers. 'If it isn't our friend the cavalry officer. Pleased to meet you again so soon, sir. We have already found your wardrobe in the bushes, and been through it. You didn't take proper care of it. And your uniform was there, too.'

'How dare you?' the man suddenly shouted. 'You can't prove anything against me.'

'Can't we, eh? It's true, you haven't harmed any of us yet, but your plans are unworthy, and according to prairie law we could get quite tough with you on that account alone. But maybe we'll let you go again.'

'You're going to have to, since you can't prove anything against me!'

'Reckon we could, though we don't have to just yet! But this Indian here would like to speak to you . . .'

The Comanche came forward. The man looked him over and snarled:

'Never seen him before.'

'You're lying!' said Tim. 'I don't suppose you know me or my brother, either! I don't suppose you ambushed two harmless Injuns! You killed the old one, and you chased his son, until we managed to lose him for you. And thanks to this little accident of your falling into our hands, we've been saved a lot of trouble. Just own up, now!'

'Ain't done nothing!' the prisoner muttered between his teeth.

Then Shatterhand put a hand on his shoulders and said:

'Now you see how things stand. What exactly did you plan to do to the settlers pious Tobias Burton is leading across the Llano? Where are those men, and why did you set fire to cactuses? I warn you, you'd better tell the truth!'

'I don't know what you want. I don't know the Indian, or these two long-nosed guys, and I've never heard of Tobias Burton. Don't know nothing 'bout any settlers, either.'

'Why were you chasing the ghost of the Llano Estacado?'

'What ghost? The guy's a bandit and he shot one of our men through the head.'

'You've no more to say?'

'Not a word.'

'Okay. But remember, your plans will come to nothing, 'cause the settlers are under our protection. And now let my red brother say what he accuses this man of.'

'Paleface shoot chief Fiery Star, my father, in stomach. Afterwards he die. I have spoken.'

'I believe you. From now on the murderer is yours.'

'For Chrissakes!' cried the prisoner. 'What kind of justice is this? You catch me with a lasso, and now this savage is going to kill me!'

The Comanche waved his hand:

'Iron Heart not need gift of scalp. He will try him like a true brave. Let brothers wait a while.'

He ran off into the darkness, but was soon back with Stewart's horse.

Then he laid down all his weapons except his knife. Finally, he jumped onto his horse, saying:

'Untie paleface and give him knife. Let him mount horse and ride where he want. I will follow, and where I catch him we will fight for life or death, knife against knife. If I do not return in one hour, seek me in the sands of the Estacado.'

The hunter agreed. He loosed Stewart's bonds, and gave him a knife, and Stewart mounted his horse, calling out:

'Not everyone's that stupid. You will not thwart my plans, gentlemen. We'll soon meet again — so long!'

The Indian rode off with a piercing Comanche war-cry, driving his horse like an arrow in pursuit of the fugitive.

THE GHOST OF THE LLANO ESTACADO

The others stood silent for a while. Then they sat down, with only a word or two spoken now and then. The suspense lay heavy on them.

Quarter of an hour or more went by, and nothing was heard. The fire was dying down. Then they heard at last the sound of two horses' hooves. The Comanche was back, leading Stewart's mount.

'Iron Heart send one murderer after his father,' he said, tersely. 'Others soon follow. I have spoken.'

The Ghost's Lair

An old lullaby drifted across the morning air, and the branches of the almond trees and laurels seemed to sway in tune. Tiny humming-birds flew around the negress as she sang at the lakeside. The sun had just climbed over the horizon, and its rays were reflected with a sparkle from the water. High in the sky a vulture circled, while on the bank a little way off a couple of horses were grazing. On the top of a cypress, head cocked to one side, a songthrush listened to the old negress's song. When her singing stopped, it gave a loud 'meeteer, meeteer', as if imitating the last words of her song.

Over the plumes of the low palm trees, which were reflected in the water, cedars and sycamores spread their protective branches. Among them huge, brightly coloured dragonflies flitted, golden flies, and other insects; and behind the house by the lakeside, a flock of dwarf parrots squabbled over a grain of yellow corn.

From the outside it was not clear what the cabin was made of, since both walls and roof were completely covered in thick white passion-flowers, veined with red. Their yellowish, egg-shaped fruit poked out from the bag-like leaves. The whole splendid scene looked as if it belonged in some valley in southern Mexico, or central Bolivia, in a region of rich tropical vegetation, yet here it was, in the middle of the dreaded Llano Estacado. It was the mysterious patch of water many had spoken of, but no one had yet seen.

'My heart leaf, my heart leaf.

My life and my star.

My hope and my delight.

My sorrow, my care!'

the old negress went on singing.

'Mycare, mycare — mycare,' the winged songster imitated the last two words.

But the woman took no notice. Her eyes were fixed on a faded photograph which she held in both hands and kissed now and again in between verses.

So many tears and kisses had rubbed at the photograph that it would have taken a sharp pair of eyes to tell what was in it — a negress with a boy in her arms. The boy's head had gone completely...

'My good, dear Bob!' the negress said, emotionally. 'My little Bob. Good missus have her picture made, and when photographer man come she have him make picture of Sanny and her boy. But when missus die, massa sell Bob. Oh, massa was a wicked man! Sanna much cry and beg for her dear little Bob, but massa he say: "What for you need him, you stupid negress?" Then massa ride off and take little boy with him. Then Sanna have only picture of Bob, and she still have it when good massa Bloody Fox bring her here... Ah, yeah, Sanna can look at picture, anyhow, until she die. And Bob now big, strong man...'

She stopped suddenly, lifting her head to listen, her snow-white hair contrasting strangely with her black face. She heard footsteps. Jumping up, she put the photograph away in the pocket of her calico dress, and called out:

'Oh Jesus, Jesus, how glad Sanna be! Good Bloody Fox here again! She bring meat right away and cook cornmeal cakes!'

She ran to the house, but had not reached it when Bloody Fox appeared among the trees. He was very pale and tired, and his horse seemed feeble.

'Welcome, massa!' the old woman greeted him. 'Mother Sanna bring food right away. Sanna will hurry.'

'No, no, mother,' Bloody Fox replied, jumping down from the

saddle. 'Better fill all the bladders with water: all of them, do you hear! Just now that most important.'

'Why the bladders? Who for? Why massa not eat?'

'I hungry, but will take what I want. You not have time. I want to set off again.'

'Jesus, Jesus! So soon? Why massa always leave old Sanna alone in middle of Llano?'

'Because otherwise many people die. Evil men lead them wrong way, mother.'

'And why massa not lead them right?'

'Could not get to them; they surrounded by many bandits, they surely get me if I try to get through them.'

'They want attack poor settlers?'

'Sure thing. But hunters come help from north . . . surely will help. But hunters need water, or will die anyway. So give me water, mother Sanna, quickly! I put bladders on all horses. Only black horse stay here; he very tired . . .'

Bloody Fox went to the hut and in through the door among the passion-flowers. There was only one room inside, surrounded by four reed walls reinforced with clay. Over the fireplace, also made of clay, an iron pot was blackening. Small windows in three walls were not decorated with flowers.

Beneath the roof a piece of smoked meat hung, and on the walls there were all sorts of weapons used in the West. The floor was covered with skins. The two beds were made of a network of straps, fastened to poles, and covered with bearskins. The most beautiful ornament of all, however, was without doubt a shaggy buffalo skin with a whitened skull. It hung opposite the door, and on either side of it on the wall there were at least twenty knives with different marks on their handles.

Apart from a table and two chairs, and a ladder reaching up to the ceiling, there was nothing else in the hut.

Bloody Fox stepped over to the buffalo skin, stroked it, and said to himself:

'The mask of the spirit, and the knives of all those who have fallen to his shots. But when will he find the one who deserves death more than all the rest? Never, maybe? Or does the evil one return to the scene of his crimes?'

Then he lay down on a bed and closed his eyes, though not in order to sleep. What thoughts went through the young man's head at that instant?

In half an hour Sanna came into the room and announced that the water skins were filled. Bloody Fox stood up and lifted one of the skins from the floor. Beneath it was a hollow containing a metal-bound box. It contained ammunition, and he filled his belt. Then he climbed up the ladder to the ceiling for meat. Finally, he went to the lake, on the banks of which lay eight large skins filled with water, strapped together in pairs. Their contents had saved many a lost traveller from death.

There were five horses grazing a little way away. One of them received the saddle Bloody Fox had taken from the tired black stallion, the others were given pairs of skins to carry. He tied their reins to the tail strap of the horse in front, and all was ready. Bloody Fox mounted.

The negress helped him a great deal in his work — it was not the first time that she had done so.

'Massa Fox hardly get back, and he leave for more danger! What poor old Sanna do when one day massa get shot and no come home?'

'I always come home, Sanna,' came the confident reply. 'I have powerful protector. Without him Bloody Fox dead many times, believe me!'

'But old mother Sanna always so alone! No one to speak to, only horses, parrots and picture of little Bob.'

'Maybe I bring you company next time. And one negro called Bob like your darling, him there, too.'

'Nigger Bob? Oh Jesus, Jesus! Him no have mammy she called Suzanna, everyone call her Sanna?'

'That I not know.'

'Him sold from Tennessee to Kentucky?'

Bloody Fox shrugged his shoulders.

'Maybe it be my darling!'

'What can you be thinking? Thousands of negroes they called Bob. Why should this one be yours? Do not think it, mother. But maybe you better speak to him yourself. I go now — look after black horse...'

'Good bye, massa! Oh, Jesus, Jesus, I left alone again. Bring me that Bob here for sure!'

He waved to her pleasantly, and set off with his horses. The whole cavalcade soon disappeared from view among the trees.

The cypresses, cedars and sycamores had always grown here, but Bloody Fox himself had planted the almonds and laurels, like the grove of chestnut trees he was just that moment riding through. Beyond them stretched the fast-growing bushes which protected this oasis from wind and sand. The young man had dug deep ditches from the lake to this place to irrigate the shrubs. Where the moist soil ended creeping cactus grew, and after that there were only the bare, barren sands of the Llano.

Here the young man drove the horses to a gallop, and the procession soon vanished like a string of dark blobs on the horizon.

Half a day's ride to the north-west of the oasis, around midday, a sizable group of horsemen could be found. In front rode Winnetou, with the chief of the Comanches; behind them the bear-hunter with his son Martin. Then came other hunters, followed by another group of Comanches.

They made no sound, as if a single word might cost them their lives. The eyes of the riders at the rear turned inquiringly from left to right, sometimes to the horizon behind them. But they often returned to the pair of chiefs, Winnetou in particular, who was literally hanging from his saddle, bending close to the ground and following some tracks.

There was nothing but sand and more sand, and the tracks were fairly clear. Only now and again did the riders reach bare rocks; otherwise the Llano was like a huge lake which had dried up thousands of years ago.

Sometimes they saw in the distance to the right or left grey-brown strips indicating patches of cactus, through which they would not have passed.

So they went on. The tracks became clearer, or younger, as the Indians say, showing that the riders were catching up on the pursued.

Late in the afternoon they finally reached a place where those who made the tracks had halted. Winnetou got down from his horse to

examine the spot. He walked northwards for a while, then turned and walked the same distance eastwards. Then he said:

'Man with water rode due north. Two pursuers wondered whether to follow, then decided to ride east. Who should I follow?'

'Best if my brother decide for himself,' the Comanche chief said.

'Then I will give my opinion. The ones who the lone horseman is going to are in the north. We could go that way and warn him. But since the pursuers turned so suddenly from his tracks, the trap is probably near. They went there to find the vultures and tell them they had seen the tracks of the man with water. Then the bandits will hurry after him and prevent him from giving water to those he wants to save. But his tracks are so fresh that we can catch him before sunset. Let my brothers decide what we should do. Should we follow the man with water to help him, or set out for Murding Bowle to deal with the vultures right away? In the first case they will probably run away as soon as they see us.'

The Comanches were quiet for a moment, until their chief spoke:

'We should rather follow the trail of the enemy. Does my red brother agree?'

Winnetou nodded and turned to follow the tracks eastwards.

More than a day's ride to the north-east of the flowering oasis, a long snake was crossing the deep sands of the Llano Estacado. Its body was made up of at least a score of covered wagons, following each other at suitable distances, and accompanied by armed riders.

The wagons were well-built and strong, so that the teams of six to eight oxen that pulled them had their work cut out. In addition the animals were tired and weary. The horses, too, looked as if they could scarcely carry their riders. Their tongues hung out, their flanks heaved, and their legs quivered at every step.

People walked alongside the exhausted animals. Their heads were hung low, and they seemed scarcely to have the strength to hold the huge whips they used to drive the teams. The whole wagon-train gave the impression that it would soon have to stop.

Only the front rider's horse still seemed fresh. He had long hair like an Indian, and wore ruddy brown, tight-fitting clothes with dark stripes, and several eagle feathers in his hair, making him look like a chief.

But it was none other than Tobias Burton, a devout Mormon missionary, or so he would have folk believe. He had offered to guide the wagon-train, and was now leading it to its doom.

Another rider appeared beside Burton's horse. It took him a great effort to catch up, and it was with a similar effort that he spoke:

'We can't go on like this! We haven't had a drop to drink since yesterday, for we were saving the water for the animals. And now the last two barrels have gone. How come they ran dry?'

'It's the heat,' Burton replied calmly. 'The hoops open up with the heat.'

'That's not true. I examined them myself, and while there was still water in them, they were tight enough. But someone drilled holes in them, so that the water ran out in the night and no one noticed. Some rogue in this train wants to destroy us!'

'Nonsense! Anyone who let out the water would be digging his own grave, too.'

'That's what I thought, but that's how it is. I haven't told anyone yet, so as not to add to their worries. The animals can hardly walk, and look up there! The vultures are circling, as if they were looking forward to a feast. Are you sure we're on the right trail?'

It was Burton who had drilled the casks in the night. When he had given his horse plenty of water and quenched his own thirst, he had insured himself by filling a tin bottle which was now tied behind his saddle, carefully covered in leather.

'Don't worry,' he replied, pointing to the posts which stuck out of the sand at regular intervals. 'You can rely on these stakes.'

'Rely? Don't you know that bandits sometimes move them, so as to lead folk to their deaths, and make them easy prey for them, and for those vultures up there?'

'Maybe that used to happen, but the days of the stakemen are past. And anyhow, I should know whether we're on the right track or not.'

'This morning you said we were in the middle of the Llano. Why do these stakes lead this way, where there isn't a drop of water, when on the edges there are whole stretches of cactuses, and the sap of their fruit could refresh us?'

'That would be too much of a detour. But you can be sure we'll reach a patch like that by this evening. And tomorrow we'll get to a spring. But we'll have to hurry.'

'Hurry! The animals can hardly walk!'

'Then we'll take a rest.'

'You know yourself we can't afford to. Once they lie down, we won't get them to move again. We'll have to keep them going, so that we can reach the cactus at least.'

'As you wish, sir. I'm as thirsty as you are, but I know that help is at hand. Look at these tracks. As you see, a fair-sized group of riders went this way, and they wouldn't ride along just like that. It'll all be over soon.'

At these ambiguous words the pious fellow smiled, and drove his horse out in front of the wagon-train.

Between the flowering oasis in the Llano and the ambush lay an impenetrable cactus field, tens of miles long and wide. That was why Bloody Fox never set out in that direction, and why he did not get to Murding Bowle. He used to hunt on the western edge of the cactus field and northwards. If he had headed eastwards at the northern edge of the cactus, he would have found the fateful place. But he supposed the settlers to be to the north-east, so he set off in that direction as soon as he left the cactus behind.

The sun blazed. He felt its heat through his clothing; the horses were sweating, but he gave them no rest. Suddenly, a number of dots appeared to the north-east.

'That's them!' the young man cried. 'I'll get to them in time!'

And he spurred his horse, so that the pack-horses had to hurry along, too.

But he soon saw that it was riders he had seen, not wagons. Still, he headed that way, thinking it was the vanguard of the train.

When he finally got a better view, he was surprised not only by the large number of riders, but by the way they behaved. They were watching him, too. But instead of waiting calmly for him to approach, they split into three groups. One of these halted, while the others approached the young man from the left and right, as if they wanted to surround him.

Bloody Fox sat upright in the saddle to take stock.

'By the stars!' he breathed in surprise. 'They have horses with posts on them. It must be those vultures themselves!'

He turned and rode off. But the other horses slowed him down, and so his pursuers got nearer all the time. Then the beasts of burden began to protest: they tugged at the reins, and kicked their hooves. Bloody Fox untied the reins of the second horse, and the four horses carrying the water ran off.

'They are lost!' Bloody Fox grated between his teeth. 'But they shall not have them for nothing!'

He calmed his mount and pulled up. In an instant his rifle was at his shoulder, and a shot rang out, then another, and the first two of his pursuers crashed into the sand.

'That'll teach you a lesson! And you'd better not come any nearer!'

Then he spurred his horse on northwards. For a little while the stakemen continued to pursue him with angry shouts, but when they saw their horses were not fast enough, they went back to where their companions lay.

Again about a day's ride from the oasis, but to the north, another group of riders headed south. It was Old Shatterhand and his friends. They, too, were following the tracks of the vultures towards the wagon-train, as they pulled up the stakes in front of it and led it into the trap.

Old Shatterhand rode out in front as usual. Alongside him was the young Comanche, Iron Heart. Fred and the Sharpnose brothers rode behind them, followed by Frank, Jemmy and the rest.

Shatterhand was silent. He never took his eyes off the tracks, and never said a word. The others were not as quiet. Frank, in particular, was noisy. At that moment he was getting excited again:

'As far as scientific matters are concerned, you are always off the track, or even in the maze of mirrors — I've known that for a long time! That's why I have the juristic right to ask you to acknowledge my mental superiority. He says the globe of light we saw came from the sky! As if the sky had nothing better to do than to illuminate those dark spiritual imaginings with balls of fire!'

'Then you explain it,' Jemmy challenged him, craftily.

'I'm not going to do that, since I should make you a couple of degrees Fahrenheit cleverer, and you are an ungrateful old so-and-so.'

'Isn't it because you don't know an explanation?'

'Aha! I can explain things just as well as King Solomon, and a ball of light like that is child's play. It is due to a sulphurous compound of phosporus with fiery fungi, which sometimes . . .'

He was interrupted by Old Shatterhand, who suddenly pointed southwards and said:

'Can you see that rider? He's on his own, and he must know the Llano very well to ride through it as carelessly as he does . . .'

'Who can it be?' Tim wanted to know. 'Look — he's riding straight for us!'

Old Shatterhand pulled up his horse, took out a spyglass, and turned it on the rider. Then he sighed with satisfaction.

'It's Bloody Fox. We must wait for him.'

In a little while the rider recognised them, too. He waved, and soon they heard his voice:

'Lucky we meet! I need help, quickly!'

'Of course we will help, but who?' Old Shatterhand asked.

'The settlers. Their wagon-train will be attacked tonight by the bandits . . .' With these words Bloody Fox reined in his horse.

'They'll be the same rogues we're looking for,' Shatterhand said. 'Where are they?'

'To the south-east of here. I think they want to get them to the great cactus field.'

'That doesn't mean much to me.'

'It's the biggest patch of cactus on the Llano. I saw about thirty riders; they were pulling up the wooden posts and driving them in to take the train to the cactus. The wagons can't cross it, and I reckon they want to attack them there.'

'How long will it take us to catch up with them?'

'At least three hours' ride, but at a gallop!'

'OK. Let's go, we're losing time. We can speak as we ride.'

So they set off across the plain like the wind. Bloody Fox rode beside Shatterhand, and told him how he had met the bandits and lost his four horses. The hunter looked at him, and then laughed:

'Five horses in the middle of the Llano? Wasn't the one the famous ghost rides with them?'

For a moment the silence was broken only by the pounding of hooves and the hard breathing of the horses. Then Bloody Fox admitted the truth:

'That is so, sir . . .'

'As I thought.'

'I will not be able to keep the secret of the ghost any more, since you will soon see his lair,' the young man smiled. 'And if we manage to wipe out the bandits, I will not have to play the part any more. It will be enough to get one of them . . .'

'Which one?' Old Shatterhand interrupted.

'The one who caused me to be the only one to survive. To stay alive with a bloody head, by which I am called to this day.'

'Who knows what has become of that good-for-nothing. But you are brave, Bloody Fox, and I have great respect for you. Later you must tell me everything from the start. But if you have several horses and can come and go with them as you wish, you must know a place in the Llano where they can find water and grazing.'

'Indeed. I live beside a lake on the other side of the cactus field.'

'By a lake, you say? Then the old legend was right! Can you describe to me more exactly where it is?'

Bloody Fox did not hesitate, but none of the others heard what he said, and Shatterhand resolved not to betray his secret.

For a while they slowed down to give the horses a rest, but then they spurred them into a gallop again.

Just as the sun was setting they saw the tracks of the wagons, and began at once to follow them southwards. It was not difficult, since the moon soon rose to light their way. After about an hour Old Shatterhand pulled up his horse, pointed forwards, and said quietly:

'There they are. I can see their circle of wagons. Wait for me — I'll try to speak to them.'

He jumped down from his horse and disappeared. After half an hour, however, he reappeared like a ghost and reported:

'There are twelve wagons in a square. In the middle, hungry and thirsty people are sitting, and can't even light a fire, since they haven't any fuel. The oxen are lying on the ground, and without water they'll not get up tomorrow. The little we have with us won't be enough

even for the people. We'll have to arrange some rain if we want to save the animals.'

'Rain?' asked Frank, incredulously. 'It won't be that easy in the middle of the Llano.'

'We'll have to do something.'

'That's true. But it's a bit too much for me. You are a remarkable man, but I don't believe you can conjure up rainclouds whenever you want to. Or are you in league with the devil?'

'Something of the sort, but there's no time to tell you the details, Frank. To get water I need fire, and as big an area as possible. Bloody Fox has told me about a big cactus field not far south of here. I hope to produce a nice heavy shower from it. But now we'll have to hurry.'

He jumped onto his horse and made for the wall of wagons. The others watched. They were still shaking their heads over the mystery of the rain, and were most inquisitive to see the poor settlers they had hurried to the aid of.

The wagons were too close to each other for a rider to pass through, but the settlers heard them coming, and when they dismounted a little way off they heard someone beyond the wagons saying:

'Can you hear that? Someone's coming. Have they come to help us, or to destroy us?'

'We've brought you some water,' Old Shatterhand replied. 'Come over here, and let us inside!'

'Zounds!' they heard another, surly voice. 'It can't be ... wait a minute, I'll take a look at these folk myself!'

The man approached, leaned over the shafts of a wagon, and asked: 'Who are you, strangers?'

'Old Shatterhand and his friends — all honest men.'

'Old Shatterhand ... the devil take you!'

The man who greeted these rescuers with such a curse was none other than the pious Tobias Burton.

'Well, now, if it isn't Mr. Burton!' the hunter said, feigning surprise. He recognised the Mormon even in the dark, in spite of his Indian costume. 'I'm pleased to see you here!'

But Burton did not hang around much longer! He knew it was time to disappear, and he dashed over to the opposite side of the camp, where the horse was tethered, unfastened a wagon shaft to let himself out, leapt into the saddle, and rode for all he was worth.

Before he was out of earshot, he heard the cries of delight with which the settlers greeted their deliverers.

'Just you wait!' he hissed. 'I'll soon be back, and then those rescuers of yours will live to regret it! And we'll get Old Shatterhand into the bargain!'

He didn't have far to ride. In a quarter of an hour he reached his companions, who were already waiting for the signal to attack and massacre the settlers.

They were unperturbed to hear that the famous hunter had joined the settlers. On the contrary, they felt that this fact added to the success they could look forward to. True, their attack would not go unopposed now, but one way or the other they would get what they wanted. But they would have to wait until dawn, so as to see what they were shooting at.

The band had been joined by the two Mexicans Winnetou had tracked. At Murding Bowle they had found the one sentry who had been left behind, and he had brought them. After what they reported, it had been decided that the bandits would first slaughter the settlers, and then deal with Winnetou and his group.

It never occurred to them that the Apache might already be close at hand.

Winnetou and his companions had arrived at Murding Bowle, but found the den empty. The place was in a rather steep ravine, with a muddy patch of water shining at the bottom. The water may have reached the place from the 'spirit's den', which was not far away, and though it was cloudy, it was a rarity in the middle of the Llano. For this reason the bandits would meet there, and when they set off into the desert, someone always stayed behind to keep watch and pass on any messages to the rest.

But today the sentry had left with the two Mexicans, and when Winnetou's party arrived there was no one there. They soon picked up the tracks again, however, and at last reached the place the vultures had their camp.

The pursuers halted. Winnetou lay down on the ground and crawled forward like a snake. Though he could not get close enough to hear what the bandits were saying, he saw clearly the arrival of a white man dressed as an Indian. He also managed to count the bandits, and then he returned.

'There are thirty-five of them. I hope that this time tomorrow the real vultures will fight for their bodies,' he said at last.

'What are their plans?' asked the bear-hunter.

'They are waiting for their prey, which must be to the north of here, for that was the way the Mexicans were heading. And just now a messenger came from that direction to announce that they can attack. My brothers and I will now go in the same direction — to help those who are ambushed.'

He jumped into the saddle, and led his men in a wide arc so as to pass by unnoticed. Only then did they head north.

Before long they reached the wagons. They were greeted by the sentries Old Shatterhand had set. To their challenge Winnetou said:

'Palefaces need not fear. I am Winnetou, chief of the Apache, and I bring you water and food.'

The chief's booming voice could be heard a long way. The moment he finished speaking, Frank could be heard to cry from inside the chain of wagons:

'Winnetou? Hurrah! Where there's the Apache, there's the bear-hunter and his son Martin! Let me out to greet them! In the middle of the desert and the middle of the night you meet all your best friends! What a coincidence!'

He leapt down from the wagon, but when he saw the troop of Comanches, he froze like a pillar of salt.

'Jiminy, what in heaven's name is this?' he cried out. 'There's a whole battalion of cavalry here! Come and look, Shatterhand — the spirits are out in force tonight!'

But at that moment Martin flung himself round Frank's neck, and the bear-hunter embraced him cordially from the other side.

Winnetou also greeted the little backwoodsman, and then he asked:

'Did Shatterhand not hear me, that he has not come?'

'Of course he did — here I am!' his old friend called, and he fell into Winnetou's arms.

Then the rest followed. There was no end to the questions and answers, and joy of reunions.

Only the young Indian Iron Heart had a serious face, as he told the Comanches of the murder of his father, Fiery Star. The braves listened without a word, but that dour silence seemed to pronounce a merciless death sentence on the vultures of the Llano.

After that there was busy activity inside the camp, which had to be enlarged to make room for the newcomers and their horses. The bandits had to be prevented from finding out their enemy's real strength. The Comanches distributed among the settlers the meat and water they had brought with them in hollowed-out gourds. But not even this new water sufficed to quench their thirst entirely.

Old Shatterhand and Winnetou, who had now taken over the leadership without question, sat next to Bloody Fox and listened as he told them of his life, and of the country they were in. Not one bandit must escape, they declared, so that there might once and for all be an end to their outrages, and the two of them were glad to hear that, apart from the large cactus field, there was another to the east which, though much narrower, was also much longer. Bloody Fox also told them that the two plains were linked by a narrow strip of sand which could be used to get to his hideout by the lake.

'In that case not one of those rogues will escape,' Old Shatterhand nodded. 'If they see us too soon and try to escape at once, we will trap them between the cactus fields and set them alight on both sides. That will make it rain, and we shall have water for the animals.'

'But then the vultures will escape past my lake,' objected Bloody Fox.

'Don't worry. Take ten Comanches and ride there at once, so that you can give them a proper welcome. You will arrive in time, for they will not attack before dawn.'

And so it was. The camp was opened up. Bloody Fox and ten

Comanches rode out, and at once there was uninterrupted silence. The sentries, posted a long way out, had orders to withdraw to the ramparts as soon as they caught sight of the enemy. Saddled horses were waiting there, and every rider had his orders.

The night passed. To the east the dawn came up, and the silhouettes of the wagons and other objects became clearer. There was no

mist that morning, and daylight came more and more quickly, until suddenly they could even see the vultures on their horses. They were standing less than a mile away from the camp.

Then, suddenly, they began to move like an ocean wave, galloping across to the camp, convinced they would find a solitary sentry there at the most.

But behind the rampart, riflemen watched them ride into range . . .

The distance between the attackers and the camp shortened rapidly. A hundred, eighty, then just fifty paces . . .

'Fire!' ordered Old Shatterhand.

At least thirty shots rang out. The troop of attackers was transformed into a confused tangle. Dead and wounded fell from the saddle, and riderless horses ran onwards. Less than a dozen horsemen remained, pulling back their reins.

'Hurrah! Hobble Frank called out at the top of his voice. 'Come along, then — Old Shatterhand and Winnetou are waiting for you!'

No sooner had these two names been added to the casualties they had suffered, than the bandits headed southwards at full tilt, led by the panic-stricken Burton, recognisable by his eagle feathers.

'To your horses! Everyone to his post!' cried Old Shatterhand.

They quickly moved aside two of the wagons so that they could all ride out. The settlers ran towards the dead and wounded, and the rest pursued the fugitives, but for the moment deliberately let them keep their lead.

Only two of them rode at top speed to the south-west, where they were to set fire to the cactus. It was Jim and Tim Sharpnose.

A dozen Comanches had long ago turned soutwards to force the fugitives to ride between the two cactus fields. The rest, led by Old Shatterhand and Winnetou, rode southwards after the vultures, who were riding at such a pace that it seemed they might escape after all.

Their flight was in silence; only an occasional curse was heard, out of frustration at the failure of their enterprise. They did not stop until they reached Murding Bowle.

'What now?' asked Burton, who could scarcely catch his breath. 'We can't stay here: the dogs are on our heels!'

'Right,' agreed Carlos Cortejo. Like his brother, he had remained uninjured. 'And we can't go through the cactus. So we'll have to head to the right. Let's go!'

They set off in that direction, but soon spotted thick smoke in the distance ahead of them.

'The devil take them!' cried Emilio. 'They have set fire to the cactus! Back, back!'

So they headed eastwards around Murding Bowle. After about ten minutes they caught sight of Old Shatterhand and his group to the left, riding to cut them off. This put the wind up them, and they rode all out to try and outstrip their pursuers. In a while it seemed they had succeeded.

They wanted, of course, to turn to the right, but they soon realised their mistake. A dozen Comanches blocked their path.

'All hell's been let loose today!' Burton said bitterly. 'Winnetou must have a hand in this. I heard his name. We'll have to go through the cactus!'

'Isn't it a dead end?' Carlos asked, breathlessly.

'I don't know, I've never been along it. But we've got no choice.'

'Come on then, or the fire'll get there first!'

They set off for the south, just where Old Shatterhand wanted them. And the hunter, too, dug in his spurs. From the left the group of Comanches closed in, from the right the Sharpnose brothers, who had done their work and set fire to the cactus. Now they all pursued the bandits along the narrow strip of sand between the cactus fields, to where the ghost had his lair.

Carlos Cortejo had been right to warn his companions of the danger from the fire. It got going slowly at first, but in a while it was roaring like a mighty river.

For centuries the remains of cactus had lain here, dry as paper. As the years passed, new cactuses grew from them, but these, too, died, making way for more. The result was material like tinder. At first the flames licked contentedly along the ground, but then they began to writhe and leap, until they reached a height of several metres. Soon the whole plain was a mass of fire, its crackling sounding in the distance like a continuous roll of thunder. The growing heat caused a flow of air which grew stronger, until a proper gale was blowing. The blaze spread further south, covering an area of several square miles. This brought nearer the effect Shatterhand was hoping for. The sky lost its blue colour, turning a cloudy yellow, then grew greyer and greyer. Soon dark blotches began to form, but this time it was not smoke from the fire. The gale had brought along thick clouds, which soon covered the whole sky.

The air was unimaginably humid; the sand burned. Lightning flashed hither and thither among the clouds, and the first big raindrops fell. The rain grew heavier, until it was pouring down like a tropical storm.

The settlers, meanwhile, had made short shrift of the wounded bandits and caught their horses, and were waiting for their rescuers to return. They were still thirsty. Then they saw the fire, and clouds in the sky. They felt the first spots of rain, which soon turned into a downpour. Quickly, they brought all the vessels they had to collet water in. The draught animals, which had lain motionless, perked up. They lowed, rolled about in the rainwater, and at last were able to drink their fill. They were saved, and with them the settlers, who would not have been able to continue without the harnessed animals to pull their wagons.

Shortly after dawn Bloody Fox and his band of Comanches reached the oasis. Sanny was not startled when she saw the Indians. On the contrary, she was pleased to see so many people again, and asked at once about the negro, Bob. Bloody Fox calmed her, telling her she must wait, and went into the house. When he emerged, he was wearing the buffalo skin.

'The spirit of the Llano Estacado!' cried Iron Heart, who had joined the group of Comanches.

The other Indians, too, were amazed to see the mystery revealed, but they said nothing. Bloody Fox remounted and led them to the south-eastern tip of the cactus field, where they took up their new position.

To the north, where the young man peered inquiringly, they could see a black wall rising skywards. Below it flames were licking.

'The fire is driving the vultures before it,' said Bloody Fox to Iron Heart. 'Maybe my red brother will find among them the murderer of his father.' They both grasped their rifles.

The fire and the dark wall grew nearer. The air got more and more humid. But the flames could not reach them, since they had to stop where the cactus field ended.

'Look!' cried the Comanche, pointing northwards. 'They come!'

Indeed, the stakemen were on their way, but there were only three of them left. The rest had been dealt with by their pursuers. Behind them they could see Old Shatterhand, Winnetou and the others. It was a wild chase, though Winnetou and Old Shatterhand were not driving their horses too hard. They wanted to leave the last of the bandits to Bloody Fox and the Comanches.

The first to appear was Burton; he had quite a start on his companions, and as soon as he saw the trees, he made straight for them. Bloody Fox rushed out to meet him. The false Mormon cried out with surprise and stuck his spurs into his horse's flanks, so the creature gave the last of its strength to try to reach the trees.

The other two drew closer. As they rode past Iron Heart, the Indian recognised them: they were the ones who had taken a hand in the murder of his father. Two shots cracked, and the pair fell from their horses. He ran to take their scalps.

Meanwhile Bloody Fox was pursuing Tobias Burton, the worst of all the rogues, who liked to put on a show of Mormon piety. He rode through the trees towards the cottage. The chase was so wild that Bloody Fox lost his buffalo skin. In front of the cottage the horse stumbled, and Burton was flung from the saddle. In an instant Bloody Fox was standing over him; he drew his knife and stretched out his hand. But then he started with amazement. As Burton fell, something had fallen from his head. It was a wig, covering his short-cropped hair! The villain's face, creased with the effort of his ride, stared up at the young man. Burton had broken his neck... And as Bloody Fox looked down at him, he suddenly understood. It was the man who long ago had killed his parents, Stealing Fox! As an eight-year-old he had heard the name when they were ambushed, but only the word fox had stayed in his memory. He had kept saying it, which is why Helmers had given it him as his own name. Nevertheless . . .

The others came riding up. The young man mounted again to retrieve his lost buffalo skin, and threw it over his shoulders again. Except for Old Shatterhand, they were all very surprised.

'The ghost — the ghost of the Llano Estacado — Bloody Fox — it was Bloody Fox!' they cried.

But the young man did not notice. He pointed to Burton's body, and said:

'Here is the murderer of my parents! That is why he looked familiar. He is dead, and now I will never know who my mother and father were.'

'It's a good thing that he is dead.' Old Shatterhand said, gravely. 'He was the last of the stakemen and the Llano can breath easily at last.'

Black Bob had also reached the oasis. But he noticed neither Burton nor the unmasked ghost. He was staring at Sanna, and she stared at him. Then she ran towards him with the words:

'Can it be that Bob?' And when he nodded, she went on: 'Is not your mother call Sanna? Did Bob seen sometime this picture of mother Sanna and her little boy?'

And she showed him the old photograph. The moment he set eyes on it, he leapt down from his horse with a cry of delight. And he hugged his mother, and the two of them were so happy they could not even speak, and only sobbed.

There is little to add. Nothing was left of the bandits, so the Comanches went back for the settlers. At the lake they could recover their strength and then continue across the Llano with an Indian escort. The fire went out, and in place of the great cactus field there were only ashes.

But the ghost's lair was a lively place. Bloody Fox was the hero of the hour: he had to tell them all about his life, answer every question which was put to him, and in the end he decided that he would stay on the Llano for ever, to protect them from all scoundrels. And Sanna and Bob said they wanted to stay with him.

The young man's tale was so fascinating that even Hobble Frank, otherwise so loquacious, did not interrupt. But when he was walking round the lake afterwards with Jemmy and the Sharpnose brothers, Jim asked him:

'You see, we got into the next world without any trouble. Do you still say the ghost of the Llano Estacado is real?'

'Fie!' the little man replied. 'If I have made an error in this respect, remember that there are other, higher realms which we can only understand, should we see them.'

'I know that you are a phenomenon,' smiled Jim.

'Stop that, now, Sharpnose. You don't know me yet, but if we stay here together a couple of months you will do, and you'll get to respect me. Everyone acquires a deep reverence for me in the end. Eh, Jemmy?'

'That's right,' the fat man replied, with an ironical smile.

'There you are, then! You owe it to me, for if I hadn't met Bloody Fox near Helmers's farm, you'd never have found out about the ghost. You have to admit it. So future generations should cast metal statues of me and the ghost. They could cut them from marble, of course. But it's more important to put the statues here by the lake and to write my name on them in gold letters. But what am I saying — not just here, but in the National Park, so that the whole world can honour my memory!'